"I th[ink] you['re] a **dangerous man,** *Emily said.*

"You're right," Mitch said. "I *can* be dangerous." *Dear God, sweet Emily, I'm the most dangerous man you know.*

"My grandmother taught me to trust my instincts where people are concerned."

"What are your instincts telling you right now?"

Swallowing, Emily held back the first response that came to mind. She'd nearly said her instincts told her that she should give herself to him, that she was meant to belong to him. Lord help her, had she lost her mind? "My instincts are telling me to be very careful where you're concerned."

When she gazed up at him, she was shocked by the look of pure lust she saw in his eyes. This man wanted her. The thought sent pinpricks of excitement rushing through her. She couldn't let this happen. He was a stranger.

She didn't even know his name....

Dear Reader,

It's month two of our special fifteenth anniversary celebration, and that means more great reading for you. Just look what's in store.

Amnesia! It's one of the most popular plot twists around, and well it should be. All of us have probably wished, just for a minute, that we could start over again, be somebody else...fall in love all over again as if it were the first time. For three of our heroines this month, whether they want it or not, the chance is theirs. Start with Sharon Sala's *Roman's Heart,* the latest in her fabulous trilogy, THE JUSTICE WAY. Then check out *The Mercenary and the Marriage Vow* by Doreen Roberts. This book carries our new TRY TO REMEMBER flash—just so you won't forget about it! And then, sporting our MEN IN BLUE flash (because the hero's the kind of cop we could all fall in love with), there's *While She Was Sleeping* by Diane Pershing.

Of course, we have three other great books this month, too. Be sure to pick up Beverly Barton's *Emily and the Stranger,* and don't worry. Though this book isn't one of them, Beverly's extremely popular heroes, THE PROTECTORS, will be coming your way again soon. Kylie Brant is back with *Friday's Child,* a FAMILIES ARE FOREVER title. Not only will the hero and heroine win your heart, wait 'til you meet little Chloe. Finally, welcome new author Sharon Mignerey, who makes her debut with *Cassidy's Courtship.*

And, of course, don't forget to come back next month for more of the best and most excitingly romantic reading around, right here in Silhouette Intimate Moments.

Leslie Wainger
Senior Editor and Editorial Coordinator

Please address questions and book requests to:
Silhouette Reader Service
U.S.: 3010 Walden Ave., P.O. Box 1325, Buffalo, NY 14269
Canadian: P.O. Box 609, Fort Erie, Ont. L2A 5X3

$\mathscr{B}$EVERLY $\mathscr{B}$ARTON

EMILY AND THE STRANGER

Silhouette®
INTIMATE™MOMENTS®

Published by Silhouette Books
America's Publisher of Contemporary Romance

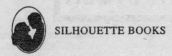

SILHOUETTE BOOKS

ISBN 0-373-07860-9

EMILY AND THE STRANGER

Copyright © 1998 by Beverly Beaver

Printed in U.S.A.

Books by Beverly Barton

Silhouette Intimate Moments

This Side of Heaven #453
Paladin's Woman #515
Lover and Deceiver #557
The Outcast #614
*Defending His Own #670
*Guarding Jeannie #688
*Blackwood's Woman #707
*Roarke's Wife #807
*A Man Like Morgan Kane #819
*Gabriel Hawk's Lady #830
Emily and the Stranger #860

Silhouette Desire

Yankee Lover #580
Lucky in Love #628
Out of Danger #662
Sugar Hill #687
Talk of the Town #711
The Wanderer #766
Cameron #796
The Mother of My Child #831
Nothing But Trouble #881
The Tender Trap #1047
A Child of Her Own #1077

Silhouette Books

36 Hours
Nine Months

*The Protectors

BEVERLY BARTON

has been in love with romance since her grandfather gave her an illustrated book of *Beauty and the Beast*. An avid reader since childhood, she began writing at the age of nine and wrote short stories, poetry, plays and novels throughout high school and college. After marriage to her own "hero" and the births of her daughter and son, she chose to be a full-time homemaker, aka wife, mother, friend and volunteer.

When she returned to writing, she joined Romance Writers of America and helped found the Heart of Dixie chapter in Alabama. Since the release of her first Silhouette book in 1990, she has won the GRW Maggie Award, the National Readers' Choice Award and has been a RITA finalist. Beverly considers writing romance books a real labor of love. Her stories come straight from the heart, and she hopes that all the strong and varied emotions she invests in her books will be felt by everyone who reads them.

To Leslie Wainger, a special lady and an extraordinary editor, and a big Thank You to Joan Parris, who saved my sanity when my old computer died—while I was writing this book!

Prologue

Darkness surrounded Emily, pressing her down, down, down. Thick, heavy smoke obliterated everything in its path, spreading throughout the room and taking away the very air she breathed. Dropping to her knees, she called out to Stuart. She could barely see him.

"Get on the floor and stay there," Stuart said. "Crawl toward the door. I'm right behind you."

He tugged on her foot. Sighing, Emily lowered herself to the carpet, careful not to bear all her weight on her stomach. Above all else, she had to protect her unborn child.

A thunderous boom shook the building. Emily screamed. Stuart reached out for her, grabbing her ankle. She gazed up into the swirling black mass above her. A burst of flames shot down from the ceiling.

Sirens sang a high-pitched, never-ending song somewhere outside. Emily prayed that help would reach them in time.

Stuart released his hold on her ankle. "Crawl, Em. Get to the door."

Following his directions, she inched her way across the living room, past the sofa, and toward the closed door. Only a few more feet. The hem of Emily's nightgown caught on the edge of the magazine rack by Stuart's recliner. Jerking to free herself, she ripped the pink silk.

Surely the firemen would find them quickly. Their apartment was only on the third floor. Any minute now their rescuers would burst through the front door and carry Stuart and her to safety.

Suddenly a shattering rumble shook the room. A hot, fiery weight hit Emily's back and flattened her to the floor. She cried out once, twice, three times. The pain! Dear God, the unbearable pain!

"Help us! Stuart! Oh, God, someone help us!"

Moaning, Emily lifted her head, then eased back down on the pillow. Tears seeped from the corners of her eyes. "Stuart? Help us. Stuart!"

She didn't have the strength to open her eyes. The fierce reality of the dream had drained her physically as well as emotionally, and the pain eating away at her flesh was as strong as it had been two years ago when burning shards of the ceiling had fallen across her back.

She had lost everything that mattered to her. She had longed to die, had pleaded with Uncle Fowler to let her die, but he had willed her to live. Stuart's uncle had prayed for her life when she had begged God to let her die. He had given her his strength when she had none of her own.

"I'm here, Emily. I'm here." Fowler Jordan leaned over his niece's bed. He placed his slender hand on Emily's head and petted her tenderly.

"It hurts, Uncle Fowler." Even the soothing touch of Fowler Jordan's hand could not ease her suffering.

Opening her eyes a fraction, Emily stared up at her husband's much loved uncle and noted the sorrow and worry in his dark blue eyes. *Uncle Fowler loves me so dearly that he can't bear to see me confined to my stomach and suffering again, after yet another operation.*

"I know how it must hurt," Fowler said. "But it'll stop hurting very soon now. I promise you, my sweet girl."

Emily gripped a piece of the sheet that lay beneath her hand, wadding it tightly in her grip. Parting her lips, she tried to speak, but emitted only a breathy moan. Her eyelids closed.

"I don't think she can hear you, Mr. Jordan," the nurse said. "She doesn't seem to be fully conscious. She's probably just talking in her sleep."

"Yes, she does that a lot these days," Fowler said. "She's reliving that horrible morning."

But I'm awake! Emily wanted to tell them. *I'm not talking in my sleep.* She tried to open her eyes once again, wanting desperately to communicate with her uncle, to tell the man who had been her lifeline these past two years that she needed more medication. How long had it been since the last injection? Dear God, it didn't matter whether it had been four hours or thirty minutes. She needed something not just to ease the pain, but to put her into a deep, dreamless sleep.

But the nurse wouldn't give her a shot if it wasn't time for one. They doled out the medication as if it were liquid gold.

Concentrate, dammit, concentrate on something other than the pain. You've endured worse than this; you can defeat the pain if you try hard enough.

Sighing heavily, Emily eased her eyelids open again and in her peripheral vision caught a glimpse of the private nurse her uncle had hired for the twelve-hour day shift. Ann Loggins. That was the woman's name. She was sweet, attentive, caring, but a bit nosy and such a chatterbox.

"That terrible fire happened nearly two years ago, didn't it?" Ms. Loggins spoke softly. "Your Emily's been a real trouper, I'll say that for her. She never complains, except in her sleep, like she just did. And to think this sixth surgery won't be enough. How on earth will she endure another one?"

"She'll endure it the way she's endured everything else that has happened to her." With his gaze centered on Emily's misty, half-focused eyes, Fowler smoothed back the dark, damp strands of hair that stuck to his niece's pale cheek. "Are you sure she's not fully conscious?" Fowler asked. "She keeps opening her eyes."

"She may be partially conscious, Mr. Jordan," Nurse Loggins said. "She's drifting in and out, but I doubt if she understands anything we're saying. She's heavily medicated."

"My poor sweet darling. When she lost Stuart and the baby, she didn't want to live. She's gone from wanting to die to unemotional acceptance of whatever comes her way."

"Someday she'll marry again and have another child. She's too young and beautiful to mourn forever." Ann Loggins opened the window blinds, letting in slivers of bright morning sunshine.

Emily blinked several times. The light hurt her eyes.

"I'm afraid Emily will never consider herself a beautiful woman again," Fowler whispered. "Dr. Morris has told us that no amount of surgery will ever completely erase those ugly scars from her back."

"The right man won't care that she's scarred. He'll love Emily for all the reasons you love her."

"The right man will have his work cut out for him." Fowler sighed. "Emily's grandmother raised her to be a bit old-fashioned. She always wanted a husband and children as much as she wanted a career. Now she's afraid to care about anyone or anything."

Emily closed her eyes and clenched her teeth, bitterness rising in her throat. Didn't Uncle Fowler understand? Didn't anyone understand that she couldn't let herself care, that she didn't dare dream of a happy future? It would have been better if she had died, too. When the apartment building where she and Stuart had lived for less than a year had collapsed and caught on fire, why had God taken Stuart and the baby and allowed her to live—to suffer so unbearably?

After Stuart's death, she had been hospitalized for months, so Uncle Fowler, on her behalf, had joined forces with the residents of Ocean Breeze Apartments. They had brought suit against the contractors who had cut corners, used substandard materials and paid off a building inspector when they'd built the apartment complex.

Consumed with grief and pain and rage, she had been determined to see Styles and Hayden bankrupted, and had rejoiced in their ruin. If she'd had her way, the two men would be rotting in jail right now. But Randall Styles had disappeared off the face of the earth before the trial. Then shortly after the jury awarded a settlement to the Ocean Breeze residents and no criminal charges were brought against him, M. R. Hayden had left town.

For months afterward, Emily had longed for revenge. She had told herself that if there was any justice in this world, the two men responsible for her torment would learn the real meaning of pain. And even now, two years later, after reading and re-reading the transcripts from the trial and learning that M. R. Hayden had been duped by Randall Styles, she could not find it in her heart to forgive him any more than she could forgive his guilty partner. She hoped they both burned in hell.

The policeman tried to hold him back, but he rammed his way through the barricade, only to be stopped by two other officers blocking the entrance to Ocean Breeze Apartments.

"Just where do you think you're going?" the young, freckle-faced cop asked. "If you've got family inside, take it easy. They've gotten nearly everyone out. There are just a few people left."

"Please, if there's anyone trapped in there, let me help," Mitchell Ray Hayden begged the policemen.

"Look, check over there," the older officer said. "Whoever you're looking for is probably in that crowd yonder."

Mitch glanced at the men, women and children huddled in small groups near the row of emergency vehicles. Most of them wore pajamas, gowns, robes or hastily pulled-on jeans. Some of the children clung to their mothers; others sat in their fathers' laps, their frightened eyes filled with tears. All their soot-streaked faces blurred together in front of Mitch's eyes.

Dear God, how had this happened? But he knew. The proof of what he had suspected for several weeks now, and had only confirmed yesterday, stood in front of him. The collapsed apartment building, in flames, its residents barely escaping death, told him more than he wanted to know about his own stupidity.

He had been a fool to trust Randy Styles. A greedy, egotistical fool! He had wanted it all, and had been willing to do whatever it took to make it big. But he'd never agreed to Randy cutting corners, using substandard material or paying off the building inspector.

Mitch had never meant for something like this to happen. If only he had uncovered the truth a little sooner, maybe, just maybe, this disaster could have been prevented.

"Please, sir, move out of the way." The redheaded policeman nudged Mitch. "They're bringing someone out now."

A fireman rushed through the front entrance, a still body lying in his arms. Medical attendants scurried toward him to take the woman and place her facedown on a stretcher.

"She's badly burned," the fireman said. "Not much flesh left on her back."

Pain hit Mitch square in the gut. *No, please, no!*

"But she's better off than her husband, I guess." The fireman shook his head. "We didn't get to him in time to save him."

I'm sorry! Mitch screamed silently as he stepped backward, his glazed stare darting back and forth from the burning building—a Styles and Hayden building—to the ambulance speeding off down the street, carrying a severely burned woman to the hospital.

He glanced at the sidewalk. A shiny spot of something pink caught his eye. Bending over, he picked it up. A tattered piece of the woman's nightgown! Mitch clutched the silk fragment in his hand.

He walked aimlessly down the street, accidently bumping into several bystanders, curiosity seekers gathered half a block away. In his mind's eye, he kept seeing the seared, soot-smeared, satin gown hanging on the woman's body, and the length of her long, dark, singed hair falling over the fireman's shoulder.

The smell of smoke filled his nostrils. The sound of weeping children and women echoed in his ears.

He was responsible for this nightmare. He and Randy. If he ever got his hands around his partner's neck, he'd strangle the life out of him.

"I'm sorry," Mitch cried out. "I'm so sorry. I never meant

for anything like this to happen. Forgive me. Dear God, forgive me for being such a blind fool!''

Mitch awoke with a start, his body drenched in sweat. He shot straight up in bed. His heart hammered at breakneck speed.

Running a trembling hand over his face, he took several deep breaths. Two years, dammit! Two years, and yet he couldn't escape. Neither awake nor asleep.

Flinging back the light covers, he crawled out of bed, then heard someone snoring. He looked back at the bed. A naked woman lay sprawled on the wrinkled yellow-and-green striped sheet. Her bleached white-blond hair spread across the pillow like thin strands of dried straw. Smeared mascara circled her closed eyes. One large breast lay uncovered, its rosy nipple staring up at Mitch.

Carly. Carly something or other. He'd known her about a week. He'd met her at the Gold Digger the night he'd ridden into town. Into Hartsville, Kentucky.

Glancing around the room, he realized he was in Carly's apartment. He had spent the past few nights here with her, the two of them drinking and messing around. He'd won at poker last night and they had celebrated with a pizza and beer.

As he made his way to the bathroom, he stepped on an empty beer can. Early-morning sunlight illuminated the tiny living room, which he could see from where he stood in the square hallway. The place was a mess. Carly might be damn good in bed, but she wasn't much of a housekeeper. The place looked as though it hadn't seen a decent cleaning in months.

He flipped on the bathroom light, raised the commode lid and relieved himself. Turning on the water faucets, he leaned over the sink, then made the mistake of glancing into the mirror. Bloodshot blue eyes stared back at him from a face he barely recognized. Three days' growth of light-brown beard stubble covered his jaw and upper lip. Deep lines marred the corners of his eyes. And he was in bad need of a haircut.

But haircuts cost money. He wondered how much of his poker winnings he had left. Enough for a haircut? Enough for a few decent meals? Enough for gas so he could ride his Harley out of town?

He splashed cold water on his face, then lathered himself with soap, cleaning the remnants of sex from his body. He wondered if Carly kept any razors and shave cream around. He thought he remembered her saying something about having her legs waxed at her cousin's beauty salon.

He opened the medicine cabinet and found it empty except for a few bandages and some cotton swabs. Without thinking, Mitch looked down at the wastepaper basket beneath the sink. He sighed. Two used condoms rested atop the trash. Thank God he hadn't been too drunk to remember to use protection.

He lived daily with the memories of a cool April morning two years ago when his successful life had come to an end—the day the Ocean Breeze Apartments in Mobile, Alabama had collapsed and burned.

He'd been lucky, he supposed, to walk away without going to jail. But it really didn't matter that the state hadn't prosecuted him; that, legally, he'd been innocent. He'd been living in a prison of his own making, trapped behind the bars of regret.

M. R. Hayden had lost everything that mattered to him. His business, his good reputation, his hefty bank account, his luxurious apartment in Mobile, his Jaguar, his closet of expensive clothes—and his fiancée. When the dust had settled and he'd been left with nothing, Loni had walked out on him. She had reinforced the bitter lesson Randy Styles had taught him. Never trust anybody.

Mitch returned to the bedroom, picked up his clothes off the floor and slipped into them. He pulled out his old, battered wallet, removed a couple of twenties and tossed them onto the nightstand. He figured he owed Carly a little something for his room and board the last few days. The sex had been free. She'd made that fact perfectly clear.

On his way out, he picked up his jacket off the back of the sofa. After closing the front door behind him, he walked down the steps to the ground floor.

Glaring sunshine nearly blinded him when he emerged from the two-story apartment building. He opened his saddlebags and stuffed his jacket inside, then lifted his helmet, put it on and jumped astride his Harley.

Revving the motorcycle, Mitch tossed his head back, took a deep breath of crisp Kentucky morning air and willed the memories out of his mind. Memories of long, dark hair cascading over a fireman's shoulder. Memories of burned flesh and scorched pink satin. Memories of a woman named Emily.

Chapter 1

Zed Banning checked the address again. Good God, had Mitch come to this—a homeless shelter in Claypool, Arkansas? Zed straightened his tie before he opened the front door and walked inside the ramshackle old building less than ten yards from the railroad tracks.

An elderly man with a weathered face and gnarled fingers looked up at Zed from his seated position behind a scuffed, army-surplus metal desk.

"You here to make a donation?" The man wheezed when he spoke. "If so, I'll go get the reverend."

"No, I'm not here to make a donation." Once the words left his mouth, Zed felt overcome with guilt. "Well...that is...I'll probably make a donation, but that's not my main purpose for being here."

Hell, why was he trying to explain to some pitiful old man his reason for flying in to Little Rock, renting a car and driving all the way to Claypool?

"You here to see Reverend Wilkes about something?"

"Yes. Could you tell me where he is?"

"Out in the kitchen, helping with lunch." With labored

breaths, the man stood, then burst into a coughing fit. "I'll show you—" Cough. Wheeze. Cough. Wheeze. Cough. "The way."

Zed's self-preservation instincts warned him to step away from the source of whatever kind of germs the man was spreading, but instead he followed him out of the entrance hall and down a narrow corridor. On each side of the middle hallway lay two large rooms filled to capacity with metal beds, every one neatly made with worn sheets and muddy-gray, woolen blankets. Two of the beds were still occupied.

Zed stopped, took a good look inside the room to his right and saw the broad shoulders and long legs of a man who was the right size for Mitch Hayden.

"Something wrong, mister?" the old man asked.

Zed walked into the room, pausing several feet away from the still body of the man he thought might be his old friend. The guy was big and had scraggly, dirty blond hair.

"Mitch?"

The reclining form turned over, his bloodshot eyes apparently unable to focus as he glared up at Zed.

"Huh?"

A breath-robbing smell of stale alcohol stunned Zed. *Dammit, Mitch Hayden, how the hell did you let yourself sink so low?* His old friend had aged ten years in five. His once pretty-boy good looks had been erased forever, his handsome face irrevocably marred by years of hard living.

Zed rounded the corner of the bed, knelt down and grabbed Mitch by the shoulders, shaking him soundly. "What have you done to yourself?"

"Zed?" Mitch raised his head up off the threadbare pillow. "What are you doing here? Did you come to have a drink with me or to get that little blonde who stole my last five dollars?"

"I haven't heard a word from you in nearly five years." Zed sat down on the edge of the cot. "I wondered if you were dead. I see now that you're worse than dead."

"Worse than dead," Mitch repeated. "Living hell. Remembering that building burning... All those people staring at me in court... That—that pink nightgown."

"What have you been trying to do—kill yourself?" Zed lifted

Mitch up into a sitting position, bracing Mitch's back against the wall behind him. "You've turned into a damn drunken bum!"

"Yep. I'm damned all right."

"Why, Mitch? Did you think destroying your life could bring back the man who died when Ocean Breeze Apartments collapsed? Did you think it would erase any of the pain and suffering those people endured? Did you think if *you* suffered enough you could somehow change what happened to Emily Jordan?"

"I had to do something to try to forget. Dream about them...all those people. Dream about her. That pink satin gown and her long, black hair."

What could he do? Zed wondered. He'd known Mitch for nearly twelve years. He'd hired him on as a construction worker on that motel down in Tampa, Florida, right after Mitch had left the marines.

Back then Mitch had been smart, hardworking and very ambitious. Zed didn't doubt for a minute that if Mitch hadn't fallen for Loni Prentice's obvious charms and allowed her to dupe him into a partnership with Randy Styles, Mitch would have been a partner in Zed's construction firm by now.

"May I help you?"

The deep, authoritarian voice came from the open doorway.

Zed turned and saw a small, slender man wearing old jeans and a white T-shirt walk into the room. "I'm Zed Banning. Are you Reverend Wilkes?"

"Yes. I appreciate your coming to see about Mr. Hayden," the reverend said. "We were fortunate that your friend still carried a wallet." He turned to the old man who'd greeted Zed when he entered the shelter. "Go to my office and bring me Mr. Hayden's wallet."

Zed offered his hand to the reverend, who accepted the greeting.

"When you phoned, you said the only name and address in the wallet besides Mitch's expired driver's license was my business card," Zed said.

"That's right. I was so relieved to know you're willing to

help Mr. Hayden. We're able to give these men a bed for a while and some food and occasionally a change of clothes, but that's about it.''

"I understand." Zed nodded. "I plan to take him back to Mobile with me as soon as I can get him cleaned up and completely sober. How many nights did you say he's stayed here?''

"Last night was his third night. He came in around midnight, banging on the door. Woke everyone.''

"Thanks for letting him stay." Zed glanced around the dismal room. "I'll mail you a check.''

"Any small amount would be appreciated." Reverend Wilkes smiled, the dimples in his cheeks softening an otherwise hard, weary face.

"I'll take Mitch off your hands. I plan to rent a hotel room in Little Rock so he can clean up before we fly home. I've got a rental car outside." Zed turned back to Mitch, who had closed his eyes and leaned his head over on his left shoulder. "Come on, let's get you on your feet.''

"Here's the wallet, Reverend." The old man held out the battered leather wallet.

"Give it to Mr. Banning, please, Homer.''

Zed took Mitch's wallet and turned it over and over in his hand. He flipped it open. Empty. Except for Mitch's driver's license, Zed's business card and a tiny patch of pink material. Zed lifted the scrap from the wallet.

"My God!" Zed recognized the pink satin. Mitch had shown it to him nearly five years ago, shortly after Ocean Breeze Apartments had collapsed and burned. Hastily, Zed returned the dirty fragment of Emily Jordan's pink satin gown to Mitch's wallet, feeling somehow that he had invaded his friend's privacy.

"What do you plan to do with his motorcycle?" Reverend Wilkes asked.

"His what?''

"Mr. Hayden donated his motorcycle to us the first night he came here, but I'm sure he wouldn't have if he'd been sober.''

Standing, Zed rubbed his forehead and grunted. "There he lies only partially sober, looking like hell warmed over, smelling like a brewery, not a dime to his name, but somehow he's managed to keep a battered old wallet—'' Zed slapped his hand over the pocket where he'd placed the wallet ''—and the Harley he bought twelve years ago when he first got out of the marines.''

''Your friend is a man being chased by demons.'' Reverend Wilkes reached in his pocket, pulled out a tarnished key chain and handed it to Zed. ''Perhaps you can help him exorcise those demons.''

Zed accepted the circular chain, the key to Mitch's motorcycle its sole occupant. ''I'll make arrangements to have the Harley shipped to Mobile. Once Mitch gets back on his feet, he'll want that old pile of scrap metal.''

Zed lifted Mitch off the bed, circling him around the waist as he draped Mitch's left arm over his shoulder. Mitch shuffled his feet when Zed took a few tentative steps.

''Let me help you with him,'' Reverend Wilkes said.

Together the two men escorted Mitch outside, the cold January wind a sobering slap in his face. Mitch groaned.

''Where are we going?'' he asked when Zed and the reverend eased him into the front seat of Zed's rental car.

''I'm taking you back to Mobile,'' Zed told him. ''It's time you came to terms with the past.''

''I don't want to go back to Mobile.''

''Tough! You're going whether you want to or not. I'm finding you a place to live and giving you a job. The rest will be up to you.''

''I can't go back to Mobile!''

''You can and you will.'' Zed slammed the door, then rounded the hood of the Lincoln. ''Don't even think about getting out of this car.''

''You don't understand,'' Mitch said. ''I dream about that building collapsing, about all those people being injured, about that man dying. About her. It's all I think about, no matter where I go or what I do.''

''Then it shouldn't matter whether you're in Hong Kong or in Mobile, should it?'' Zed got in the car, started the engine and drove away from the homeless shelter.

''Why the hell did you bother to come get me?''

"Because I think everybody deserves a second chance," Zed said. "And you've obviously punished yourself more than enough for something that wasn't really your fault."

"It was my fault. If I hadn't been such a fool. If I hadn't—"

"Stop feeling sorry for yourself. I'll give you a couple of weeks to pull yourself together and then you'll start work on my job site in Gulf Shores. It'll be a laborer's job, just like the first job I gave you twelve years ago. Use an alias if it'll make things easier for you. Believe me, you've changed so much that only your closest friends would recognize you now."

"I sure could use a drink."

Zed glared at Mitch. "What you need and what you're going to get is a bath."

Mitch grinned. "What's the matter, old pal of mine? Do I stink?"

"You smell like you fell into a mixture of rum and cow manure."

Zed glanced at Mitch and the two men broke into hearty laughter.

God, what a sorry sight Mitch was. The years since the Ocean Breeze disaster had changed him, aged him, hardened him. Zed couldn't help wondering how long it had been since Mitch Hayden had truly laughed about anything.

Zed was determined to help Mitch. He could give him a job; that was easy enough. And Mitch could live, rent-free, in one of the apartment buildings he owned.

Yeah, he could provide his friend with a job and a place to live, but it would be up to Mitch to straighten out the mess his life had become and find a way to put the past behind him.

"You've done what?" Fowler Jordan frowned at his niece.

"I've bought half ownership in an art supply store in Fairhope. While my partner takes care of the business details, I'm going to teach art classes."

"My dear girl, I know you had mentioned that it was time you began rebuilding your life, but I had no idea that you'd rush into anything so foolish as investing your money in some little art store." Fowler laid down the *Mobile Register,* pushed his wire-frame glasses upward on his nose and stared disapprovingly at his nephew's widow.

"I've put my life on hold long enough," Emily told him. "I've allowed you to pamper me—coddle me, really—for much too long. I should have been out on my own a couple of years ago. I can't spend the rest of my life hiding away here with you."

"Is that what you think you've been doing, Emily? Hiding away?"

Fowler couldn't bear the thought of his precious little Emily leaving his home, the sanctuary of his protection. For the past five years, ever since Stuart's tragic death, Fowler had—gladly, joyously—devoted his life to her. She had become as dear to him as a child...as a sister. The very thought that anyone or anything would ever harm her again created a burning rage inside him. But how could he keep her safe if she went back out into the cruel world, a world her fragile sensibilities weren't prepared to encounter?

Easing back her chair, Emily rose from the dining table and went over to Stuart's uncle. She placed her hand on his thin shoulder. "Yes, I've been hiding away from the world ever since Stuart died and you know it. I used the operations on my back as an excuse not to start living again. I've imposed on you for five years. You've given up far too much to take care of me. It's time I gave you back your life and it's way past time that I had a life of my own."

Fowler laid his hand over Emily's where it rested on his shoulder. Turning his head sideways, he gazed up into her beautiful face and patted her hand affectionately. Didn't she realize, he wondered, that he had given up nothing, that before she had come to live with him here in his family's big old Victorian house, he had been alone and very lonely? Didn't she know that she had given his life meaning? Surely she knew how much he loved her.

"Well, my dear, if this is what you want, of course I won't try to stop you." Fowler brought Emily's hand to his lips and placed a fatherly kiss on her knuckles. "I suppose a forty-five-minute drive from here to Fairhope every day won't be that bad.

You'll need a new car, of course. I'll call Harry and have him bring over a new Mercedes for—''

Emily kissed Fowler's forehead. "You will do no such thing. My LeSabre is only six years old. Stuart and I bought it new. Besides, I won't be making a trip every day.''

Fowler snapped his head around and glared at Emily. "What do you mean?''

"Now, don't go getting all upset." Emily gave his shoulder a gentle squeeze. "But I've decided to move into Grammy's Point Clear beach cottage. You know I've been redecorating it for the past year.''

"Yes, I know you have, but..." Fowler let his words trail off as his mind considered the reality of Emily's announcement. She intended to move out of his house, away from him, to live on her own. How could he bear to live alone again, to live without Emily's sweet smile and loving presence? "Hannah's cottage was built as a summer retreat, not as a year-round residence.''

"Dozens of families have turned the old summer cottages on the eastern shore into year-round homes. I love Grammy's cottage. Some of the happiest days of my childhood were spent there with her. I think that's why she left it to me in her will.''

"But you'll be all alone out there. Aren't the two nearest cottages both still rental houses?''

"Oh, Uncle Fowler, you're such a worrywart.''

Emily smiled and Fowler thought his heart would break. She was the most beautiful creature on earth. He'd thought so the first time he'd seen her, when Stuart had brought her home and introduced her as his girlfriend. He'd been so pleased when his nephew had married Emily and they had generously made him a part of their lives. Stuart's death and Emily's miscarriage had destroyed their happy family. But he had moved heaven and earth to help Emily. He had forced her to live when she wanted to die. He had held her hand and wiped her tears through countless surgeries that had been unable to erase the hideous scars from her back. He wanted her to be happy again, to live again, but...

"Have you told Charles that you're moving?'' Fowler asked.

Emily groaned. "No, of course I haven't told Charles. Why should I? It's not as if—"

"He's very fond of you, you know. And I certainly approve of him as a...a suitor for you."

Charles Tolbert was an up-and-coming young accountant in Fowler's firm, a man Fowler had taken under his wing. He had chosen Charles as his protégé, after Stuart's death, and it was his heartfelt wish that someday Emily would agree to marry Charles. They had been dating on and off for the past year. Charles was quite smitten, but Emily's feelings for Charles remained rather lukewarm.

"You can tell him today," Emily said. "There's no reason Charles and I can't continue being friends. After all, I'm just moving across the bay."

"I wish you had discussed this with me before you decided to move out on your own. It isn't too late for you to change your mind. We could—"

"Everything is settled," Emily said. "I've signed the papers. I am now co-owner of the Paint Box. I start work next Monday, so I'm going to move into the cottage this weekend."

"So soon?"

Emily laughed. Fowler loved her warm, genuine laughter. He would miss everything about Emily, but most of all, he would miss her laughter.

"I shall miss you terribly, my dear." He sighed. Tears glazed his eyes. "But of course, you know what's best for you. I want only your happiness, and if buying into this business and giving art lessons will make you happy, then I'll support you one hundred percent. But I thought you were happy working on your children's book—your Hannah book."

"I'm not going to give up work on my Hannah book," Emily said. "As a matter of fact, living on the beach, in the cottage where the book is set, will make doing the watercolors much easier. I won't have to do them from memory."

"I see. Well, you seem to have everything planned." If he thought he could talk her out of leaving, he would, but he knew Emily well enough to know that once she set her mind to do something, she did it. He saw no alternative but to go along with what she wanted, even though he felt it was a mistake for her to leave him. "If you're determined to move, I'll help you. And it goes without saying that if there's anything here at the house you'd like to take with you..."

Leaning over, Emily grabbed Fowler and hugged him tightly. "You're wonderful. You know that, don't you? I love you, Uncle Fowler."

"And I love you, my dear."

"Well, what did he say?" Nikki Griffin asked, peering at Emily over a stack of boxes in the middle of the storeroom floor. "Does he know that I'm the person you're going into business with?"

Emily looked directly into Nikki's hazel brown eyes, expressive eyes that gave away Nikki's feelings far more readily than she ever did by word or action. "No, he doesn't, but I didn't see any reason to tell him...yet. After all, he's having a difficult enough time adjusting to my leaving his house, after my living there the past five years."

"Well, he's going to throw a fit when he finds out that you and I are partners in the Paint Box," Nikki said. "Your Uncle Fowler doesn't approve of me. He thinks I'm a shameless hussy."

"Well, you have to admit that you didn't make a very good impression the first time he met you."

"Ah, yes." Nikki sighed dramatically, then threw back her head and laughed, shaking her short, saucy red curls. "That was what...eight months ago? I'd just moved back to Alabama and I went to that charity do with Chip Walters." Biting down on her bottom lip, Nikki grinned mischievously. "It wasn't my fault that Chip and Lance Dunham got into a fight over me."

Emily couldn't control the tiny curving of her lips, the almost smile. "I thought Uncle Fowler would die when I told him that the woman at the center of the ruckus had been one of my best friends in college."

"Oh, Em, college seems like a lifetime ago, doesn't it?" Nikki lifted the top box off the stack. "I don't like to think about the past. It's too painful."

Emily knew a little about her old friend's past, just as Nikki knew a little about hers. They hadn't seen each other in nearly eight years when they'd run into each other at the infamous charity function. Since then, they had renewed their old friendship and a few weeks ago decided to go into business together. For entirely different reasons, both she and Nikki wanted to put their pasts behind them.

"I brought a bottle of champagne," Emily said. "Why don't we postpone opening these supplies and go open the bubbly? I think we should make a toast to new beginnings. Yours and mine."

"Well, I can't say it'll be the first time I've had champagne before noon." Nikki lowered the box back down on the stack, came over to Emily and laced their arms together. "But it will be the first time I've shared champagne before noon with another woman."

Emily chuckled. "Nikki, you're awful—you know that, don't you? No wonder Uncle Fowler thinks you're a hussy. And no wonder people assume you're a...a..."

"A loose woman?"

"What an expression! Let's say a woman of the world." Nikki escorted Emily over to the compact refrigerator in the corner of the makeshift kitchen in the back room of the store. "We're a pair, aren't we?"

Emily opened the refrigerator and removed the chilled bottle of Dom Perignon.

Nikki whistled. "Ah, the good stuff."

"What do you mean, we're a pair?" Emily handed Nikki the bottle, then opened a cupboard and retrieved two plastic cups.

"We've both been hiding from the pain of the past, protecting ourselves from ever being hurt again. You in your way, by living in that Victorian mausoleum with your dead husband's uncle. And by refusing to date anyone except the most nonthreatening types like Charles what's-his-name. And me by moving around all over the country and dating every eligible man in sight."

"A serious relationship really isn't an option for me." Holding the bottle over the sink, Emily uncorked the champagne.

The overflow spilled down the side of the bottle and across Emily's hand. "Dating someone other than a nonthreatening type like Charles leads to romance and romance leads to sex and—"

"The right man won't care about the scars on your back," Nikki said quietly. She held out the plastic cups.

Emily poured the effervescent liquid, then set the bottle on the countertop. Nikki handed a cup to Emily.

"I didn't think you believed in the existence of Mr. Right or Prince Charming."

"I don't believe in a Mr. Right for me," Nikki said. "But for a princess like you, there's bound to be another Prince Charming just around the corner."

"I'd like to make a toast." Emily lifted her cup in a salute. "Here's to dreams coming true. To my finding a Prince Charming who won't even notice the scars on my back...and to your finding that Mr. Right you don't believe exists."

"Ah, Em, what a stupid, romantic toast." Nikki saluted with her glass, then downed the cup of champagne.

Chapter 2

She picked up the telephone receiver. "The Paint Box. Emily Jordan speaking. May I help you?"

"Emily," the husky, muted voice said.

Every nerve in Emily's body froze. It was *him* again. The same man who had been calling her for the past few days. If he persisted, she'd have to call the police. Right now the phone calls were annoying, but not really threatening.

"What do you want?" Emily asked.

"To hear your voice."

"Please stop harassing me!" Emily slammed down the receiver.

"Oh, God, it was him again, wasn't it?" Nikki rushed to Emily's side. "What did he say?"

"He said he wanted to hear my voice."

"I don't see why you don't call the police." Nikki squeezed Emily's shoulder reassuringly.

"He hasn't actually broken the law. He never threatens me." Emily sighed.

"Well, this guy may be doing nothing more than bugging

you with annoying phone calls right now, but what if he does more? What if he starts stalking you?"

"I pray that doesn't happen, but if he shows his face, at least we'll know who he is."

"I say it's Charles Tolbert." Nikki's button nose crinkled when she frowned. "You said yourself that he was very upset when you told him that you two shouldn't date anymore because your relationship had no future."

"Charles isn't the type to make husky-voiced phone calls. He's a nice man. In some ways, he reminds me of Stuart." Emily's thoughts drifted back to seven years ago when she'd first fallen in love with Stuart. Happy days, filled with the promise of a perfect future. A future that died a tragic death the morning the Ocean Breeze Apartments collapsed.

"Then why stop dating Charles?"

Emily shook her head. "I don't know. Maybe because he does remind me of Stuart. And maybe because...well, to be honest, Nikki, I'm just not attracted to Charles. Not in that way." Emily gave Nikki a you-know-what-I-mean glance.

"He doesn't make your juices flow, huh? I can understand. But Charles isn't the only man interested in you. What about Rod Simmons? Talk about a hunk."

Emily laughed. "Rod Simmons is twenty-two years old! And he's one of my art students."

"So? It's obvious he has a major crush on you."

"Yes, I know. And it's the major crush he has on me that's convinced Uncle Fowler that Rod is my secret caller."

Nikki idly drummed her fingers on the countertop. "I suppose it could be Rod. But my money is on Charles. Or..."

"Or?"

"What about your new neighbor? The blond Adonis you told me about? Maybe breathy phone calls are his way of introducing himself. Hey, is that guy the reason you aren't going to see Charles again? Have you got the hots for the 'boy' next door?"

Emily laid her hand over Nikki's, silencing the repetitive tapping. "My new neighbor doesn't even know my name, let alone my unlisted phone number. Besides, I'm not sure he even knows

I'm alive. Just because I've noticed him a few times doesn't mean he's noticed me.''

"Well, have you ever thought of just walking over to his cottage and introducing yourself?'' Nikki asked. "We both know that Mr. Big, Blond and Gorgeous has gotten your juices flowing more than once.''

Emily's cheeks flushed, then she smiled sadly. "He is a very intriguing man. Very virile. And yes, I do find him attractive, but...something tells me that he's not the type who'd be interested in a woman like me.''

A woman whose back and buttocks are hideously scarred. Emily suspected her new neighbor was the type of man who wanted his women physically perfect—as physically perfect as he was.

"Ah, Em, you're going to have to get over this hang-up you have about your scars,'' Nikki said. "You're a beautiful woman. And any man worthy of you isn't going to be turned off by your scars.''

"I'd like to believe you're right, that my scars wouldn't matter. But I—I'm afraid to run the risk. I'd die if a man I cared for turned away from me in revulsion when he saw my naked back.''

Before Nikki could respond, Emily picked up a stack of envelopes off the top of the counter, handed them to Nikki and said, "You go ahead and take care of the new bills that came today and I'll keep an eye on the shop until my next art lesson.''

Nikki grasped the mail, nodded agreement and headed for the storeroom that doubled as kitchen and office space. Emily took a deep breath, then exhaled slowly. She knew Nikki meant well when she encouraged her to get to know her new neighbor, when Nikki assured her that the right man wouldn't care about her scars. But she just wasn't ready. Not yet. She had been living out on her own for only a few months and she and Nikki were trying to get their business off the ground. And for the past week, she'd had to deal with some whispering Romeo aggravating her with lovesick phone calls. No, most definitely, positively, no! Despite her attraction to the Viking god who'd moved into the cottage next to hers, the last thing Emily needed at this point in her life was to fall in love.

"Have you lost your freaking mind?" Zed Banning asked, his dark eyes glowering at Mitch. "You've rented a cottage next door to Emily Jordan!"

Mitch glanced around the restaurant and grimaced when he noticed several nearby patrons staring pointedly at Zed and him. "Calm down, will you? Hell, you'd have thought I just told you that I'm sleeping with her. All I did was move in next door, to sort of keep an eye on her. That's all. For now."

"For now?" Grunting in disgust, Zed shook his head. "The woman has survived for five years without any help from you. I think if she's made it this long, she's all right."

"You told me that she'd lived with her husband's uncle up until a few months ago," Mitch said. "She hasn't been living out on her own since... Dammit, all I want to do is make sure she really is all right. And if there is anything I can do to help her, to make up for... Well, you know what I mean."

"You want Emily Jordan's forgiveness." Zed lifted the cup to his lips, hesitated momentarily and looked Mitch square in the eye. "You're playing with fire here, buddy boy. You want something from the lady she might not be able to give you. What then?"

"I don't know," Mitch admitted. "I haven't thought that far ahead."

Zed finished off his coffee. "Look, you've turned your life around these past few months. You're sober. You're clean. And you've got a job. Don't screw things up now by getting involved with Emily Jordan. I have some idea how you feel about her, but—"

"You have no idea." Mitch's knuckles turned white as he gripped the table's edge with both hands. "I've spent five years being driven crazy with the memory of that woman's lifeless body thrown over a fireman's shoulder. Even when I came out of my drunkest stupors, thoughts of her were always the first thing that entered my fuzzy brain."

"You're obsessed with Emily Jordan, with redeeming your-

self in her eyes. And I'm afraid you're setting yourself up for
a fall. If you follow through with your plan, you're going to get
hurt. And so is Emily Jordan.''

"I know you think I'm nuts, but I'm not. I have to do this.
I don't have any other choice.''

"We always have other choices,'' Zed told him.

"I don't,'' Mitch said. "Not about this. Without Emily Jordan's forgiveness, I'll never be able to live any kind of normal
life.''

Emily watched the stranger. He stood alone on the porch of
the beachfront cottage, his gaze riveted to the boundless horizon.
He didn't look at the beauty before him, the soft glimmering
sand, the Gulf waters, the clear blue sky overhead; instead his
vision seemed trapped, almost spellbound by something he
could not see, except in his mind's eye.

Was he remembering something he could never forget? Emily
wondered. She understood, only too well, the galvanizing effect
of memories.

She had watched the man for the past month, ever since he'd
moved into the house on the beach next to hers. Not being
naturally nosy, she hadn't deliberately set out to spy on him.
But she couldn't help being curious.

The stranger came outside every morning, wearing a pair of
tattered jeans and no shirt, despite the chill of the spring breeze.
As usual he held a mug in his hand, occasionally taking a sip
as he stared out at the bay.

Emily did not want to find the man attractive. But she did.
He was brutally masculine. Big, tall and muscular. A bit heavier
and even more muscular than he'd been when he'd first moved
in. He was tanned and powerful in the way only a man who did
manual labor could look. Pure feminine instincts told her that
his hard body hadn't been perfected in an athletic club nor had
his tan been acquired from spending leisure hours lying in a
tanning bed.

Although Emily had seen him only from a distance, on his
porch early in the morning or late at night, and once in a while
walking alone on the beach, she could tell his features were

sharp, chiseled perfection. High cheekbones, slanting eyes, square chin. His blond hair was golden in the sun and a bit shaggy, but not overly long. And brown stubble shadowed his face. Obviously, he didn't shave every day.

She wasn't quite sure why she was so drawn to the man. Her feelings defied reasonable explanations. As crazy as the notion was, Emily thought she could feel the man's bitter loneliness, could sense some horrible guilt that ate away at his soul, and she was actually sharing the deep aching hurt inside him.

Foolish thoughts! A lonely romantic's daydream. Nothing connected her to this man, this stranger, except the proximity of their dwellings along the beach. It's your own loneliness and pain you feel, not his, she told herself. Five years. Five long, lonely, painful years. And this was the first man since Stuart's death she had noticed—truly noticed—in that stomach-turning, breast-tightening, femininity-clenching way.

Why this man? And why now? Because she was a woman, who, more than anything, wanted to love again, to marry again, to have...to have a child again. Stuart, her college sweetheart, had been the only man in her life, and since his death, there had been no one in her heart or in her bed. Despite Uncle Fowler's hopes that their relationship would blossom into love, Emily and Charles Tolbert could never be more than friends.

But this stranger's overwhelming masculinity beckoned to her on some basic, primitive level, frightening her by the very strength of her own almost uncontrollable needs.

But he hadn't seemed to notice her—not once during the month she had been watching him. It was as if he looked right through her, as if she were invisible to him. She wondered if there was some woman in his life. Even though he lived alone and she hadn't seen a woman at his cottage, that didn't mean anything. Since he left every morning before seven and returned late in the day, always wearing jeans, cotton shirt and heavy work boots, she assumed his job to be blue collar and physical. A man like that wasn't likely to go long without a woman.

Emily had mentally devised different ways to meet him, always pretending that he would find her beautiful and desirable, that he would sweep her into his arms and make mad, passionate love to her. But that could never happen. No man would ever find her desirable. No man would ever want her. Certainly not this rugged stranger.

Mitch Hayden downed the last drops of black coffee as he stared sightlessly out at the bay. Four months. Four long months on the Gulf, working from morning till evening on the Gulf Shores resort project, pushing himself to exhaustion in the hope that he could sleep without dreams. He had sworn he would never come back to South Alabama, had hoped he could escape the past by staying on the run. But he'd spent the past five years running, trying to find peace, forgetfulness and absolution. No matter where he'd gone or what he'd done, he had found nothing but loneliness and pain and the never-ending guilt from which he could not escape.

Zed Banning had brought him back to the Gulf, back to face the past, to start anew. Mitch had always thought Zed was overly optimistic. Could a man actually build a new life on the cold ashes of other people's lives?

But for five years he'd tried everything else, traveling across the country, bumming around, drinking himself into stupors that would give him a few hours of sleep without haunting dreams. Nothing worked; nothing helped. Nothing could change the past. Nothing could bring the dead to life or undo the damage that had been done.

There wasn't a construction firm in the South that would give him a job after what had happened. Everyone knew his name, even if few recognized his face anymore. Zed had told him that he'd aged ten years in five. Mitch accepted the fact that the slender, cocky young man with the movie star mustache, pretty-boy good looks and tailor-made suits no longer existed. He had been replaced by a hard-as-nails, muscular construction worker, with a rugged, lined face.

All those years ago, before disaster struck, Zed had tried to tell him that he had made a bargain with the devil, that no good would come of a partnership with Randy Styles. But Mitch hadn't listened. He'd been too eager, too greedy, too determined to prove himself to the world...and to Loni. Zed had cautioned him about Loni, too. Dear God in heaven, if only he'd taken heed of his friend's warnings.

But he had ignored Zed. He had listened to Randy's big plans, the promises of wealth and power. And he'd allowed his love for Loni to overshadow his common sense. The woman had twisted him around her little finger and made a fool of him. He had paid dearly for his youthful ignorance. After the Ocean Breeze disaster, Mitch had accepted the price he'd had to pay as his rightful punishment. What he could never accept was the price the innocent had had to pay.

Mitch laughed, the sound a mixture of self-loathing and hindsight. He had wanted too much, too fast, and he had disregarded every warning sign. When he had finally realized what was going on, it had been too late. The Ocean Breeze apartment building had crumpled like a house of cards, killing Stuart Jordan and injuring countless others. And destroying Mitch's dreams as his conscience hurled him into an endless nightmare of guilt and torment.

He had come damn near close to dying more than once in the past five years. He'd drunk too much, driven too fast, gotten into too many fights and had too many one-night stands. It wasn't so much that he'd had a death wish, he just hadn't given a damn whether he lived or died.

He was sober now; he hadn't had anything stronger than a beer in four months. And for the first time in five years, he had a steady job, he ate three square meals a day—and he hadn't had sex since he'd done some nameless, faceless little blonde back in Kentucky.

When Mitch turned to go inside the cottage and finish dressing before leaving for work, he noticed Emily Jordan standing on the porch of her cottage. He'd seen her numerous times over the past month. Sometimes she'd be on the porch the way she was this Friday morning; other times she'd be sitting on the beach under a huge umbrella, a sketch pad in her hand. Zed had called him a fool when he'd told his old friend that he intended to rent a cottage next door to Emily Jordan. He'd tried to explain to Zed why he needed to be near Emily, why he needed to get to know her, to make sure she was all right, to find a way to

help her if he could. He didn't think Zed understood. Hell, he
wasn't sure he really understood his motives himself. All he
knew was that without Emily Jordan's forgiveness, he'd never
be able to forgive himself and truly move forward with a new
life.

Zed had warned him that he was playing a dangerous game.
Zed was right. If he had a lick of sense, he'd stay as far away
from Emily as he could. But that was the problem. He couldn't
stay away from her. In the years since the collapse of the Ocean
Breeze Apartments, Emily had become a symbol of his guilt,
an obsession in his heart. She was a stranger to him, and he to
her, and yet not one day in five years had gone by that he hadn't
thought of her, wondered about her, worried about her.

Since his breakup with Loni, there hadn't been a woman in
his life he'd cared about and certainly no one who'd really cared
about him. Hell, there never had been a woman who had truly
loved him. Loni had used him, betrayed him and left him high
and dry.

But this woman—the sad and lovely Emily Jordan—was as
different from Loni as diamonds are from cut glass. There was
a certain genteel air about his neighbor, a casual elegance. He
knew that she'd been raised with money, the kind that had been
in the family for generations. Yeah, that's what this woman
reminded him of. Good breeding. A Southern lady. She somehow seemed out of place in this modern world, a woman in her
ankle-length, flowing skirts, her wide-brimmed straw hats and
her long, dark hair secured with satin ribbons.

He didn't want to find Emily attractive, but he did. The sorrow in her life had slowed her pace and changed her youth into
maturity before its time. But there was a strength in her that had
helped her survive a tragedy that would have destroyed a weaker
woman.

He had been living beside her for a month and still hadn't
worked up the courage to face her, to tell her who he was. He
needed her forgiveness. But more than anything he needed to
do something—anything—to help make amends for the havoc

Styles and Hayden Construction Company had created in her life.

Somehow, someway, he would make atonement to Emily Jordan. If she asked for his head on a silver platter, he would kneel at her feet and hand her the sword.

Chapter 3

He had made up his mind to speak to her. Today. It would be so simple. All he had to do was walk out on the beach and say hello. But what would she say, what would she do, when he told her he was M. R. Hayden? Common sense warned him to stay away from her, not to ask for the impossible. His own gut instincts told him he was a fool. Emily Jordan didn't need him in her life.

But he needed her.

He needed to hear her say that she forgave him, that he should stop punishing himself, that it was time for him to move ahead and let go of the past.

Mitch was restless and lonely today, more so than most days. Sunday was his only off day. The Banning Construction Company worked six days a week on the Gulf Shores resort project. He should be taking it easy on his one off day, but he couldn't. He had seen Emily leave around nine-thirty this morning with the middle-aged man he'd seen visiting often. He was sure the guy was Fowler Jordan, her late husband's uncle, the man who hadn't missed a day of Mitch's trial. From the way they'd been dressed, Mitch assumed Emily and Jordan were headed for church. Emily was a good little girl, the type the old Mitch Hayden had avoided like the plague. That alone should have been enough warning. But no, it had simply increased his desire to know her, the hauntingly beautiful woman who often watched him from her porch.

She had no idea who he was, of course. Even if she had seen the few newspaper photographs of him taken during the trial, she wouldn't recognize him. He'd changed so much in the past five years, he doubted his own brothers and sisters would recognize him. The man he was now bore little resemblance to the man he'd once been.

When he had rented the cottage on the beach, he hadn't meant to become so fascinated by Emily, hadn't meant to think of her as anything more than a victim to whom he owed recompense. He had told himself all he wanted to do was make certain she was okay—really okay—and find out if there was anything he could do to help her.

Hell, it wasn't as if he needed a woman's company so damn bad. If he did, all he had to do was take up the offer he'd seen in that waitress's eyes, the bosomy blonde at Andy's, where he often ate supper after work.

Getting a woman wasn't his problem. A sexual relationship with Emily wasn't the reason he was here. Guilt and remorse motivated him, and the hope for redemption.

The spring sunshine warmed his face and heated his body through his jeans and shirt. Cottony white clouds filled a brilliant blue sky, and the tawny white sand crunched beneath his feet. A soft breeze floated in off the Gulf as the murky blue-gray water of Mobile Bay drifted in and out to the rhythm of the ocean's heartbeat.

There was a dreamlike serenity to this private stretch of beach, and only the sound of a piano could be heard over the lapping surf and mild wind. Slow and soft, gentle music filled the air. Mitch listened carefully, not recognizing the tune, but immediately aware that it was something classical. It figures, he thought. Emily Jordan looked like the classical type. He wasn't surprised that the melody coming from her small cassette player would be something written hundreds of years ago.

Even though he was standing a good twenty feet away from
his neighbor, he could make out her delicate features as she sat,
concentrating on the sketch pad in front of her. Her oval face
was as golden tan as her slender arms and legs. Her nose was
small and slightly tilted at the end. Her chin held a hint of a
dimple. Her mouth was full and pouty—the kind of mouth that
made a man want to taste it.

She had tied her pink cotton blouse in a loose knot at her
waist and hiked her full floral skirt up to her hips. She'd bent
her legs at the knees so she could use them as a makeshift prop
for her pad. Mitch had a perfect view of her long, trim thighs
and shapely calves.

Fabric in the same design as her skirt draped around the wide-
brim straw hat she wore. Long tails of flowery pink material
cascaded down her back and covered part of her sun-streaked,
dark-brown ponytail. Loose tendrils of hair curled about her
face, clinging to her forehead where perspiration dampened it.

When he was within a few feet of her, Mitch stopped. She
seemed totally oblivious to his presence as she continued using
the charcoal in her hand to create a sketch of the bay. When
the music ended, she didn't stop drawing; she merely reached
down with one hand to where the cassette player lay on the quilt
beneath her and turned over the tape. Another tune, completely
alien to Mitch, permeated the air, mixing the sound of harp with
the light spring breeze.

He felt like a fool standing there staring at her. He wasn't
some insecure teenage boy hoping to impress a girl. He was a
thirty-five-year-old man who had learned the hard way the price
a man had to pay to impress a woman. If he had any sense,
he'd run like hell. Obviously he didn't have any sense.

He couldn't stop looking at Emily, couldn't stop wanting to
reach out and touch her. The afternoon sun glistened off the
locket that hung from a thin gold chain around her neck. She
doesn't look real, Mitch thought. Wearing that long skirt and
straw hat, she looked like someone from an era when ladies
never went out in the sun without their parasols. Hell! He shook
his head to dislodge such idiotic nonsense.

He was acting like a romantic dreamer, and that was the last thing on earth Mitch Hayden was. He was a realist, and often a pessimist, and God knew he was a fool. But there wasn't a sentimental, romantic bone in his body.

He'd been too long without a woman. That had to be the problem. Otherwise he'd never be attracted to this gentle-looking creature. He preferred his women sexy, earthy and a lot less a lady. Yeah, lady. That was the first word that came to mind, and that's exactly what she was, a lady, and by the looks of her, an old-fashioned one. So, why did he find her so appealing, so intriguing? Ladies had never been his type.

And if she realized who he was, she wouldn't find him appealing in any way. If he introduced himself, would she run from him screaming?

Halting directly in front of her, he blocked her line of vision. Glancing down at her just as she tilted her chin and raised her gaze to meet his, Mitch noticed that her eyes were brown— dark, rich, cinnamon brown—and framed by long, thick black eyelashes.

She was beautiful.

Somehow he'd known she would be. On that April morning five years ago, he hadn't gotten a good look at her face. But as long as he lived, he would never forget her singed dark hair and tattered pink nightgown.

The moment their eyes met, she gasped. "Oh, hello." Her voice fit her feminine image perfectly. Soft. Sweet. Slightly sexy.

"Hello," he replied.

When she smiled, he felt the warmth of it spread through him. The bottom dropped out of his stomach. Dammit, this wasn't supposed to happen.

"It's a beautiful day, isn't it?" Stretching out her legs on the quilt, she laid her sketch pad aside. "I was hoping it wouldn't rain this weekend, so I could stay outside and sketch."

"What are you drawing?" He wasn't a man used to idle chitchat, and for the life of him he couldn't figure out why he was bothering with it now. *Because she is Emily Jordan and you want to get to know her. You want to find out if there is*

*some way you can repay her for the life Styles and Hayden
Construction Company destroyed.*

Lifting the pad, she turned it so he could see the sketch.
"What do you think?"

"I'm no art critic, but I think it's good." He pointed to the
sketch. "There's a child in your drawing."

"Hannah." She ran her fingertips lightly over the sketch of
the little girl. "I'm working on illustrations for a children's
book. Hannah is my main character."

"Is your story a fairy tale with a phony happy ending?"
Mitch well remembered his mother reading to him from the
ragged book she'd saved from her own childhood. His mother
had been a hopeless romantic, his father a lazy dreamer. Together they had almost ruined the lives of their five innocent
children.

Clutching the edge of the pad, Emily sighed heavily. "If
you're asking whether or not all my stories will have happy
endings, then the answer is yes."

"Adults shouldn't lie to children. Kids shouldn't be taught
that life always ends happily ever after."

"I disagree." She saw the skepticism on his hard, lean face,
and knew it would be useless to argue. Somewhere along the
way, this man had lost his ability to wish for the impossible.
"Simplistic as it sounds, life is a roller coaster ride filled with
ups and downs. Sometimes we'll have our hearts broken and
our dreams destroyed, but we have to dry our tears and dream
new dreams."

If Emily Jordan was still this much of a romantic optimist
after losing her husband and living through a horrible nightmare,
then perhaps her life hadn't been ruined. Perhaps she had found
happiness again. "You're obviously a romantic. Your books
must fill children's heads with a lot of pie-in-the-sky ideas."

"Not really. At least not yet. I'm still in the preparation stages
for my Hannah books."

"So you're not published?"

"Not yet, but hopefully, someday." Laying down the pad,
she punched the Off button on the cassette player. "Would you
like to sit down and get out of the sun?" Emily patted the large

tulip quilt on which she sat. She had wanted to meet this man for over a month, and now here he was standing beside her, talking to her, looking at her with the most incredible blue eyes she'd ever seen.

Was she a fool to be so friendly to a stranger? She knew nothing about this man—absolutely nothing. Was it possible that he was her mystery caller? Had he somehow found out her name and phone numbers at home and at work? Was the typed ''love letter'' she had received yesterday from him?

Her common sense told her to be cautious, but her feminine desires told her to throw caution to the winds.

''Are you asking me to share your quilt?'' He watched her closely for a reaction.

Smiling, she looked him directly in the eye. ''Yes.'' There was something about this man, about the way he looked at her, that unnerved her, but didn't frighten her.

When he sat down beside her, she turned and reached inside her small cooler to retrieve two chilled bottles. ''Would you care for some apple juice?'' She offered him a bottle.

Apple juice? He looked down at her gift. He didn't think he'd ever drunk apple juice in his entire life. His fingers grazed hers when he accepted the bottle, and a sizzling sensation ran up his arm. Touching her, even briefly, alerted his senses to trouble. ''Thanks.''

Emily studied the big, blond man sitting beside her. Muscular, tanned, robust, and sexy to the point of being dangerous to any woman who crossed his path. She found him extremely appealing. Had she let the overwhelming attraction she felt dull her senses? Was that the reason she had ignored her common sense and allowed her feminine desires to guide her? Was that the reason she had decided to trust a perfect stranger, when she had doubts about Charles Tolbert and Rod Simmons, two men she knew and liked?

The stranger turned and smiled at her, his searing blue eyes focusing on her face. When she felt the warmth of a blush creeping into her cheeks, she abruptly looked down, hoping he wouldn't notice.

Was she blushing? Mitch wondered. He couldn't believe it.

As a general rule, modern women didn't blush. Hell, was it possible that Emily felt the attraction between them as strongly as he did? Was that what was bothering her?

"My Hannah character was based on a real person," Emily said in an effort to distract herself from concentrating so intensely on her neighbor's obvious physical attributes. She took a sip from the chilled bottle of juice before she picked up her sketch pad.

"Is that right?" Following her lead, Mitch put his bottle to his lips and took a giant sip. Much to his surprise, he found the fruity liquid quite refreshing.

"My grandmother's name was Hannah. She spent many happy days of her childhood in that house." Turning, Emily pointed to the white clapboard cottage nestled on a grassy knoll above the beach. "When I was a little girl and came here in the summer, Grammy used to tell me the most wonderful stories about vacations at the cottage when she was growing up."

Mitch set the bottle of juice between his legs. He knew very little about Emily Jordan. Only what Zed had been able to find out from various sources. After her husband's death in the fire, she'd had eight surgeries on her back. Until recently, she had lived in Mobile with her husband's uncle, Fowler Jordan, the respected head of a prestigious accounting firm. Then a few months ago, she'd moved into the beachfront cottage on Scenic Highway 98 that she had inherited from her grandmother. And with a partner, she had opened an art supply store called the Paint Box in the nearby town of Fairhope.

"You were close to your grandmother?" Mitch asked.

"My grandmother raised me. At least for the most part." Emily had loved Hannah McLain more dearly than either of her own parents. "My father was killed in an accident when I was twelve, and my mother remarried shortly afterward. I chose to live with Grammy."

"How long have you lived in your grandmother's cottage?"

"For a couple of months. But this—" she spread out her arms in a loving gesture as if she could encompass the house, the beach, the bay and the sky in her arms "—has always seemed like home to me for as long as I can remember."

"I've never felt like that about a place. I haven't had a real home since I was a kid." He leaned back, propping himself up with his elbows. "I've spent the last five years bumming around the country."

"And before that?" She looked at him and couldn't help noticing that his eyes were the coldest, palest blue she'd ever seen.

He didn't reply at first, only stared at her. He was incredibly good-looking and almost too masculine. His height and powerful build gave him an air of rugged strength. His clothes fit his body with a snug casualness, his shirt outlining every well-developed muscle in his chest and shoulders. For some odd reason, Emily had the strangest urge to reach out and run her hands over his broad shoulders.

"Before I started bumming around, I had a steady job." He didn't want to tell this woman anything about his past—not yet. She probably held him responsible for her husband's death; and he didn't blame her. Even if when he told her who he was she didn't run away, how would he ever be able to convince her of his innocence, when in his very soul he felt guilty?

Emily flipped over a page in her pad, picked up her charcoal and began drawing.

"Do you live alone?" he asked, trying to think of something to say to keep himself from taking her face in his hands and bringing her mouth close enough to kiss. Dear God, she was a sweet temptation, a temptation to which he could never surrender.

"Yes." She knew by the way he was looking at her that he wanted to kiss her, and oddly enough the thought of his lips on hers didn't frighten her. "You're living alone, too, aren't you?"

"Quite alone."

"No family? Wife? Children?"

"No." He finished the last drops of apple juice and set the empty bottle next to the cooler.

"You must get lonely." She instinctively felt that this man was unbearably lonely.

"What about you—are you lonely? Or is there someone in

your life?'' He wanted her to say that she wasn't lonely, that she was happy and her life was good.

"There isn't a special man, if that's what you're asking, but my life is filled with people. A special uncle, a dear friend and my art students."

"You're a teacher?"

"An art teacher," she said. "I own an art supply store in Fairhope. And I teach art classes. Mostly to children, but I do have some adult pupils."

"You must like children if you can endure teaching them."

"I love children." If only she hadn't lost her baby the night Stuart died, her child would be nearly five years old. "Don't you like children?"

"Kids don't fit into my life in any way." He'd grown up in a household overrun with children—crying, fighting, hungry brothers and sisters with bare feet and hand-me-down clothes and Mississippi red clay under their fingernails.

"You don't plan to have children of your own someday?" She didn't think about how personal the question was until she'd already blurted it out. "Oh, forgive me for asking. It's certainly none of my business."

"No, I don't plan to have any children. I helped raise several younger brothers and sisters. That pretty much got the fathering instinct out of my system." When he'd been climbing the ladder of success and he and Randy had been raking in the big bucks, Mitch had helped his younger siblings. Now he was doing good just taking care of himself. He didn't have anything to offer a woman, let alone anything to give a child.

"I was an only child." Emily lay back and stretched out on the quilt, then looked up at Mitch. "I've always wanted children."

"Then I hope someday you have them." From out of nowhere the thought of this lovely woman's very pregnant body drifted into his mind. She would look beautiful all round and full, her feminine form nurturing a child. His child. "Damn!" Mitch sat up quickly, cursing himself for a fool.

"What?" She'd heard his outburst, but had no idea what had prompted it.

Deliberately he turned away—to avoid her searching gaze. Reaching out, he punched the Play button on her cassette player. A somewhat somber tune began, an elegant blend of strings and brass. Very gradually the music built, then dropped away, only to rebuild again and again. "Classical music, huh?"

"Yes." Instantly she realized he was fighting to control his emotions, and she knew instinctively that it wasn't something he had to do often. "That's Tchaikovsky's Symphony no. 5 playing."

"I don't know anything about that kind of music. I prefer good old rock 'n' roll or some hot jazz." He clinked the side of the empty juice bottle with his fingernail.

"I love all types of music, but I must admit I'm a sucker for classical." She watched the way he kept fiddling with his empty bottle, his hands nervously caressing the glass surface. "Grammy's influence. She used to take me to concerts when I was a child. And the ballet. And the opera."

"My old man listened to the *Grand Ole Opry* when I was a kid." Mitch supposed that was why, to this day, he couldn't stand country music. "We weren't very cultured, to say the least."

"Culture isn't everything," Emily said. "I think honesty and integrity and compassion are far more important."

He couldn't resist turning toward her, his gaze traveling the length of her slender body. For five years this one woman had haunted his dreams, had tormented him day and night. When he returned to the Gulf, he had wanted to meet Emily, to make sure she was fully recovered from the tragedy his construction firm had caused. That's all he had wanted. Just to check on her. Make sure she was all right. To see if he could do anything to help her.

But now, after meeting her, all he could think about was what it would be like to make love to her.

He looked at her with such undisguised longing in his eyes that Emily wanted to weep. What would this devastatingly handsome man think of her if he could see her scars? Would he be repulsed? Would he cringe at the sight of her imperfect back covered with disfigured flesh that could never be restored to its former perfection?

Lured by the undeniable attraction that pulsated between them, Mitch found himself reaching out to touch the locket that hung from a thin chain around her neck. His big finger circled the round gold pendant. "Lady, are you what you appear to be, or are you some illusion I've dreamed up?"

Her breath caught in her throat when his hand accidently brushed against her breast as he continued fondling her necklace. "And just what—what do I appear to be?"

"A very beautiful, very delicate, very sensitive lady." He wanted to pull her into his arms, to see if she would melt against him. She gazed at him as if nothing would please her more.

Emily eased away from him, but smiled as she stroked the gold chain about her neck. Only moments before, his fingers had caressed the thin metal, and she could almost feel his touch. She had never met anyone like this man, had never reacted so strongly to another man's look or touch or the sound of his voice.

"I think you could be a dangerous man," Emily said, admitting that he posed a threat to her self-control. Had she been wrong about him? Was it possible that he was her mystery man? Had he been the one who called "just to hear her voice"? Was he the one who had quoted Shelley and Byron in the love letter? "Any woman would be a fool to trust you too quickly."

"Did your Grammy teach you to be wary of strangers? If she did, she was a smart lady." Mitch sat beside her, unmoving, but within his own mind, he withdrew from her. "You're right. I can be dangerous."

Dear God, sweet Emily, I'm the most dangerous man you know.

"My grandmother taught me to trust my instincts where people are concerned."

"What are your instincts telling you right now?"

Swallowing, Emily held back the first response that came to mind. She'd nearly said her instincts were telling her that she should give herself to him, that she was meant to belong to him.

Lord help her, had she lost her mind? "My instincts are telling me to be very careful where you're concerned."

When she gazed up at him, she was shocked by the look of pure lust she saw in his eyes. This man wanted her. The thought sent pinpricks of excitement rushing through her. She couldn't let this happen. She had no idea who he was. He was a stranger. She didn't even know his name.

Mitch told himself to get up and walk away. The last thing he needed was a relationship with a woman who would feel only hatred for him if she knew his name. He was having a difficult enough time trying to rebuild a life that his own stupidity had destroyed, without succumbing totally to his desperate need for Emily's forgiveness.

Mitch lowered his body onto the quilt, lying down beside her, propping himself up on one elbow. *Run, you damned fool. Run now!* he told himself.

Emily drew in a deep breath. This man was a stranger, perhaps a dangerous stranger. Why didn't she tell him to go away? Why didn't she gather up her belongings and return to her cottage? Staying here, so close to him, was bound to lead to trouble. As ridiculous as the notion was, she wanted him to kiss her...this man she didn't know. She longed to feel his lips on hers.

He leaned toward her, his face so close that she tasted his breath. "I—I don't think this is such a good idea," she said. "We're strangers."

"Are you always so friendly to strangers on the beach?" he asked, somehow knowing she had never reacted this way to any other man.

"No," she admitted, closing her eyes, wanting to escape the nearness of his body, the smell of his musky aftershave, the feel of his breath mingling with hers. "Strangers don't usually intrude on my privacy."

"Why didn't you ask me to leave when I first approached you?"

"Because I... You're my neighbor. I didn't want to be unfriendly."

"I've been watching you for weeks now," Mitch told her.

"I'm no good for you, pretty lady, but I couldn't stop myself from coming out here to meet you."

He'd been watching her? Emily's heart skipped a beat. All the while she'd been spying on his privacy, he'd been doing the same thing. "I've watched you, too, and wondered about you."

"You're as lonely as I am, aren't you?" Why would a woman with so much charm and beauty and intelligence not have a man in her life? Mitch wondered. It didn't make sense. Was it possible that she was still in love with her dead husband?

"Yes, I'm lonely. My husband died five years ago, and there's been no one...." And there never can be anyone, she told herself. No man would want such an imperfect woman.

"I'm sorry about your husband. I lost someone about five years ago, too." Had he ever really loved Loni? he wondered, or had she just been a part of his big plans to get rich, to be important, to once and for all prove to himself and everyone else that there wasn't any Mississippi red clay left under his fingernails?

"She died?" Emily asked.

"No." Mitch chuckled, admitting to himself that losing Loni wasn't the worst thing that had happened to him. "My fiancée ran off with my former business partner."

"Oh." His business partner? How could that be? She'd assumed he was a manual laborer—had he once owned his own business?

"I think it's about time we introduce ourselves, pretty lady, don't you?" He held out his hand. "I'm Ray Mitchell. My friends call me 'Mitch.'" He gave her the same name he had decided to use at work. He'd chosen it hoping that if he'd ever worked with any of the laborers in the past, no one would recognize him.

His common sense told him he was a fool to lie to Emily, to hide his true identity from her. But his heart told him that there would be time enough to tell Emily who he really was. Later. When they knew each other better.

Watching the play of emotions on Mitch's face, Emily wondered what he was thinking. He was a million miles away.

Somewhere she couldn't reach him. Someplace he obviously didn't want to be.

She touched his arm. He turned to her. "I'm Emily Jordan."

Emily. He repeated the name in his mind as he had done countless times in the past. The name suited her. Old-fashioned and ladylike. "Would you go out to dinner with me sometime, Emily?"

She wanted to say yes, to scream her acceptance, but she couldn't. It was obvious that Ray Mitchell was the kind of man who would expect a physical relationship. She could never offer him her body. Her scarred, imperfect, ugly body.

"If you're looking for a friend...someone to ease the loneliness, then...well, I'd like to be your friend," she said.

"I need a friend." *I need for you to be my friend.*

Emily wanted to touch Mitch, to run her fingers down his craggy, beard-stubbled face. There was so much pain in his eyes, so much loneliness. Perhaps that was why fate had thrown them together. Perhaps she could ease Mitch's pain and end his loneliness, and he could do the same for her.

She had lost so much, suffered so greatly, that she often wondered why she'd been severely punished for sins she'd never known she committed. She and Stuart had been so happy in their new apartment at Ocean Breeze. She'd been five months pregnant and they had already begun decorating a nursery for their baby boy. And then their apartment building had collapsed. Fire had broken out, spreading quickly throughout the expensive, newly constructed complex. She and Stuart had been trapped. Stuart had died. And when she'd awakened to learn of his death and the loss of their child, she had wished she'd died with them.

But she'd lived to suffer endless agony as her severely burned back healed, and then more pain when she endured eight operations on her seared flesh.

Emily had lost her husband, her child and any hopes of ever loving and being loved again. And all because an unscrupulous construction firm had been more interested in saving money than in people's safety. Even though she'd been too ill to go to court, to face the monsters responsible for the destruction of her life, she would never forget their names. Randall D. Styles and M. R. Hayden.

"Are you all right, Emily?" Mitch asked.

"Sorry. I was just remembering...things I'll never be able to forget."

"Yeah. I understand. I have a few demons chasing me, too."

Emily smiled at Mitch, accepting him into her life, telling herself that he needed her friendship as much as she needed his. "Why don't you stop by the Paint Box tomorrow after work. We can pick up some fresh seafood and a bottle of wine. I can cook dinner for us at my house."

"Pretty lady, you've got yourself a deal."

Chapter 4

The morning had been hectic for both Emily and Nikki. Emily taught classes for senior citizens on Monday mornings, and today she'd also tried to help Nikki with the inventory. Her partner had been tied up with the distributor who provided the store with their art books, and with a disgruntled customer, Mrs. Hendricks, who came by at least once a week to complain.

Emily checked her small diamond-studded gold watch, the last birthday gift Grammy had given her. Twelve forty-five. Emily noted the number of children's watercolor sets on the shelf, recorded it on the inventory sheet, then slipped her pencil into the breast pocket of her yellow, paint-smeared smock. Her stomach rumbled, reminding her that she'd skipped breakfast this morning, something she often did when she overslept and had to make a mad dash to arrive at the store on time.

This morning she'd overslept by nearly two hours, and arrived for work thirty minutes late. She'd been unable to go to sleep last night. Her mind had been filled with Mitch. Mitch with the sexy, ice-blue eyes. Mitch with the Viking-warrior body and golden hair. Mitch who had brought to life the sexual urges she'd laid to rest with her husband.

And tonight she was cooking dinner for him. He'd said he'd drop by the store, pick her up, help her shop, then run home for a shower before supper. All morning she'd kept picturing Mitch in the shower, rivulets of warm water caressing his big, hard body. Emily ached with wanting, and that was something she hadn't experienced since Stuart's death.

But what frightened Emily even more than the passion Mitch had brought to life within her was the fear of allowing herself to get too close to this man, to want too much, to build castles in the air. Had she been foolish to offer him friendship, to think that they could settle for a nonsexual relationship? And was she crazy to trust a man she didn't know, to believe in her instincts that told her he wasn't the man harassing her?

Mitch was a man in pain, one who, by his own admission, was being chased by demons. She understood what that felt like, what it meant to be haunted by the past, to live with a heavy weight of sorrow surrounding your heart.

If only she weren't hideously scarred. If only she could go to him beautiful and perfect and unblemished. But she couldn't. Nothing and no one could ever erase the damaged flesh that covered her back. Lord knew that the doctors had tried.

"Food!" Nikki shouted from behind the checkout counter. "I'm starving. Let's eat now while no one's here but the two of us."

"Good idea." Emily dusted off her hands on her smock. "Today was your day to bring lunch, wasn't it?"

"Yes, today was my day." With her bright hazel brown eyes open wide, Nikki gave Emily a what's-up-with-you? look. "Something's going on. You haven't been yourself all morning. Even Mr. Daily noticed in class, and asked me if you were sick or something."

"Just because I wasn't sure if today was your turn to bring lunch or not, you're accusing me of—"

"Hold it right there." Nikki rounded the corner of the counter and headed toward Emily. "I know what it is. I know what it is!"

"You know what what is?" Turning away from her friend, Emily walked toward the back of the store to the rest room.

Nikki followed, and the two women shared the sink to wash their hands. "You've met him, haven't you?"

"Met who?" Emily dried her hands on the soft, seafoam-green towel hanging from the round brass rack on the wall.

"Your neighbor, the golden god." After drying her hands, Nikki grabbed Emily by the shoulders. "Tell Aunt Nikki everything. Did he confess? Is he the man who's been writing you love letters and doing all that heavy breathing over the phone?"

Emily rolled her eyes upward and sighed. "Let's eat lunch." She went out of the bathroom and into the storage room, where a makeshift kitchenette had been put together along the back wall. "What did you bring today?"

"Tuna salad sandwiches, dill pickles and cherry vanilla yogurt for dessert." Nikki opened the compact refrigerator and retrieved the items, one by one, then placed them on the small, wooden table near the lone window in the storage room. "You can change the subject a dozen times, but it won't work. You are going to tell me about meeting *him* and we both know it."

"Did you make some fresh tea?" Emily asked.

Nikki pulled a large pitcher of iced tea from the refrigerator. "What's his name? What did he say? Where's he from? What does he do for a living? Did you speak first or did he?"

Emily seated herself and arranged the pink napkins, plastic spoons and paper plates that Nikki had laid on the table. "I wish I'd never told you about him."

"The first man since Stuart that you've been attracted to! Of course you had to tell me about him." Nikki sat down, then tucked her feet back on the bottom support round of her chair. "Weeks of watching him, and now you've met him. It must have happened yesterday because you didn't say a word about it Saturday."

"I was on the beach yesterday afternoon, doing some sketches, when he just came walking along." Emily unwrapped her sandwich and pulled the two cut halves apart. "He watched me for a while, then came closer and closer."

"Does he look as good close up as he did at a distance?"

"Better."

"Better!" Nikki's expressive hands waved about in the air, slamming into the pitcher.

Emily grabbed the iced-tea container, sighing when she realized she had avoided a minor disaster. "I'll pour the tea."

"Forget the tea. Tell me more about our muscle-bound blonde. Is he or is he not your mystery man?"

"I really don't think he is," Emily said. "He doesn't seem the type. I doubt he knows anything about poetry and the letter I received quoted Byron and Shelley. Besides, Ray Mitchell could probably have any woman he wanted without resorting to secret phone calls and letters."

"Any woman?" Nikki asked. "Does that include you? Just what happened between y'all?"

"We talked for a while. That's all."

"You're holding back." Nikki bit into her large dill pickle.

"We have a date for dinner tonight. I'm cooking."

Nikki choked on the pickle. She spit it out on her napkin, her watery eyes opening wide. She stared at Emily's smiling face. "You have a date with a stranger? You, Emily McLain Jordan?"

"I can't explain it, Nikki. I've never felt anything like this before in my life. Mitch is so...so...so much a man."

"Uh-oh. Are you ready for that? I mean, you've said you'll never...that is—"

Heat spread up Emily's neck, flushing her face a warm rose beneath her tanned complexion. "Even if I'd like to have sex with Mitch, I won't. I can't."

"I've told you a thousand times that you cannot cut yourself off from life, from a future with a husband and kids, just because of your scarred back."

Reaching across the table, Emily patted Nikki's hand, then gave it a tight squeeze. "I wish you were right about that, but... I've offered Mitch friendship and he's accepted."

"If he's anything like you've described him, then a man like that isn't going to settle for hand-holding."

"Did I do the wrong thing by inviting him to dinner?" Emily wondered if she wasn't asking for trouble, asking to be hurt when Mitch wanted more and she rejected his advances. Or even worse, when she agreed to more and he rejected her. She couldn't bear the thought of Mitch seeing her scarred back and being repulsed by it.

"No, you did the right thing. It's long past time you were dating someone besides Charles Tolbert. And there's no law that says you have to have sex. Look at me, I've dated half the eligible bachelors in the world and I haven't had sex with any of them."

Emily knew that Nikki's reluctance to have sex was based on her memories of her abusive stepfather. Warner Richards had been wealthy, ruggedly handsome and very macho. He'd also been a wife beater and a child abuser. His treatment of Nikki had made her fear most men, especially rugged, powerful, macho men. And although Nikki flitted from one boyfriend to the next, like a love-starved butterfly, she had never given her heart to any man.

"Someday, Nikki, you'll meet a man...a man like Mitch, and you'll want him to make love to you."

"Maybe." Nikki sighed, shaking her head, tossing about her short reddish brown curls. "I'm just glad that you've finally met someone special, and that he's living right next door. It makes me feel better knowing you aren't out there all alone."

Emily lifted her sandwich to her lips. "Do you think the person who has called me and sent me a love letter could actually be dangerous?"

"Who knows? Maybe it is just Charles Tolbert or Rod Simmons or some other guy who has the hots for you," Nikki said. "But what if whoever this guy is, he wants more? He could turn out to be a stalker or a rapist or... Em, are you sure you trust this Ray Mitchell guy?"

"Pretty sure. He didn't even know my name until we introduced ourselves. Besides, there's no evidence pointing to him. And if it was Mitch, then now that I've agreed to a date, there shouldn't be any more phone calls or letters."

"I tend to agree with you. So, if it had been him, then there would be no need for him to send another letter, would there?"

"Well, yes, I suppose not. Why?"

Nikki drew an envelope from her pocket. "This came in the morning mail. I should have given it to you sooner, but—"

Emily snatched the letter out of Nikki's hand, ripped open the end of the envelope and drew out the plain white sheet of paper. "'My beloved Emily,'" she read. "'I arise from dreams of thee, in the first sweet sleep of night...'" Emily's hand trembled. The letter fell from her fingers, floating downward like an autumn leaf in the wind.

Nikki reached out and caught the romantic missive in midair. She scanned the page. "Whoever he is, he's smitten." Nikki laid the letter on the table. "Maybe you should call the police."

"And tell them what? That I've received another love letter?"

"Yeah, you're right. Maybe we're worrying about nothing. Maybe there's nothing more to these letters and phone calls than a guy too shy to tell you how he feels face-to-face." Nikki picked up her sandwich and bit into it, then chewed and swallowed quickly. She tapped her fingertips nervously on the table. "All the same, since you're sure this Mitch guy isn't the mystery man, I'm glad he's living next door, in case you need him. And I'm very glad that you're having him over for dinner. You could ask him, point-blank, if he's the one who's been writing to you and calling you."

"It's not him," Emily said. "But if you'd feel better, why don't you ask him yourself when he stops by the shop this evening?"

"I'll give him a thorough inspection and let you know what I think."

"You do that."

"Oh, don't worry, I will."

Mitch stood outside Zed Banning's office wondering what the hell he was doing there. He had a date with Emily, had promised to pick her up at her art supply store immediately after work. But his foreman at the construction site had given him a message from the big boss. Zed Banning wanted Mitch to drive over to Mobile to his office as soon as he left work.

Mitch shifted uneasily in the leather chair in the waiting area outside Zed's office. Zed's secretary had just left, telling Mitch that Mr. Banning was on a long-distance call and would be ready to see him momentarily.

He wasn't sure why Zed had sent him a message that he needed to see him. Was his old friend having second thoughts about hiring a man with a ruined reputation, whom no one else would touch with a ten-foot pole? Or had word reached Zed that Mitch was having problems with another worker, a real jerk named Buddy Crowell?

Or was Zed going to preach him another sermon on staying away from Emily Jordan?

Mitch knew that if Emily discovered the truth about his past too soon, she wouldn't want to be his friend. He needed a chance to win her trust before he told her that he was M. R. Hayden. He prayed that she would understand. If he could change the past he would.

Strange thing about Emily—she was the first woman he'd truly cared about in all the years since Loni had betrayed him. Once he'd met Emily, talked to her, touched her, he'd been afraid to tell her his real name. Afraid he'd lose her. Of course, he would have to tell her the truth—sooner or later. Ray Mitchell was really M. R. Hayden, a man hated by so many people— a man who'd lost his hard-earned construction firm along with every dime he had to his name, not to mention his reputation in the business and social worlds.

"Come on in, Mitch. Sorry to keep you waiting." Zed Banning stood in the doorway of his office, his broad shoulders almost touching each side, his big body filling the space.

"No problem," Mitch said. "But if this isn't a life or death situation, could we get this over with in a hurry? I've got a date tonight."

Zed raised his dark, bushy eyebrows, giving Mitch an is-that-so? look. "This won't take too long, but if it's going to run you late, give the lady a call."

"I gave her a quick call from a pay phone before I came over." Mitch followed Zed into his large, airy office. "I was supposed to pick her up right after work."

Zed eyed Mitch's appearance, the sweat-stained shirt, the

grime-covered jeans, the day's growth of beard. "Is the lady into bums?"

Mitch grinned. "We're going to pick up the fixings on the way home, and then while she gets dinner started, I'm going to run home and take a quick shower."

"The lady must live close." Zed motioned for Mitch to take a seat, then sat down behind his enormous black metal desk.

"As a matter of fact she lives in the cottage next to mine," Mitch said.

"Dammit man, what have you done?" Emitting a furious growl, Zed slammed one big hand down on his desk. "Have you lost your mind?"

Mitch sat down in a white leather chair strategically located in front of Zed's desk. The inquisition chair. The interview chair. "She's lonely, Zed. Very sad and very lonely. And very beautiful."

"A sad and lonely lady," Zed said. "Old buddy, you're asking for trouble. My advice is to stay away from her. You've got enough problems without sticking your neck in that particular noose."

"Yeah, you're probably right." Mitch eased his body to the edge of the chair, spread his legs and dangled his hands between his knees. "But I'm afraid I can't take your advice. I need Emily in my life right now."

"You didn't tell her who you are, did you?"

"I didn't tell her I was Mitchell Ray Hayden. I told her that I was Ray Mitchell."

"Secrets have a way of coming out. If you won't take my advice about staying out of Emily Jordan's life, then at least don't wait too long to tell her who you are."

"I can't believe she's lived in the Gulf area all her life and the two of you have never met. I thought you were acquainted with every beautiful woman in South Alabama." Mitch knew for a fact that Zed Banning had a reputation when it came to women—lovely, sophisticated women. But to Mitch's knowledge, his friend hadn't been involved in a serious relationship since his divorce. Zed had been in the middle of a messy settlement when Mitch had first worked for him twelve years ago.

"Maybe it's lucky for me that our paths haven't crossed. I don't think she's my type. And she's not your type, either," Zed said. "From what I've learned about Emily Jordan, the woman isn't the type for one-night stands or brief affairs. There doesn't seem to have been anyone special in her life since her husband died."

"If you're trying to tell me that I can't be that special man in her life, don't bother. I already know. All I can be is her friend. And once she knows who I am, I'll probably lose her friendship."

"Keep that in mind, and make sure you don't lead her on and wind up breaking her heart. You've already got enough guilt to handle."

"For a man who's never met the lady, you seem awfully concerned," Mitch said.

"I knew that once you saw her, you'd find a way to meet her, but it never entered my mind that you'd ask her for a date."

"I didn't plan it. It just happened."

"Being her friend is a mistake," Zed said. "Becoming more than a friend would be suicidal."

"Don't you think I know that?"

"You'd be better off and so would she if you found yourself some bosomy blonde."

"I've had my fill of cheap blondes and meaningless one-night stands." Mitch glared at his old friend. "For the last five years there hasn't been one meaningful thing in my life. As crazy as it sounds, I want Emily Jordan's friendship. I need to know what it's like to go out on a real date, to be with someone honest and decent and—"

"Tell her who you are. Don't wait. If you wait too long, you'll regret it." Zed leaned back in his chair, his dark eyes riveted to Mitch's face, then abruptly changed the subject. "Tatum has called me more than once about your run-ins with Buddy Crowell."

"So that's what this little visit is all about." Mitch jumped up, balling his hands into fists at his sides. "The guy's a troublemaker. He stays on my case all the time."

"Yeah, well, try to stay out of his way. If Tatum has to fire the guy, I don't want him having cause to fire you along with him.''

"I knew it wasn't going to be easy starting all over again as a construction worker. I was never very good at being just one of the Indians. I always wanted to be chief. Hell, maybe I was a fool for ever letting you talk me into coming back to work for you.'' Mitch rammed his fist into his open palm.

Zed slid his feet off his desk, letting them drop to the floor. "You had to come back to the Gulf and face your ghosts, confront all the guilt that's been eating away at your insides for the past five years. You couldn't go on the way you were. You were well on your way to becoming an alcoholic. You were already a bum on the streets, wondering where your next meal was coming from.''

"And what have I got now?''

"A job, a place to live, a chance for a real life." Zed stood, walked around his desk and stopped directly in front of Mitch. "And a date tonight with a beautiful lady.''

Mitch sucked in his breath. Emily. "I should get out of her life now, while the gettin's good.'' Mitch laughed, a mixture of disgust and pain. "But dammit all, Zed, I can't walk away from her.''

"Just be up-front with her. Tell her who you are.'' Zed gripped Mitch's shoulder in his huge hand.

"I'll tell Emily who I am and all about my past just as soon as we get to know each other a little better.''

"Don't wait too long. Someone else will tell her if you don't.''

"You?''

"No, not me. But despite how much you've changed physically, sooner or later, you'll run into someone who'll recognize you.'' Zed hesitated momentarily. "You may not remember this, but Fowler Jordan, Stuart Jordan's uncle, came to court every day of your trial. The man memorized your face. If you ever meet him, it's possible that he'll know who you are.''

"Then I need to avoid Fowler Jordan until after I've told Emily the truth," Mitch said.

When Mitch rode up in front of the Paint Box and saw Emily's champagne-beige Buick LeSabre, he realized that when they'd made arrangements to meet, neither of them had thought about the fact that they'd be in separate vehicles. Of course, some people might not call his Harley-Davidson low-rider a vehicle.

The Paint Box was located in a small, two-story building in the middle of Fairhope. The outside walls were painted a pale yellow and boasted dark-green awnings over the front door and display windows. Canvases of various sizes had been hung in the windows, along with a variety of imaginatively displayed art supplies.

He glanced into the shop and saw Emily waiting for him just inside the full-glass front door.

He pulled off his helmet, hung it on his cycle and swung his legs over and off. When he neared the entrance, Emily opened the door, her eyes bright with greeting, her mouth curved into a welcoming smile.

"Sorry, I'm late," Mitch said. "Like I told you when I phoned, I had a call from my boss, so I had to run over to Mobile."

"No problem." Emily stepped aside to give him room to enter. "I just realized when I saw you drive up on your motor-cycle that we have separate means of transportation."

"So we do." He loved the look of her, the soft, feminine curves of her body, the sweet, warm smell of her skin and hair, the slow, syrupy drawl with which she spoke. "I guess we were just too eager to see each other again that we didn't think this thing through."

"Why don't you ride on his motorcycle?" Nikki stepped out from behind the counter and offered Mitch her hand. "Hi, I'm Nicole Griffin, Emily's business partner and friend."

"I can't go with Mitch," Emily said. "I have my car."

"So, I'll leave my old clunker here. Nobody would steal that pile of junk. I can drive your car home tonight, then stop by and pick you up in the morning."

For such a petite woman, Nikki shook Mitch's hand with a firm grasp. Mitch assumed she was around Emily's age since they seemed to be close friends, but she looked like a teenager with her slender curves, wide hazel eyes and cropped cinnamon hair.

"I think your friend has a good idea there," Mitch said.

"I don't know." Emily hesitated, wondering if she had the nerve to ride on the back of Mitch's motorcycle. A motorcycle!

"Come on, pretty lady, live dangerously." Mitch grinned at her, that devastatingly sexy grin she was finding more and more irresistible.

"How are we going to carry a grocery bag on that thing?" Emily pointed outside to the Harley.

"No problem," Mitch said. "We'll just put the stuff in my saddlebags."

"Oh. Well, all right...I guess."

Nikki picked up Emily's straw bag off the counter. "Mitch, could you excuse us for just a minute?"

"Sure, I'll take a look around the store." Amused by the elflike Nikki, Mitch watched out of the corner of his eye as he walked away. Nikki grabbed Emily and pulled her behind the counter. He wondered what was going on. Girl talk, no doubt.

Nikki lowered her voice to a breathless whisper. "He's gorgeous. I mean drop-dead gorgeous!"

"I know," Emily said.

"Here, take your purse and give me your keys. I don't want him to know we're talking about him."

"I have a feeling he's already figured that out."

"Em?"

"What?"

"I think you're right. A guy like that isn't going to waste time writing silly love letters or making breathy phone calls." Nikki glanced at Mitch and sighed dramatically. "I'm sure he knows that if he wanted a woman, all he'd have to do is snap his fingers and she'd come running."

"So I have your unequivocal approval to date Mitch?"

"You have more than that," Nikki said. "I want you to have a wonderful time tonight. If the subject of sex comes up, don't dismiss it too quickly." Nikki grabbed the keys Emily pulled out of her purse.

"Just take the car keys. I'll need my house key to get into the cottage for my wild night with Mitch," Emily said teasingly.

"I sure hope there's a tender, gentle lover beneath all those bulging muscles." Nikki squeezed Emily's arm. "Have fun. Live a little for a change. But be careful."

"I will." Emily walked over to Mitch and placed her hand on his back. He felt warm and hard, and Emily wished that she were touching his naked flesh instead of his cotton shirt. She jerked her hand away.

"Ready to go?" he asked.

"I guess, but...what about a helmet for me? Isn't it against the law to ride without one?"

"I've got an extra."

"Oh. Okay." Why did he carry an extra helmet? For whatever woman with whom he chose to share the ride? Emily scolded herself for the raw feelings of jealousy that cut through her heart. She had no claims on Mitch. They were little more than strangers.

Just as Mitch and Emily headed for the door, a lanky young man walked down the steps that led to the upstairs rooms Emily used for her art studio. He held a stack of books in his hands. "Emily, do you mind if I take these books home with me?"

Emily pivoted slowly, smiling as she faced her student. "No, of course not, Rod. You're always welcome to borrow any of my books."

Mitch noticed the way the boy was staring at Emily, a shy but hungry look in his gray eyes. The young man was far too good-looking with his curly black hair and lean body. Who was this kid? And exactly what was his relationship to Emily?

"You need to hurry and finish up in the studio, though," Emily said. "Nikki will be closing the shop very soon."

"I didn't mean to stay so long," Rod said. "I just got busy and forgot the time. I'll clean up and head on out." Rod glanced meaningfully at Mitch. "Are you in a hurry, Emily? I'm sorry if I—"

"Go on, you two," Nikki told Emily, then turned to Rod. "Emily has a date tonight, so she's leaving—right now. But I'll hang around a few more minutes. Long enough for you to get squared away."

"Yes, ma'am. Thanks." Rod took several steps backward, up the stairs. But he watched while Nikki Griffin ushered Emily and Mitch out the door.

Mitch glanced back at the boy who glared at him, anger and jealousy marring the perfection of his handsome face. The kid had it bad for Emily. Mitch wondered if she knew. Surely she did.

"Bye, you two. See you tomorrow, Emily." Nikki stood in the open doorway, watching while Mitch helped Emily onto his cycle and handed her a metallic green helmet, then adjusted the strap under her chin.

When the Harley roared to life beneath them, Emily slipped her arms around Mitch's waist, leaning into him, absorbing the security of his strong back. As they pulled out of the parking spot, Emily turned, her gaze catching sight of Nikki in the doorway. She was smiling.

As they rode along the highway, Emily clung to Mitch, wondering all the while if she'd lost her mind. Emily McLain Jordan had never done anything so wildly exciting in her life. She had always preferred walks on the beach, classical music, poetry, art, good literature and men as gentle and cultured as Stuart had been. But Mitch was a man with rough edges, aggressive, possessive and earthy. With him the music would be earsplitting loud, jazz or hard rock. And she didn't doubt for a minute that his taste in literature ran to more basic male interests—sports, cars and adventure.

For five long years she had isolated herself from life. And now, for the first time, she was reaching out to embrace the joy of being alive, the thrill of sexual attraction, the danger of risking her life and her heart to a stranger.

Dear Lord, please don't let me regret this night.

Chapter 5

The sun lay on the horizon like a giant orange ball nestled against multicolored layers of cotton. Rays of twilight sunshine melted into the earth to the west and sent soft shadows across the waters of Mobile Bay and to the south. Boats of all sizes lined the docks of the Fair Harbor Marina.

Mitch drove his Harley up in front of the Fly Creek Fish Market. Once he'd dismounted, he turned to Emily, lifted her up and off, then lowered her slowly to her feet. Their bodies touched intimately as they stood together, alone in their own little world of sexual awareness. He removed her helmet and hung it on the Harley, then took off his.

Emily stared at Mitch, into his stark, ice-blue eyes, and her breath caught in her throat. A tremor of sexual longing rippled through her. Mitch was so big and tall and utterly masculine, and his casual attire of jeans and cotton knit shirt enhanced his rugged, blond good looks.

Mitch dressed like the man he was—a laborer, a blue-collar worker, who drove a motorcycle and drank beer straight from the bottle. But Emily didn't mind that his social position didn't equal hers. His athletic, tanned body and ruggedly handsome face couldn't be bought at any price. He was the most fascinating man she'd ever met.

"I'm glad you weren't in the mood for steaks," Mitch said, nodding at the naturally aged wood structure behind them. "I've been told that this fish market sells some of the best seafood in Alabama."

"I make a wonderful clam linguine." Emily stepped back away from Mitch, deliberately putting some distance between them. "Would you be insulted if I offer to pay for the groceries?"

Mitch glared at her, realizing she suspected he had just enough money in his wallet to cover the cost of their dinner, which would mean he'd be eating bologna sandwiches the rest of the week. Paying rent for the cottage next to Emily took a hefty chunk out of his paycheck.

"Call me old-fashioned, pretty lady, but on a first date, I consider it my privilege to pay for dinner. I'll buy the fixings and clean up afterward if you'll prepare our feast. I'm afraid I'm not much of a cook."

"I'd say that's a fair deal."

Mitch couldn't keep himself from inspecting the elegantly slender woman standing so close to him. Emily had pulled her dark hair away from her face and secured it with a pale-yellow ribbon that perfectly matched her long-sleeved yellow blouse and skirt. The soft fabric clung to her curves in a flattering yet seductive way. The golden locket lay atop the middle of her chest, dipping into the hollow between her breasts.

Emily eyed him suspiciously, then took a tentative step toward him. "You make me wonder what you're thinking when you look at me that way."

"What way?" Mitch slipped his arm around her waist, and smiled when she didn't try to pull away from him.

"Like you're wondering...well, you know...about—"

"You're a very suspicious woman, Emily. I agreed to be your friend. If you think I have an ulterior motive for asking you for a date, why did you say yes?"

"Because I'm very attracted to you." The warm flush of embarrassment crept into her cheeks.

He knew Emily's honesty shouldn't have surprised him, but it did. His past experiences had left him skeptical about the entire female sex. Loni's betrayal had taught him not only that he shouldn't trust a woman's pledge of undying love and devotion, but that he didn't dare trust his own emotions. Mitch couldn't help wondering if he had the guts to be as honest with Emily.

"I'm very attracted to you, too." He guided her toward the market. "You're different from any woman I've ever known."

They entered the seafood market, the odor of the ocean's bounty ripe in the air.

"I'm quite old-fashioned, aren't I?" Emily asked. "I suppose it comes from having been raised by my grandmother."

"You're an old-fashioned lady who's attracted to me, yet wants only friendship," he whispered into her ear. "I'm a guy down on his luck who hasn't wanted anything from a woman but a good time in a long while."

Feeling the touch of his hand on her back in every nerve ending of her body, Emily swallowed. Her cheeks flared crimson. "They say that opposites attract."

"In our case that old idiom seems true." Mitch took a deep breath, aware that the conversation was getting a bit too heavy. At this rate, he'd be telling her that he wanted to make love to her tonight. "Come on, let's get our clams and head for home."

The last fading rays of sunlight spread a soft riot of color across the horizon just as they turned off Scenic 98 and drove up Emily's long, tree-lined driveway. Mitch parked his Harley, helped Emily off, removed their helmets and carried the groceries inside through the back door. He had wondered what the interior of her house looked like. Now he knew. The inside of Emily's beachfront cottage was every bit as classy, as elegant, as feminine as the woman herself.

Emily lifted the items from the small sacks Mitch had set on the kitchen counter. "I can handle things from here if you want to run home and shower."

"Yeah, thanks. I won't be long." He reached out and touched her face, running his knuckles across her cheek, brushing his fingertips under her chin.

The corners of her mouth quivered. Her lips parted on a sigh. She simply couldn't believe the heady effect the mere touch of his hand against her face had on her.

"Take your time, Mitch. I need to freshen up, too."

Circling the back of her neck with his big hand, he pulled her gently toward him, burying his face in the soft dark tendrils of hair that the wind had freed from their confinement. "Don't freshen up too much." He breathed in her sweetness. "You smell like the wind and the sea and woman."

Emily's heart fluttered inside her chest like a trapped bird trying to escape. His lips grazed her ear. She sucked in her breath.

"I'll be back." Mitch stepped away from her, smiled, turned around and walked out of the kitchen.

Emily tried to return his smile, but all she could manage was a weak nod. This isn't going to work, she told herself. No matter what he said, Mitch wanted more than friendship from her. His every look, his every word, his every touch was a form of seduction.

If only she weren't so afraid. But how could she not be? No man would want to make love to a woman whose body was hideously scarred. How could he run his hands over her damaged flesh and not cringe?

After dinner tonight, she would have to end their relationship before it went any further, but she wanted—no, she needed—the pleasure of one beautiful evening with Mitch.

Emily had set the table with her best—Royal Doulton china, sterling silver flatware and Swedish crystal. She had arranged the centerpiece hurriedly, using the spring flowers from her small flower bed in the yard. The tapering candles, four all together, in their crystal double holders, flickered like twinkling stars, casting a warm glow over the room. Nervously, Emily patted the sides of the pastel-green cushion in the antique French cane-back chair on which she sat.

The last man for whom she'd prepared dinner had been her husband. The night before he died. The night before her whole world had been destroyed.

Emily looked across the table at Mitch, smiled when he smiled at her, then forced her gaze away from his. Glancing around the room, she absorbed the atmosphere she had created. The romantic, intimate mood she had set. Her dining room was small, but she had redecorated it during the past year, using many of Hannah McLain's treasures. Uncle Fowler had encouraged her in every way possible to renew her interest in the world, to embrace life again. This house, this summer cottage on the eastern shore of Mobile Bay, had come to mean more to Emily than a home. Each room was a precious part of the sanctuary she had created for herself. Each picture on the wall, each lamp, each piece of furniture, had been selected and installed as therapy for a woman who hadn't cared whether she lived or died.

A stylized draped fabric wallpaper wrapped the dining room. A room-size needlepoint rug covered the floor. And an antique Country French hutch held her collection of *trompe l'oeil* plates. The pewter chandelier was an antique and matched the one in her living room.

"I'm afraid I'm not dressed appropriately." Mitch cast an apologetic glance at his clean but faded jeans and his best shirt, the long-sleeved cream cotton shirt he'd bought with his first paycheck.

"Don't be silly. You look fine." Emily couldn't imagine a man more handsome than Mitch. Certainly not one more masculine.

"I look out of place at your dinner table. You're wearing silk and I'm in old denim."

"I think silk and denim make an interesting combination, don't you?" Sadness and longing combined with the sympathy Emily felt for Mitch. "I didn't dress this way or serve our meal in the dining room to make you feel uncomfortable. I did it to impress you, to present myself and my home in the best light. I wanted tonight to be special."

Mitch uttered a rather unpleasant oath under his breath, then made a sound halfway between a grunt and a laugh. Hell, he didn't know what to believe. Had she said that because she felt sorry for him or had she really wanted to impress him? He didn't want her pity. He hadn't allowed anyone to pity him since...since he'd been a kid and his parents had often taken charity from the church in the small Mississippi town where they'd lived.

"You didn't have to wear that expensive pink silk dress or lay the table with your finest to impress me, pretty lady." Reaching across the table, he laid his palm open, extending her an invitation. "You're impressive enough all by yourself."

Emily stared at his hand for several seconds, listening to the drumming of her heartbeat. She laid her hand in his. "And you're impressive enough all by yourself, too."

"I don't ever want your pity, Emily. I grew up on pity and charity. The two always seem to go together, and believe me, they have a way of eroding a person's self-worth."

Emily understood all too well what he meant. She'd been given enough pity in the past five years to last her a lifetime. Pity did erode a person's self-worth. She was a prime example.

"Let's promise each other that, no matter what, pity for each other will never play a part in our friendship," Emily said.

Damn, why hadn't he thought before he'd spoken? He'd been touchy all his life about being pitied and often his first reaction to anyone's kindness was to suspect that they felt sorry for him. But Emily, who, no doubt, had been smothered with pity after the Ocean Breeze tragedy, would understand the damaging effects of pity on a person's pride.

"You have my promise," Mitch told her.

The intoxicatingly bluesy warmth of Stan Getz's "Who Would Care?" permeated the house, the saxophone's mellow tone weaving a sexy magic spell. Mitch had brought over a couple of his favorite jazz CDs, borrowed from Zed Banning's collection. He'd told Emily that they were mood music.

Mitch gazed into her warm brown eyes and saw the gentle softening of her expression, the easing of the tension he sensed had dominated her from the moment he'd returned to her cottage tonight.

Was the emotion in her eyes concern or something more? Dear God, he had no right to want it to be something more. But he did.

He held her hand securely, his gaze focused on her beautiful face. She didn't try to remove her hand from his, where it rested on the pristine white tablecloth.

Emily felt a nervous excitement spiral through her body when he continued staring at her with such absolute intensity. "Perhaps we should enjoy our dinner." She pulled her hand away from his, then removed the silver covers from one chafing dish and then another. "You said you liked clam linguine."

"I do."

He watched while she spooned the linguine onto their plates, then covered it with the cheesy clam sauce. She was very adept with her hands, every move deliberate, practiced.

"Should I pour the wine?" he asked, and when she nodded affirmatively, he uncorked the bottle and tilted it over her crystal glass. "I wasn't sure whether or not an old-fashioned lady like you would drink."

Emily couldn't stop herself from laughing at his comment. "On the contrary, old-fashioned ladies greatly enjoy wine with their meals. My grandmother even preferred a shot of straight whiskey from time to time."

"Then she was nothing like the God-fearing, churchgoing ladies in Sutra, Mississippi, where I grew up. Ladies there never drank anything stronger than coffee."

"So that's where you got all your strange notions about old-fashioned ladies, huh? Sutra, Mississippi?"

"And you got all of your old-fashioned notions from your grandmother. Obviously a very different source."

Emily tasted the clam linguine. "Delicious, if I do say so myself." She sipped the wine. "Quite good."

During the course of their meal, Mitch and Emily's conversation turned mundane, each intently aware of the other in a disturbing way.

Mitch wasn't sure where this evening would lead.

Emily tried to convince herself that she shouldn't see Mitch again.

He couldn't seem to think of anything except what it would be like to make love to her.

She prayed that her common sense would overrule the sensual emotions warming inside her, heated by every look he gave her.

"Do you want some of that pecan pie we picked up at the bakery?" Mitch asked.

"I couldn't possibly eat another bite right now," Emily said. "But you go right ahead and indulge, if you want."

Mitch stood up quickly, tossed his linen napkin on the table and waved his hand toward the living room. "I'd rather take you outside on the porch and look at the stars."

Emily's heart raced wildly. Her breath caught in her throat. Hesitantly, she allowed Mitch to assist her to her feet. When she felt his hard, strong arm circle her waist, she shivered, a combination of fear and desire rippling over her nerve endings.

Without a word, she followed him out of the dining room, through the living room and onto the front porch. Overhead the night sky shimmered with a bevy of twinkling stars and a three-quarter moon spread a golden glow over the bay. From inside the cottage, the soft strains of the George Shearing Quartet's rendition of "Isn't It Romantic?" drifted out and mingled with the spring breeze and the lulling melody of the Gulf waters caressing the shore.

They stood on the porch, gazing at the bay, while the warm night wind stroked their bodies. Mitch let his hand drop from Emily's waist to her hip. She leaned into his side, cuddling her head against his shoulder.

"You're very beautiful in the moonlight." Mitch reached out, fingering a strand of her dark hair where the gentle breeze had curled it about her face.

Emily wondered how many times he'd used that same line, and how many women had believed him. She desperately wanted to believe him, to believe that she was special to him. But she didn't dare. He might think she was beautiful right now, but what would he think if he could see her scars?

But neither fear nor common sense could stop Emily from responding. It had been such a long time since she had allowed herself to get this close to a man, and it felt good. It felt like sheer heaven to be held, to be told she was beautiful.

"Tell me about yourself," Emily said, glancing up at him.

He looked down at her uplifted face and wanted nothing more at that precise moment than to kiss her. "What do you want to know?"

"Tell me about your life, about who Ray Mitchell is."

He hesitated, gazing longingly at her. God, how he wanted this woman! "Dance with me." The words were a command, not a request.

Before she could reply, he turned her against him and pulled her into his embrace. The music from inside enveloped them in its sultry, sweet cry, the mellow expertise of Shearing at the piano. "None but the Lonely Heart" filled the two listeners with an intensity of emotions neither could deny.

Loneliness had become a way of life for Mitch. He couldn't remember a time when he hadn't been lonely. Even when Loni had lived with him. And even as a child in a full house, he had felt a sense of loneliness so great at times that he had choked on the tears his youthful masculinity never would have allowed him to shed.

"My father was a drunk and a gambler." Mitch's tone was so steady and unemotional that its very calmness made the words a declaration. "He tried to farm, but he failed at that, the way he had everything else in his life. He kept waiting for his luck to change, but he never did a damn thing to help himself."

Emily sighed. "My memories of my father are of a big, handsome man who was always smiling, laughing, enjoying life. My mother was a great deal younger and I think she married him mostly for his money."

Emily knew for a fact that her mother hadn't had any qualms about allowing her only child to live with her grandmother once she herself had received her share of Burke McLain's legacy.

Mitch ran his hand up and down Emily's back, then rested it just below her waist. With his other hand, he held her fragile fingers in a gentle grasp.

"My mother didn't give a damn about money," he said. "She believed that the best things in life were free, that money wasn't necessary for happiness."

"Then how on earth did she raise such a cynical son?" Emily could smell the faint fragrance of Mitch's spicy aftershave, a

scent so subtle that it blended perfectly with the raw, powerful
scent of manliness that emanated from him.

"You know the old saying about actions speaking louder than
words. Well, my mother's unconcern about material things kept
me and my two brothers and two sisters in ragged clothes and
with hungry bellies most of our childhoods."

A cold shiver sliced through Emily at the thought of Mitch
as a boy, perhaps hungry and cold and lonely...so lonely. Somehow she felt that little boy's loneliness as strongly as she could
feel the man who held her in his arms.

"Mitch—"

Placing the tip of his index finger over her lips, he stilled
their swaying bodies. "Hush. We made a bargain. Remember?
No pity. So, don't feel sorry for me. That isn't why I told you
about my childhood. I just... I don't usually bore my dates with
stories about my white-trash upbringing."

"You didn't bore me." Tears gathered in Emily's eyes. She
wished them away, but they stayed.

Mitch saw her tears. His body tensed. "Dammit, Emily, don't
cry for me!"

But Emily couldn't help feeling for him. She had been raised
in the lap of luxury, with every material possession at her fingertips. Yet she had been a lonely little girl after her father died
and her mother deserted her. If it hadn't been for her grandmother, she might be as bitter as Mitch was.

"What do you want from me, Mitch?"

"I want to make love to you," he said truthfully.

"Oh."

When he pulled her tightly against him, she could feel the
evidence of his desire. Flushed and trembling, she succumbed
to the temptation of his nearness when he lowered his head and
claimed her lips, tentatively at first, and then with a wild aban-
don that took her breath away.

He held her close. She lifted her arms to circle his neck, her
fingers threading through his thick, blond hair. With unerring
accuracy, his tongue delved into her mouth, seeking and finding
every soft, vulnerable spot. His exploration of her mouth continued while he caressed her, allowing his hands to roam up and

down her arms, then her back and finally her hips. He clutched her buttocks, drawing her hard against his arousal, rubbing her seductively into the pulsating warmth of his body.

"I ache with wanting you." His ragged-edged voice proclaimed the precarious hold he had over his emotions. "Since we first met on the beach, I've thought of little else but easing your clothes from your body and running my hands over every beautiful inch of you."

Emily froze in his arms. "Please, Mitch, you mustn't say such things to me."

His whispered seduction claimed her heart, but her rational mind reminded her that this man would be repulsed by the sight of her not-so-beautiful body. He had no way of knowing that ugly scars covered her back. She tried to pull away from him, but he restrained her.

"Why shouldn't I say such things to you? I want you to know how I feel. You make me crazy, pretty lady." *Crazy to be inside you.*

"Please let me go." Emily tried again to free herself of his hold, but he refused to release her.

"Give me a chance. Give us a chance." He brought her hand to his lips, kissing the top of her fingers. "Don't try to deny that you feel what's happening between us just as strongly as I do."

Emily submitted momentarily, laying her head on his chest. Loving the hard, hot comfort of his big body, she listened to the savage beat of his heart. "I feel the attraction between us, but I can't... I'm not going to give in to what I feel. I thought you understood that all I can offer you is my friendship."

Mitch dropped his hands from her body. He hated himself when he looked into her bourbon-brown eyes and saw the truth staring back at him. Emily was scared.

"I'm sorry." He cupped her chin in his hand. "Don't be afraid of me, Emily. I would never hurt you. I pushed a little too hard tonight, went a little too fast. I'll slow down. We'll move at your pace."

Dear God, he was an idiot. He hadn't meant to confess how

much he wanted her, how desperately he longed to make love to her. Their first date should have been less intense.

"Mitch, I... Please don't expect—"

"I expect you to forgive me for wanting more than you're ready to give." Leaning down, he kissed her on the forehead. "There hasn't been anyone, has there, since your husband died?"

"No. There hasn't been anyone." *And there never will be.* The tears that fell from her eyes came from self-pity, from the depths of her soul, which had endured so much to survive despite her heart's desire to die.

Mitch couldn't bear to see her upset, to know that she still felt her husband's loss so intensely. "Don't cry, Emily. Smile for me. Tell me that you forgive me. Tell me you'll be my friend."

Emily swallowed hard. Mitch wiped away her tears with his fingertips. She looked at him and smiled.

"There's nothing to forgive." More than anything she wanted to tell him the truth, to explain why she'd turned away from him, why she was afraid to become his lover. "I want us to be friends, Mitch. I want that very much."

Chapter 6

"This isn't turning out the way I'd thought it would," Mitch said. "All I had planned on doing was making sure she was all right and seeing if I could do something—anything—to help her."

Zed Banning glanced down into the glass of bourbon he held, grunted, then lifted the liquor to his lips and took a sip. "I tried to warn you. I told you to stay away from her, but you wouldn't listen to me. Then I told you to tell her who you are, but you didn't do that, either." Zed slammed the glass down on the coffee table, sloshing the contents up to the rim. "You're obsessed with Emily Jordan. You have been for the past five years. And now that you've met her, you're more obsessed with her than ever."

Mitch paced the floor in Zed's condo living room. He felt like a trapped animal. Trapped by his own unwanted emotions. Trapped by his desire for a woman he had no right to claim. "She's not like any woman I've ever known. She's so honest and—"

"Ladies never were your type, Mitch." Zed dropped his big body down into a plush navy leather chair.

"It's more than that." Stopping dead still, Mitch glanced at Zed and saw the concern in his old friend's eyes. "I'm about as confused as a man can get. I want to help Emily. I'd like to make everything up to her, to see that nothing bad ever happens to her again. But at the same time, I want her more than I've ever wanted anything in my life." Mitch raked his fingers through his hair and groaned a vulgar curse. "Go ahead and tell me I'm crazy. Tell me that I've screwed up again, that I've gone and painted myself into a corner."

"There's only one way out of this, only one decent thing to do."

"Tell Emily who I am."

"You've been seeing her for a couple of weeks now, and from what you've told me, things are getting pretty serious." Zed lifted one leg, crossing it over his other knee, then he reared back in the chair and crossed his arms over his chest. "If you're not honest with her soon, you're going to wind up breaking her heart, and you've already got more than enough guilt to deal with."

"I didn't plan on getting involved with her." Mitch walked behind the bar, reached into the liquor cabinet beneath and brought out the bottle of bourbon. "Not romantically involved. But I swear, Zed, if you ever saw her...if you ever talked to her...touched her..."

"Are you in love with her?"

Mitch laughed, the sound edged with pain. "Hell, I don't know the first thing about love. I wouldn't know it if it jumped up and bit me on the ass. But I know a lot about lust, about wanting a woman until you hurt with the wanting."

"So you just want to sleep with Emily, is that it?"

"No! Yes! Dammit, Zed, I told you that I'm confused. I feel so many different things when it comes to Emily that I can't straighten out all my emotions." Mitch gripped the bourbon bottle with white-knuckled tension.

"Maybe part of the confusion is that you know you've lied to her and that when she finds out the truth, anything can happen. She might hate you. She might forgive you. Hell, for all you know, she might already be in love with you. But one thing's for certain—you're going to wind up hurting her, whether you tell her the truth tonight or tomorrow or next month.''

Mitch poured the whiskey into a glass, recapped the bottle and shoved it aside. He lifted the glass, saluted Zed with it and then downed the bourbon. It blazed a trail down his throat and hit his stomach like a hot coal.

He caught Zed glaring at him and knew his friend was concerned about his drinking. ''Don't worry. This is my first drink tonight and it'll be my last. I've found out that drinking myself senseless doesn't solve my problems.''

''I'm glad you've made one right decision since coming back to the Gulf. I was beginning to wonder if you were incapable of learning from your mistakes.''

''Yeah, well, I've learned something else, too. Something I should have learned five years ago.'' Mitch took a deep, cleansing breath. ''When you give me advice, I should take it. If I'd listened to you, I would have told Emily that I was M. R. Hayden the day I introduced myself to her on the beach.''

''Better late than never.'' Zed glanced down at his gold Rolex. ''It's only eight o'clock. You can be in Point Clear in forty-five minutes. Tell her tonight.''

''She's not at home tonight. She's having dinner with her uncle here in Mobile. At his house. She's very fond of Fowler Jordan. She told me that he kept her alive when she wanted to die, after her husband's death....'' Mitch's voice trailed off. He couldn't bear to think about how much Emily had lost because of Styles and Hayden. ''Emily said that Jordan wouldn't let her give up. She thinks she owes him her life.''

''From what I've heard, she gave him five years of her life.''

''And he gave her five years of his.''

Zed lifted his arms up and behind his head, leaning back into the soft, thick cushion. ''I don't know Jordan personally, but we do have several friends and associates in common. And they say that Jordan is more than devoted to Emily. They say...'' Zed hesitated, focusing his attention directly on Mitch ''They say he's obsessed with her, and that when she moved out of his house, he was distraught. It seems Jordan had picked out a new mate for Emily, someone he knew he could control. Someone willing to take his nephew Stuart's place not only in Jordan's accounting firm, but in his home, as Emily's husband."

"Sounds like Jordan didn't intend to lose a niece when she remarried—he just planned on gaining an obedient replacement nephew."

"Be prepared for Jordan's wrath when he finds out about you," Zed warned. "Make no mistake about it. Jordan hates M. R. Hayden, and he'll do his damnedest to make sure Emily never forgives you."

Mitch stared at the whiskey bottle, badly wanting another drink. He was in an untenable position and he had no one to blame but himself. He had walked into this relationship with Emily Jordan with his eyes wide open, knowing full well he had no right to keep his identity from her. He had unintentionally helped ruin her life five years ago. But this time his common sense had told him that he was going to hurt Emily if he lied to her, and still he had gone with his gut emotions—his damn male desires—and pursued Emily like a lover.

Zed was right. He *had* been obsessed with Emily for five years and now that he'd gotten to know her, he was more obsessed than ever. If only he'd never talked to her, never touched her, never looked into her whiskey-brown eyes, never tasted her sweet, hot mouth.

What the hell was he going to do? He didn't want to lose Emily. Not as a friend. Not as a... As a what? A lover? They weren't lovers. Not yet. But Emily felt the sexual attraction between them as strongly as he did. He knew that she wanted him. With every look, every shy smile, every kiss, she told him silently of her desire. In spite of her declaration to the contrary, Mitch knew that sooner or later, she would allow him to become her lover.

But not if she knew he was M. R. Hayden.

Emily shifted uncomfortably in the carved mahogany Chippendale chair. She covered her mouth to hide a yawn.

"Are we boring you, my dear?" Fowler Jordan asked, his dark-blue eyes focusing on Emily.

"I'm sorry, Uncle Fowler." She smiled at him apologetically, her look beseeching his forgiveness for her rudeness. She knew one of the things Uncle Fowler had always liked about her was her old-fashioned Southern good manners. Grammy had set great store in good manners. As a child, Emily remembered countless times Grammy had said, "We don't do that." Or, "We prefer this." Always using "we" in the royal sense. Other people might be allowed to forget their good manners, but not the McLains.

"It appears that we've bored her so badly that we've taken away her appetite." Charles Tolbert glanced at the food on Emily's plate. "You've barely eaten a bite. All you've done is play with your food."

Emily cringed. Charles was such a fussbudget. When she had described his personality to Nikki, she'd said, "He's as fussy as a crotchety old woman." He wasn't really. It was just that he was so highly organized, his life so structured, his habits so predictable, his opinions so set, that he made little allowance for mistakes—in himself or others. And Uncle Fowler doted on Charles, as he had once doted on Stuart. She couldn't help but wonder if Stuart had been as straitlaced and uptight as Charles was and she simply had been too young and too in love to notice.

"My dear, you don't seem quite yourself tonight." Fowler neatly folded his linen napkin and laid it beside his plate. "Is there something wrong? Something bothering you?"

Telling Uncle Fowler about Ray Mitchell would be easier if Charles wasn't sitting across the table from her. She supposed she should have known that her uncle would invite Charles to join them tonight. After all, he was determined to see her marry Charles and the two of them resume the life that he'd planned for Stuart and her. Although she had dated Charles on and off for months before she'd moved out on her own, there had never been anything romantic between them. At least not on her part. And she'd never said or done anything to lead Charles on. She was fond of him, thought of him as a friend, but she certainly didn't love him. And marriage to him was out of the question. She had tried to make Uncle Fowler understand, but he'd told her to give herself time, that he knew Charles was the perfect man for her.

"There's something I think you should know." Avoiding eye contact with either man, Emily glanced across the room at the English Regency sideboard topped by a pair of bronze Chinese vases. "I—I've been seeing someone for a couple of weeks now."

Charles strangled on the sip of coffee he'd just taken into his mouth. His pale-brown eyes rounded in shock. Fowler straightened, stiffening his back.

"You've been seeing someone?" Fowler's jaw tightened; his eyes narrowed questioningly. "For a couple of weeks, and you're just now mentioning it to me?"

"I didn't want to give you something else to worry about," Emily explained, well aware that no matter how she handled this, her uncle would not be pleased. "I know you've been unhappy about my moving into Grammy's cottage and I know you think I'm insane for going into business with Nikki...and you've been so upset about the letters and phone calls. I just wanted to wait until I knew my relationship with Mitch was going to...to—"

"To what?" Charles asked. Pink stain splotched his pale face.

"Mitch? Mitch who?" The pulse in Fowler's throat throbbed. "Not that beach bum neighbor of yours? My God, girl, don't you realize he could be your tormentor."

"When you say 'seeing' him, do you mean 'dating' him?" Charles fiddled nervously with the handkerchief folded neatly into the front pocket of his navy blue blazer. A fastidious dresser, Charles always looked as if he'd just stepped from the pages of a *GQ* ad. But despite his attractive appearance, Emily found his light-brown hair and faded-brown eyes as boring as his personality.

She faced Charles. "Yes, I've been *dating* Mitch." She turned to her uncle. "Yes, Ray Mitchell is my neighbor. And he isn't a beach bum. He's a construction worker. He's helping build a new resort in Gulf Shores for the Banning Construction Company. He and Zed Banning are personal friends."

"A construction worker?" Charles gasped. "You're dating a

manual laborer? Whatever could you possibly see in a man like that?''

Emily groaned internally and tried not to allow her aggravation with Charles to show on her face. What did she see in Mitch, a common manual laborer? Neither Charles nor her uncle would want to hear her honest answer to that question. Mitch was the most devastatingly masculine man she'd ever known, and the most intriguing. And he made her feel like a woman. Not a lady. A woman. With deep, hungry desires and burning passion.

"You say this Mitchell is a personal friend of Zed Banning?'' Fowler asked.

"Yes. They've known each other for twelve years.''

Fowler rubbed his forefinger and thumb up and down his chin. "Perhaps I should call Banning and ask him a few questions about this man. After all, we don't know anything about—''

"Don't you dare!'' Emily knotted her hands into fists and held them in front of her, trying desperately not to jump up and run. "I appreciate your concern for me, but I'm perfectly capable of making my own friends and choosing whom I want to date.''

"Yes, of course you are,'' Fowler said. "I didn't mean to imply that you weren't. I simply thought that a good word about Mr. Mitchell from a man of Zed Banning's reputation would put all our minds at ease.''

"My mind is at ease.'' Relaxing her hands, Emily folded them together and placed them in her lap. "Mitch is a wonderful man. He's kind and considerate and caring.''

"Have you told him about the phone calls and letters you've been receiving?'' Fowler asked.

"No, I haven't. You and Nikki are the only two people I told.'' She glanced meaningfully at Charles. "And you told Charles.'' Against my wishes, she wanted to add, but didn't. "But I'm going to tell Mitch, now that I've decided to continue seeing him.'' She glared directly at Charles. "Yes, that means I'm going to continue dating him.''

"Well, you certainly can't be serious about this man,'' Fowler said. "After all, you barely know him. I'm sure that whatever...physical attraction...you feel for him will diminish when you realize the two of you have nothing in common."

"You could be right, Uncle Fowler. But for now, I'm not going to stop seeing Mitch. As a matter of fact, I've decided to—"

"You aren't going to sleep with him!" Charles looked pleadingly at her.

"What I was trying to say is that I've decided to give my relationship with Mitch a chance to develop into something more than friendship."

"I suppose Nikki Griffin has been encouraging you in this relationship with Ray Mitchell." Fowler's slender fingers clutched the napkin beside his plate, his hand forming a fist around the linen.

"Nikki wants me to be happy," Emily said. "And she knows Mitch makes me happy."

"Then perhaps I should meet this young man." Fowler glowered at Charles when Charles cleared his throat loudly. "Why don't you bring him to the house for dinner this weekend?"

"Thank you, Uncle Fowler. I'd like that very much. I'll ask Mitch."

Emily said a silent prayer of thanks. Fowler Jordan was as dear to her as her own father had been. She wanted and needed his approval. Once he met Mitch, once he saw for himself how happy Mitch made her, then surely he would accept their relationship and cease his efforts to pair her with Charles. But whether he did or not, she wasn't going to stop seeing Mitch. She wasn't going to let anything come between her and the man she was falling in love with.

Emily tossed her handbag and key ring down on the mahogany-and-walnut bowfront commode in the small foyer, then turned and locked the front door. She had left lights on in the foyer, hallway and living room, as she always did. Ever since being engulfed in heavy, black smoke during the fire five years ago, she had what some people would call an unnatural fear of the dark.

She unzipped her dress before she reached her bedroom, then the moment she opened the door, she flipped on the light switch and kicked off her heels. When she sat down on the edge of her bed and slithered out of her panty hose, she noticed the light on her answering machine blinking. She punched the Message button and listened to Nikki reminding her of their plans to meet and have breakfast in the morning with the manager of the French Quarter Art Gallery in Fairhope.

Emily stripped out of her slip and bra and pulled a pair of lavender silk pajamas from the top drawer of her cherry armoire.

The next message began. The moment Emily heard the muted voice, she stilled instantly, apprehension shivering through her.

"'Nothing in the world is single; all things by law divine, in one spirit meet and mingle. Why not I with thine?'" The voice quoted Shelley. "If you need someone, sweet Emily, why not me? Why him? He isn't worthy of you. He could never care for you the way I do."

Oh, God! It was her mystery man again. And he knew about Mitch. Only a handful of people knew she was dating Mitch. Nikki. Uncle Fowler. Charles. And Rod. And Mitch's friend Zed Banning. But she hardly thought her secret admirer would be Mr. Banning, since she'd never even met the man. But she knew her uncle wasn't harassing her, and she didn't want to believe that Charles or Rod was tormenting her with these phone calls and "love" letters.

The second message ended and a third began. "Where are you, Emily? Are you with him?" the voice asked. "I can't bear to think of you with him. You should be with me, in my arms. I should be the one kissing you, caressing you. Not him."

Emily clasped her hands together tightly in a prayerful gesture, took a deep, calming breath and reminded herself that whoever the man was, he hadn't really threatened her in any way. He sounded more like a lovesick suitor than a stalker. But she couldn't help feeling a little scared whenever he telephoned or whenever she received a letter from him. He'd made no move to harm her physically, but nevertheless, his unwanted attention was taking a toll on her nerves.

Several loud, heavy knocks at the front door gained Emily's

immediate attention. She jumped and gasped simultaneously. *Get a grip. Stay calm. Go see who's at the door.* She retrieved a thin, lavender silk robe from the closet, slipped it on and walked down the hallway. She saw a man's silhouette through the half-glass front door. A big man. When she reached the foyer, she hesitated momentarily before she walked over and looked outside. Mitch! Thank goodness. Breathing a sigh of relief, she unlocked and opened the front door.

Bracing one hand on the outer door frame, Mitch leaned forward. "Hi."

His broad, devilish grin created butterflies in Emily's stomach. She had never reacted to another man the way she did Mitch, on a purely sexual level. "Hi yourself."

"Is it too late?" He inspected Emily from head to toe. His grin widened. "This is the first time I've seen you in your pjs. Very sexy sleepwear for a lady who sleeps alone."

"I wear them for myself. I like nice things. Besides, I hardly call what I'm wearing sexy. Every inch of me from shoulders to ankles is covered."

Mitch reached out and placed his finger in the hollow of her throat, then slowly ran his finger downward, stopping at the top button. "Not quite everything is covered."

Emily's breath caught in her throat. Her heart pounded wildly. "How—how was dinner with your friend?"

Mitch removed his finger. "Is it too late for me to come in for a while?"

"Oh, no. Forgive me. Where are my manners?" *Every time that man touches you or even looks at you, your good sense goes out the window,* she scolded herself. "Please, come in." She stepped back to allow him entrance.

When he came inside, he slipped his arm around her waist and drew her close. He kissed her on her forehead, then released her and walked into the living room. "Zed and I called out for pizza, then we just sat around and talked. How was dinner with your uncle?"

Emily groaned inwardly, knowing she didn't dare tell Mitch about Uncle Fowler and Charles's cross-examination of her and their efforts to persuade her to stop seeing him.

"Uncle Fowler wants me to bring you to dinner one night soon. This weekend, if you're free."

Mitch tensed, every muscle in his body freezing. Fowler Jordan wanted to meet the man Emily was dating. Give him the once-over, no doubt. But Mitch couldn't meet Jordan. There was a good chance he might recognize him as M. R. Hayden. No, he had to tell Emily the truth himself. And soon.

"Could we put off dinner with your uncle until later?" Mitch asked. "I had special plans for us tomorrow night."

"What sort of special plans?" Emily sat down on the sofa and motioned for Mitch to join her.

"I booked us a dinner cruise."

"You did? Oh, Mitch, how roman— How very nice."

"Weren't you going to say, 'how romantic'?" He sat down beside her, placed his arm across the back of the sofa and eased his body close against hers.

"Yes, I was, but...I feel sort of silly. I'm the one who set the rules. We were going to be friends. Nothing more. Friends don't go on romantic dinner cruises."

Mitch slid his arm down and around her shoulders, turning her toward him in the process. "I think we both know that we're past the friends stage of our relationship, if we were ever in that stage. I think I've been in the...uh...'romantic' stage since the first day we met."

"I suppose, if I'm honest with you and with myself, I'll have to admit that I've never been able to think of us as just friends, either."

Mitch ran his hands up and down her arms, caressing her tenderly. "Before our relationship goes any further, there are some things you need to know about me. Things that could make a big difference to you."

"I can't imagine anything that could change the way I feel about you." Emily lifted her hand to his face. Looking into his blue, blue eyes, she stroked his cheek. "I've become very fond of you in a very short period of time. I can hardly believe we've known each other only a couple of weeks."

"I feel the same way." Mitch laid his hand over hers and pressed her palm against the side of his face. "I've never known

anyone like you. Anyone as kind and loving and honest. Don't
you see, Emily, that's why I have to be honest with you. You
have a right to know the kind of man I am.''

"I think I already know." She placed her arms around his
neck and drew him to her, his lips a hairs breadth away.
"You're strong yet tender. Rough yet gentle. Loving, understanding, honest—"

"Not honest, honey. Not honest with you about..." Dear God
in heaven, how could he tell her? How could he bear to see that
sweet, trusting look wiped off her beautiful face? She cared
about him, truly cared about him, in a way no other woman ever
had. And he cared about her, more than he'd ever cared for
another human being.

"You're scaring me a little bit," she said. "You make it
sound as if you're an ax murderer or something."

"Not quite that bad, but... That's why I booked the dinner
cruise tomorrow night. I want us to have one special night together before I tell you all about who Ray Mitchell really is.
When I bring you home tomorrow night, I'll tell you everything
and pray you can understand and forgive me."

She cupped his face in her hands. His strong, masculine face.
His rough, rugged, handsome face. "No matter what it is, I'll
try my best to understand. I promise. And I can't believe you've
ever done anything that I couldn't forgive."

Mitch swallowed hard. If only he could believe her. If only
she *could* forgive him once she knew he was M. R. Hayden. "I
want you to remember something. Will you, Emily? Will you
remember that I'd rather die than ever hurt you, that I'd do
anything to make you happy?"

"Oh, Mitch." She leaned into him, taking the initiative,
pressing her lips to his, wrapping her arms around him.

He responded instantly, catching fire like kerosene exposed
to a lighted match. Crushing her against him, his embrace surrounding her, Mitch thrust his tongue into her mouth and leaned
her backward slowly. Pressing her down on the sofa, he covered
her body with his.

He wanted her—wanted her now! But he couldn't—
wouldn't—take her. She had a right to know the real identity

of the man making love to her. If he took her now, before she knew who he was, she really would hate him. If there was any hope for them, any slight chance that she might one day give herself to him—to Mitchell Ray Hayden—then he had to tell her the truth. It was the only way.

Emily trembled with desire. Mitch knew the signs. Just a little more good loving and she'd be his for the taking. He drew her up and onto his lap, ending the kiss. He nuzzled her neck. She sighed.

"I'd better go before I...before we... I don't want to go," he said. "I'd like nothing better than to stay here and make slow, sweet love to you all night long. But we aren't ready for that yet. You aren't ready."

Her breath labored, her insides quivering with desire, Emily nodded in agreement, then slid off Mitch's lap and onto the sofa. "I—I have a couple of things I need to tell you, before we move forward with our relationship." She stood up and held out her hand to him. "Let me walk you to the door."

"Emily, whatever you have to tell me probably won't matter once I confess my deep, dark secret."

Mitch stood and followed her out into the foyer. When she opened the door, he walked past her and stood in the doorway, his gaze focused on her face. He didn't touch her again. He didn't dare. It had taken every ounce of his willpower not to give in to the desire he'd seen in her eyes, the desire that still smoldered just beneath the surface.

"I'll come over about six o'clock tomorrow evening."

"Six o'clock." Her voice was breathy.

Emily watched Mitch leave her porch and walk up the beach toward his house. She watched him until he was out of sight, then she went back inside, making sure to turn the lock. Leaning back against the door, she closed her eyes and willed her raging senses to calm. Thank goodness Mitch had called a halt before things had gone any further than a heated kiss. She was quaking inside with a yearning so strong it frightened her. What if Mitch hadn't ended things so quickly? What if things had gotten out of hand? What if he'd seen her scarred back? That couldn't happen. She had to tell him about her scars, had to let him see

the imperfect woman that she was. And she had to tell him about
her mystery man, someone who might pose a threat not only to
her, but to him, too.

Well, it seemed tomorrow night was going to be a night of
revelations. She hoped and prayed that once there were no secrets standing between them, she and Mitch would have a
chance for a future together. Even though he hadn't been specific about the sorrows from his past, Emily knew that Mitch
had lived through as much torment and loneliness as she had,
that whatever his deep, dark secret, she would understand and
forgive. And if he could accept her flawed body and still want
her, there wasn't anything that could ever keep them apart.

Chapter 7

Emily couldn't remember a time when she'd enjoyed herself so much, when she'd been so alive and happy, when she'd felt so cherished. She had grown up on the Gulf, her time divided between the family's home in Mobile and their cottage in Point Clear. No one appreciated the beauty of land and sea and sky more than she did, but sharing the splendor with a man like Mitch highlighted how truly romantic an evening cruise could be.

Emily had persuaded Mitch to drive her car tonight, and they'd both dressed up. She wondered if he'd bought himself a new sports coat and slacks or if he'd borrowed them from Zed Banning.

She'd been down Highway 90 numerous times, had visited the USS *Alabama* once with her father, once with her grandmother and again with Stuart.

The tour boat, the *Captain's Lady,* docked near the historical battleship, boarded promptly at six-thirty for the dinner cruise. She and Mitch had chosen their dinner from a three-entrée buffet and danced to the live music, then joined other couples to stroll the huge deck.

They stood on the deck, enjoying the sights that blended the past with the present. The breeze off the bay ruffled Emily's long, dark hair. She'd allowed it to fall freely down her back, secured only with a set of pearl combs that had belonged to her grandmother.

Mitch draped his arms around Emily, holding her in front of him as they gazed out at the last remnants of the May sunset. Long, white-tipped gray clouds spread across the horizon, floating over the coral red sky.

"I don't want this night to end." Emily rested the back of her head against Mitch's chest. "It's all been so perfect."

"Well, the cruise will end around nine-thirty, but the night doesn't have to end until you want it to." Mitch kissed her neck, his lips warm, moist and infinitely tender.

Emily shivered. "The magic of this night will end when we drive home. We can't go on pretending that...well, that we have no pasts and no futures, that our relationship can stay the way it is now."

"You're right, pretty lady. We're going to have to face the truth, and I'm afraid some of my truths aren't very pleasant."

Emily turned in his arms, holding him about the waist as he did her. "I have a couple of things to tell you, too," she said. "One can wait until later. It's something more serious, something that could affect our...our ever... Anyway, the other thing has been bothering me for a while now. I should have already told you, but I wasn't really worried about it. But now that we're involved, you've become a part of it."

Mitch felt her tense in his arms, saw the frightened look in her eyes. "It's all right, Emily. Whatever it is, tell me."

"Before I tell you anything, I want you to understand that I'm not afraid. Not really. It's just that the phone calls and the notes—"

"What are you talking about?" Mitch didn't like the sound of this. His instincts told him that despite her denial of fear, Emily was afraid. But of what? Of whom?

"Maybe I should begin at the beginning."

"Best place to start."

"Several weeks ago, I began receiving strange phone calls."

"Threatening phone calls?" Mitch asked.

"No, not actually threatening. Just disturbing. He says things like he just wants to hear my voice and...he quotes poetry to me. Last night, he left two messages on my answering machine. He knows about you, Mitch. He told me that you weren't worthy of me, that you could never care about me the way he does."

"Damn! Do you have any idea who he is?"

"He disguises his voice, so if he's someone I know, I don't recognize him."

"You have contacted the police, haven't you?"

"No. Not yet. I just didn't think that there was anything they could do. Somehow he found out what my unlisted home telephone number is. But he usually calls me at work. And the numbers that showed up on my caller ID were numbers for pay telephones." Emily ran her hands nervously up and down Mitch's arms. "A couple of weeks ago, the letters began—love letters. He quotes poetry to me in the letters, too."

"And you have no idea who might be doing this to you?"

"Not really. Everyone has a theory," Emily said. "There's Charles Tolbert. He works for Uncle Fowler in his accounting firm and we dated on and off for several months. And there's one of my art students, Rod Simmons, who has a crush on me. And..."

"And?"

"Uncle Fowler thought it might be you," Emily admitted, shivering when she saw the deadly look in Mitch's cold blue eyes. "Before I got to know you, the thought crossed my mind that it might be you. But I never seriously thought it was you. I told Uncle Fowler that you would never—"

Mitch's insides tightened into painful knots. He gripped Emily's shoulders. "It isn't me, pretty lady. I swear. I'd die before I'd cause you pain, of any kind."

"Oh, Mitch." Tears glazed her eyes. "I know that. I trust you. Besides, why would you call and tell me I should stop seeing you?"

Mitch felt as if his guts had been ripped open. Emily trusted him! Dear God, if she knew the truth, knew who he really was, he'd be the last man on earth she'd trust.

He gently grasped Emily's face in his hands, holding her securely as he gazed into her trusting brown eyes. "Whoever this guy is and whatever his motive, I promise you that I'll protect you from him. I won't ever let anyone hurt you." His voice lowered to a whisper. "Not ever again."

Wrapping her arms around Mitch's waist, she hugged him, then stepped backward, separating their bodies. "This man probably isn't a real danger to me. After all, he hasn't done anything threatening, except—"

"Except warn you against me." For one brief instant Mitch's heart stopped. Good God, did someone know who he was? Did they know he was M. R. Hayden?

"I'm glad you told me about the situation. I'll always be only a phone call away." Mitch slipped his arm around Emily and led her from the deck's edge. "Let's walk."

"I didn't tell you before now because I didn't want you to think it was a big deal. But Nikki's been trying to convince me that my secret admirer might be a mass murderer or something."

A cold chill raced up Mitch's spine. "Nothing's going to happen to you as long as I'm around." *If you'll let me stay around once I tell you who I am.*

Sighing, Emily cuddled closer to Mitch's side. He slowed their walk, turned and gave her a brief, gentle kiss.

The cooling night breeze swept into the Buick through the open car window. The smell of the sea and sand and springtime saturated every breath Emily took. Neither she nor Mitch had spoken a word for the last few miles. She suspected that Mitch was cocooned in his own private thoughts and secret emotions, just as she was.

When they neared the cottage, Emily sat up straight, lifting her head from Mitch's shoulder. She gasped. "The lights are off."

"You must have forgotten to leave them on," Mitch said as he pulled the car into the drive at the side of the cottage.

"No, I didn't forget. I never forget. I always leave several lights on inside the house, day and night, whether I'm home or not." How could she explain to him about her deathly fear of the dark? Would he understand if she told him that ever since she'd been trapped inside the burning, smoke-filled Ocean Breeze Apartments, the darkness of night frightened her as nothing else in her life ever had? No one could truly understand unless he, too, had been enveloped in the evil, smoldering dark that had crept through her home, blotting out the light, absorbing the oxygen.

When Mitch touched her on the shoulder, Emily jumped and cried out.

"It's all right, honey. Give me your key and I'll go turn on the lights."

"No, you don't understand." Emily clutched Mitch's arm. "Something's wrong. I left the lights on this evening." Her heart raced. The palms of her hands moistened. Her body trembled ever so slightly. "I have an abnormal fear of the dark."

Mitch reached over and pulled her into his arms. "It's okay, Emily. We're all afraid of something, if we'll just admit it."

"I almost died in a fire once, years ago. Ever since, I've been irrationally afraid of the dark. The lights are always left on in my house."

For a split second the vision of long, dark hair draped over a fireman's shoulder, of a tattered pink satin nightgown, flashed through Mitch's mind. He forced the memory from his thoughts. This wasn't five years ago. This was here. Now. And this time he *could* do something to help Emily.

"Are you saying someone turned the lights off after we left?" he asked.

"Unless the power is out, then yes, that's exactly what I'm saying."

"You stay here in the car." Leaning across Emily, Mitch popped open the glove compartment and looked inside. "Good. Just what I need." He removed a yellow flashlight, closed the glove compartment, then lifted his head and smiled at her. "Don't worry, pretty lady." He kissed her cheek. "I'll go take a look around." He swung open the door and stepped outside.

"Mitch, please, be careful."

"I will." Leaning back inside the car, he kissed her on the nose.

Mitch moved cautiously around the house to the closed front door and found it locked. Then suddenly, as if it had been months instead of years, his military training came back to him. He slipped around the side of the cottage and into the back door, which stood wide open, one of the glass panes broken. Emily was right. Someone had been in her house.

He listened for any sound of an intruder, but only a still, almost eerie silence surrounded him. He crept into the kitchen and stopped to listen. No sound except the ticking of a clock.

Running his hand along the wall by the back door, he sought and found the light switch. Just as he flipped the light on, he heard someone run up behind him. Jerking around, he grabbed Emily in a stranglehold.

"What the hell do you think you're doing sneaking up on me like that?" Loosening his deadly grip, he pulled her into his arms. The thought that he might have harmed her shook him badly. "I told you to stay in the car."

Coughing several times, Emily regained the breath Mitch had momentarily cut off when he'd grabbed her around the neck. She breathed deeply in and out, in and out. "I'm not very good at taking orders. Besides, I couldn't sit out there not knowing what was happening to you."

"The back door was open. A pane is broken out. So I assume you've had a visitor. I'm sure whoever it was is long gone by now."

"I don't see anything out of place in here." Emily glanced around at the undisturbed orderliness of her sunny-yellow kitchen.

"Follow me and we'll check each room." When she moved in front of him, he grasped her by the shoulders, halting her. "You follow me."

"Why?"

"Just in case I'm wrong about the intruder being long gone."

"Okay." Emily allowed Mitch to walk in front of her.

He flipped on light switch after light switch as they moved down the hallway, checking in the bedrooms and the bathroom before reaching the living room. Emily gasped and grabbed Mitch's sleeve.

"Oh, my heavens. Look at my living room!"

The cotton jabots that crowned twelve-over-twelve pane windows had been ripped. Two peach wingback chairs lay turned over on each side of the small trunk used as a coffee table. And the camelback sofa's green-and-cream print upholstery had been slashed in several places. The handmade hooked rug that covered a large area of the room was littered with sand, obviously hauled from the beach and deliberately dumped. An antique secretary's contents had been scattered. A pair of Staffordshire dogs lay broken on the wooden floor.

Mitch's gaze wandered around the room, slowly taking in all the random destruction. He sucked in his breath when he saw the message printed on the large mirror over the unused fireplace.

"'Don't ever see him again! He's the wrong man for you!'" Emily read the message aloud.

"Come on, Emily. Let's go back in the kitchen. I'll call the police while you make us some coffee."

He'd never felt so protective of a woman in his life. The thought that someone was harassing Emily made him want to kill. And knowing that his relationship with her had prompted her poetry-quoting admirer to become destructive made him more determined than ever to take care of her. Whoever was wreaking havoc in her life would have to answer to him.

When they walked into the hallway, Mitch placed his hand on Emily's shoulder. "After the police take a look at things here, do you want me to drive you over to spend the night with Nikki?"

"I'm not going to let anyone force me out of my own home. I'm staying here, and tomorrow I'll start cleaning up that horrible mess in the living room."

"Then I'll stay here with you tonight," he told her.

"Mitch, that isn't—"

"I'll sleep in the guest room."

"Thank you."

She smiled at him, obviously grateful for his concern, and that shy, sweet smile of hers turned him inside out in a way nothing and no one ever had.

The police came and went, giving Emily little hope that they would ever find her intruder, unless he struck again. And although he hoped he was wrong, Mitch didn't doubt that whoever was harassing Emily wouldn't give up easily. Was her mystery man only a jealous want-to-be-lover, or was there more to his warnings? Did he know who Mitch really was? If so, why hadn't he already told Emily?

"His phone calls and letters weren't threatening, until...until he found out about you," Emily said. "My soft-spoken secret admirer has become dangerous, hasn't he?"

Emily talked to Mitch briefly about what had happened and about her fears, then she told him she needed to be alone. He wanted to take her in his arms, to hold and comfort her, but she shut him out, and he felt he didn't have the right to intrude on her private thoughts.

Hours later, Mitch tossed and turned in the natural wicker bed in Emily's guest room. He'd listened to Emily stirring about in the adjoining room, and when she'd quieted, he'd tried to sleep, but sleep wouldn't come. His mind had shifted into overdrive—all he could think about was the possibility that someone posed a threat to Emily. But who? And why? Rod Simmons, her love-struck art student? Or Charles Tolbert, the guy she'd said she had been dating on and off for the past year? Or was it someone else? Someone who knew Mitch?

Hell! He might as well get up. He wasn't getting any rest this way.

Mitch flipped on the wood-and-brass bedside lamp sitting in the middle of the unfinished-pine nightstand. The long, wide windows, covered with wooden shutters, overlooked the front of the house, giving a clear view of the beach in the daytime.

He flopped down in the twig chair and propped his feet on the matching ottoman, both covered in a muted beige animal print. Rubbing his eyes and yawning, Mitch leaned back in the chair.

At first, he thought he was imagining the sound, but when he cleared his mind and listened carefully, he could make out the muffled cries. Emily's cries.

He jerked upright in the chair, his body tensing as he listened to her quiet little sobs. Was she crying into her pillow, trying to keep him from hearing her?

Standing, Mitch reached down to the foot of the bed, picked up his slacks and slipped into them. He opened the bedroom door and walked down the hall. Hesitating outside Emily's room, he listened at the door.

He knocked lightly. The crying stopped. He knocked again.

"Yes?"

"Emily, may I come in?" He grasped the doorknob.

"I—I guess so. Yes."

Mitch opened the door slowly, uncertain what to expect, unsure what he should do. The room was alive with light, soft light coming from several different lamps—a white, wrought-iron floor lamp placed beside a chaise longue, etched glass hurricane lamps flanking the bed and a tiny crystal boudoir lamp sitting on the dressing table.

Mitch took a tentative step into the room. Emily sat on the chaise longue. She stared at him, her eyes red and swollen, her face damp with tears.

"Please, come in, Mitch." She scooted to the edge of the chaise and stood. "Is there something wrong? Do you need anything?"

Did he need anything? Yes. He needed her. Was something wrong? Yes. He wasn't holding her in his arms.

"I heard you crying. I was worried," he said.

"I'm sorry if I woke you. I tried... It's just that I'm scared, and I don't want to be scared."

"You didn't wake me. I couldn't sleep."

"You're in a different house. A bed you're unaccustomed to sleeping in. I understand."

Mitch stared at her. She stood there looking like a lost child who only moments before had been crying for her mother. Only, Emily wasn't a lost child, and his instincts told him that if she'd been crying for anyone, it had been for him.

"I can stay with you." He saw the uncertainty in her eyes, the hesitation before she spoke.

"Mitch...I..."

"Wouldn't it be appropriate for friends to sit and hold each other, to comfort each other, to talk the night away if they wanted to?''

He couldn't remember the last time he'd seen anything as lovely as Emily Jordan standing there wearing a pair of dark-gold pajamas, the feminine contents of her lacy bedroom surrounding her.

He'd never seen so much lace. At the windows. On the tables. Covering the bed, creating a canopy with curtains that dropped down from the top of each bedpost. White and cream and ivory combined in a room that whispered the word *lady* ever so softly.

An ivory damask chaise by the windows basked in the moonlight. The wooden floors had been painted a plush cream and delicate striped wallpaper in shades of white and cream decorated the walls. Etched crystal lamps sat on each side of the bed, one on a round, lace-draped table and the other on a cherry Victorian bedside table. Watercolors that he felt certain Emily herself had painted hung in gilded frames, punctuating the walls in shades of palest pink, blue, lavender and green.

''There hasn't been a man in my bedroom since...since...'' Emily held out her hand to him.

Her hand trembled. Damn! He wanted to sweep her up into his arms and lay her down in that big, lacy bed of hers and give her the kind of relief a night of lovemaking could provide for them both. But Emily wasn't asking for sex; she was asking for comfort.

God help him, he hoped he had the strength to give her what she wanted and needed, without demanding more.

Emily had tried not to cry, and when she'd failed, she'd tried to mask her sobs by crying into a pillow. Now she wondered if she'd wanted Mitch to hear her, if she'd subconsciously cried out for him to come to her.

He stood only a few feet away, wearing nothing but his unbuttoned slacks. The brown hair on his broad chest glistened like golden silk curls in the warm light of her bedroom. He looked so big and hard and totally male in the midst of all her feminine lace.

He didn't make a move toward her, standing rigid as a statue, as if he were afraid to reach out and touch her. Emily took a step forward, then another. Mitch waited for her to come to him. She raised her hand to his face, touching his cheek with her fingertips.

"Will you come and sit with me?" she asked. "Will you hold me in your arms? Will you spend the rest of the night talking to me?"

Every nerve in Mitch's body came to full alert. Control! Control! he told himself. Give her what she's asking for. Prove to her that you're the man she can count on. You need this woman as much as she needs you.

After lifting her off the floor and into his arms, Mitch carried her across the room. He sat down on the chaise, bracing his shoulders against the back, positioning her between his legs. Circling her arms, he clasped his hands across her waist. Emily leaned back, resting against his chest, her head on his shoulder.

Mitch kissed the side of her face, brushing his lips against her hair directly above her ear. "Talk to me, pretty lady. I'll listen to every word you say."

Closing her eyes, Emily breathed deeply, absorbing the feel of Mitch's strong arms holding her, his hard body protecting her. Turning her head, she buried her nose against his flesh, loving the clean, masculine smell of him. She kissed his shoulder. He tasted hot and salty and delicious.

"You aren't talking," he said.

Snuggling into his embrace, Emily sighed. "I can't ever remember feeling so safe, and so very special. Thank you, Mitch."

"And I can't ever remember looking forward to spending the night just talking to a beautiful woman." Mitch chuckled, and felt warm relief spread through him when he heard Emily's quiet laughter.

"Have you ever had a dream, Mitch? Something you wanted so very much?" she asked.

"Yeah. Once. A long time ago."

"Did your dream ever come true?" She rubbed her fingertips across his clasped hands, caressing his knuckles.

"In a way." Was now the right time to bare his soul and tell her about his past, as he'd planned on doing after their date last night? "I wanted to be a successful businessman and make a ton of money. I accomplished that goal, but I made a lot of mistakes along the way, and not only did I pay dearly for my mistakes, a lot of other people did, too."

Opening her eyes, she tried to turn around in his arms, but he held her in place, nuzzling her neck with his nose. "What about you, Emily, do you have a dream?"

"You don't want to tell me, do you? About what happened to your dream? Is what happened to you that painful?"

"I'll tell you everything, honey." He tightened his hold on her. "I had planned to tell you last night, but that was before we discovered someone had broken into your house. What I've got to tell you can wait another day. You don't need anything else to make you unhappy tonight."

"Have it your way. We'll talk only about happy things tonight." She held both of his hands. He turned her hands over, twining his fingers through hers.

"Is your dream something that makes you happy?" Mitch asked.

"Yes."

"Tell me."

"I want to publish my Hannah books. You know. I've told you about my little heroine, Hannah, whom I based on my Grammy. I've almost finished the first book, watercolors and charcoal sketches and the story itself."

"I think you'll sell your book," Mitch said. "I've seen your work, you know. You're very talented."

Emily sighed. "It's been my dream to write and illustrate children's books ever since I wasn't much more than a child myself."

"You really do love children, don't you?" He knew that many of her art students were children, a few of them physically and mentally handicapped. She often spoke about individual students. A little boy who liked to paint everything in his pictures various shades of red. A little girl who talked incessantly and giggled every time Emily scolded her. And always, there was a wistful look in Emily's eyes when she talked about children.

"That was my other dream." Emily willed the tears to stay

inside, willed the pain not to come. "I've always wanted children of my own."

"Then someday—"

"I lost a baby."

Inadvertently, Mitch slipped their entwined hands down over Emily's flat stomach. She quivered. He gripped her hands tightly.

The pain in her voice was almost his undoing. She had lost a child when Ocean Breeze had collapsed and caught on fire. She had lost more than a husband that fateful morning in April five years ago. Both deaths weighed heavily on Mitch's conscience. If only he'd realized sooner what Randy was doing. If only...

"Do you want to tell me about the baby?" Mitch asked.

"No. Not tonight. Only happy talk. Remember?"

He remembered. "Tell me some more about your Hannah books, and about your Grammy."

Mitch held Emily in his arms for hours, talking a little, but mostly listening to her as she told him every detail of her Hannah books and countless stories of her life growing up with her beloved Grammy. He'd never spent a night just holding a woman, comforting her and loving her with only his thoughts.

When dawn broke, spreading a thin coat of pale pink across the horizon, Emily slept in Mitch's arms, there on the chaise longue. Safe. Secure. Cherished.

And finally, Mitch slept, too. Hopeful for the future for the first time in a long time.

Chapter 8

Emily stood in the doorway looking at the destruction in her living room. Somehow it appeared even worse in the cold, hard light of day. She had decorated this room with the same loving attention with which she had decorated the entire cottage. The project had helped save her sanity in the days after Stuart's death and her recuperation from the surgeries. Almost everything could be replaced, even the pair of Staffordshire dogs that Grammy had given her as a Christmas gift. But the replacements would never be the same.

Turning around and leaving the wreckage behind her, Emily made her way to the kitchen, where fresh coffee was brewing. She'd set the machine shortly after Mitch had left to run home for a shower and shave. She poured herself a mug of Southern Pecan coffee, then nudged open the back door and went out onto the porch that wrapped all the way around the cottage.

As she strolled along the porch, Emily's thoughts returned to last night. To the anger and fear she'd experienced when she realized someone had broken into her home. To the desperate need to protect herself and to punish the culprit. And to the sense of safety and peace she'd found throughout the night as she lay in Mitch's arms.

Come what may, she didn't have to face it alone. Whoever was behind the phone calls, the notes, this break-in, they would have to bear Mitch's wrath. No matter what lay ahead, Mitch would be at her side. Mitch would help her find out who had broken into her home, and Mitch would make sure...

Mitch. Mitch. Mitch. Emily sat down in the wooden rocker on the side porch, sipping her coffee and smiling. She had been falling for the man since the day they met, but last night she had toppled over the edge and fallen head over heels in love with him. She'd never known the feelings she experienced during the hours they sat together, his arms draped lovingly around her, the two of them alone on her chaise longue. His understanding, his comfort, his gentle care had taught her that she could give her heart to this man and he would cherish it. She could trust Mitch. She could count on him to be there for her.

When other men might have pressured her for sex, when other men might have taken advantage of her vulnerability last night, Mitch had known exactly what to say and do to help her through the traumatic experience. His every thought had been for her happiness and well-being. In her heart of hearts, she knew the day would come when she would trust Mitch enough to show him her back, and he would not turn away from her.

For the first time in five long years, she had hope for the future—a future with Mitch.

When Emily heard the car coming up the drive, she stood and walked down the steps to meet her best friend. Nikki ran up the stepping-stones walkway that led from the drive to the porch. Throwing her arms around Emily, Nikki hugged her close.

"Thank God, you're all right. When Mitch phoned this morning to tell me what had happened, I wanted to strangle the SOB who broke into your house. The police are going to have to do something. This has gone beyond phone calls and letters!"

Emily led Nikki up the steps and onto the porch. "Calm down. The police have no evidence against anyone. They can hardly arrest someone without proof of guilt."

"They need to question Charles Tolbert and maybe even Rod Simmons."

"I can't believe either of them would break into my home and cause all this destruction," Emily said. "I could possibly see either one of them making the phone calls or writing the letters, but not wreaking havoc in my house."

"Then who?" Nikki asked.

"I don't know."

Nikki glanced toward the front door. "Is Mitch still at his house? When I talked to him he told me that he'd spent the night here with you."

With her arm draped through Nikki's, Emily led her around the porch. "We didn't sleep together last night, if that's what you're wondering. Well, actually we did, but we didn't do anything. Well, we did. We talked. But nothing happened. No, that's not true, either. Something did happen."

Grabbing Emily by the shoulders, Nikki shook her. "Stop babbling. You're not making any sense."

Emily smiled. "Mitch held me in his arms all night. We lay on the chaise in my bedroom. We talked and talked. Well, mostly I talked and Mitch listened. And we fell asleep like that."

Nikki released her hold on Emily, shaking her head from side to side. "You're in love with him, aren't you? I mean all the way in love with him."

"Yes, I am."

"Oh, Em. Did y'all get around to confessing your secrets to each other last night, the way you told me y'all were going to do?"

"After the break-in, last night didn't seem the appropriate time." Emily led Nikki into the kitchen. "He's coming back over for breakfast. I was going to clean up the mess in the living room, but Mitch said my insurance agent wouldn't want us to bother anything until the adjuster came out and took a look at the damage."

Nikki pulled down a mug from the rack hanging beneath one of the white cabinets and poured herself a cup of coffee, then added two teaspoons of sugar. "Em, I want you to promise me that you'll tell Mitch about what happened to you. About being burned in the fire that killed Stuart. And ask him about his past. You need to know.''

"Nikki, I don't understand why you've been so persistent about my telling Mitch about my past and about my finding out every detail of his life. After all, what difference does it make? I'm in love with him, no matter what sort of life he lived before we met.''

"What if he's—''

Mitch knocked at the back door. Nikki jumped. Emily turned and smiled. He opened the door and walked into the kitchen.

"Good morning again.'' Slipping his arm around Emily's waist, he pulled her close and kissed her cheek. He turned and smiled at Nikki. "Hi, Nikki. Are you having breakfast with us?''

"Uh...I don't know.'' Nikki widened her eyes in a questioning pose as she looked at Emily.

"Yes, she's having breakfast with us.'' Emily opened the refrigerator, pulled out a carton of eggs and handed it to Mitch. "You promised to fix me an omelette.''

"So I did.'' Mitch took the eggs, then told Emily what other ingredients he'd need to prepare his one and only culinary speciality—a western omelette.

All the while he was showing Emily how proficient he was in the kitchen, he felt Nikki watching him, her hazel eyes filled with a look that Mitch finally decided was suspicion. Why was Nikki Griffin suspicious of him? Had she figured out who he was? If so, why hadn't she told Emily?

During breakfast and the cleanup following, Emily didn't seem to notice how oddly her friend was behaving, but Mitch was well aware of Nikki's scrutiny. He realized that he couldn't put off telling Emily the truth. If he didn't tell her first, and if Nikki did know, she was sure to tell her.

"Let's take our coffee and go out on the porch,'' Emily said. "It's a perfect day for sitting outside.''

"I can't stay.'' Nikki grabbed her purse off the countertop. "You two need some privacy to talk.''

"You just got here,'' Emily said.

"What do you think Emily and I need to talk about?" Mitch asked.

"Oh, Nikki's got herself in a snit because we still don't know a lot about each other," Emily said. "She's worried about me because she doesn't trust men and she's not sure I should trust you."

"Em, could I talk to Mitch for a few minutes? Alone?" Nikki asked, then tossed her purse on the table.

"Oh, for goodness sakes. First you're leaving so Mitch and I can talk and now you're staying to talk to him yourself." Emily threw up her hands in disgust, then lifted her coffee mug and stood. "I'll go sit on the porch and rock and look at the bay, but you make this little talk quick and don't you dare say anything unkind to Mitch."

The moment the back door closed behind Emily, Nikki turned to Mitch, who still sat at the kitchen table. "Your name isn't Ray Mitchell, is it? You're M. R. Hayden, the guy who owned half of Styles and Hayden Construction Company."

Mitch's stomach clenched; a sour taste coated his tongue. This was what he'd feared—that someone else would find out his true identity before he revealed himself to Emily. "How long have you known?"

"Fowler Jordan came to my house late last night. It seems that when Emily mentioned you to him, that you were her neighbor and she liked you—liked you a lot—Fowler hired a private investigator to find out about you. It didn't take the PI long to discover who you really are. Just a few phone calls. The guy brought Fowler his report last night and then Fowler came to see me."

"My God, is he in the habit of having every man Emily meets investigated?"

"There haven't been any men in Emily's life since Stuart died. Unless you count Charles Tolbert. And Fowler handpicked Charles for Emily. Your coming into Emily's life sort of messed up Fowler's plans."

"Why would Jordan come to you?" Mitch asked. "I thought Emily said that he didn't like you."

"He doesn't. But he knows I love Emily like a sister. He

wanted me to be here today, to be here for Emily, when he told her who you are."

"Nikki, give me a chance to explain—" Mitch spread out his hands across the table, his palms open, beseeching her.

"You cannot imagine how much Emily lost and how terribly she's suffered. How could you, of all people, cause her even more pain?"

"I didn't want to tell Emily about my past until we became better acquainted. I wanted her to know the real Mitch Hayden before she judged me based on the man I used to be." Mitch took a deep breath.

"Do you have any idea what you've done?" Tears filled Nikki's eyes. "You know who Emily is. You've known all along. You deliberately sought her out, didn't you?"

"Yes, I know who Emily is, and yes, I sought her out. I hadn't intended to wait so long to tell her who I am. But once I met her, once I found myself caring for her..." He looked directly at Nikki and noted a combination of anger and pity in her eyes. "I've spent five years hating myself, punishing myself for what happened. Zed Banning realized that I was killing myself by slow degrees. He brought me back to the Gulf to face the past and start all over again."

"My God, Zed Banning knows who you are, who Emily is, and he didn't try to stop you!"

"No one could have stopped me from finding Emily and making sure she was all right. Can't you understand how important it was to me to try, in some way, to make things right for her?"

"Make it right for her?" Nikki stared at him, an incredulous look on her face. "Are you out of your mind? Your construction firm was responsible for her husband's death, for her unborn child's death and for her— And you walked into her life and made her fall in love with you. How could you have done something so cruel?"

"Nikki, please understand. I need Emily's forgiveness. I need—"

"You need! You need! What about what Emily needs? She needs to be loved, not used. Once she finds out the truth, she'll be devastated. She'll hate you. She'll never forgive you. Never!''

His Emily. His beautiful, sweet, loving Emily would hate him? She would never forgive him? Of course she would hate him and never forgive him. If he'd been honest with himself, he would have known all along how this would turn out.

Mitch closed his eyes against the pain, trying to blot out the rage inside him. Perspiration broke out on his face. His palms moistened with sweat.

''I'll tell her the truth myself, if you'll let me.''

''I wish she never had to know,'' Nikki said. ''Tell me this, Mitch, are you the one?''

''The one what?''

''The one who's made all the phone calls, sent all the letters? Are you the one who wrecked her living room?''

''How the hell could I have wrecked Emily's living room when I was with her when it happened? We had a date, remember?''

''Maybe you hired somebody to break into her house while you were with her. So you'd have an alibi. So no one would suspect you.''

''Nikki, just listen to yourself. You're not making any sense.'' Every muscle in Mitch's body tightened painfully at the thought Emily might believe her friend's frantic ravings. ''What motive would I have? I came into Emily's life to help her, not hurt her. I want to take care of her, to make amends for the past. I'd never hurt her. Please believe me.''

Nikki glowered at Mitch, her eyes narrowing to slits. ''You have to tell her who you are. Today. Right now.''

''Thank you,'' he said, his voice a ragged whisper.

Mitch stood up, walked to the back door, opened it and went out onto the porch. When he didn't find Emily, he made his way around the porch to the front of the cottage.

A small, slender man, with thinning gray hair approached Emily with open arms. Fowler Jordan! Mitch would never forget the man's face as long as he lived. Stuart Jordan's uncle had come to the courtroom every day of the trial. He had stared at Mitch, his gaze filled with loathing.

Emily greeted her uncle warmly, readily going into his embrace. "Uncle Fowler, what are you doing here?"

"Nikki called me this morning and told me what had happened." Fowler slipped his arm around Emily's waist. "You shouldn't have stayed here alone last night. I wish you had telephoned me. I would have driven over immediately and taken you home. You know your room is always ready. I haven't changed a thing since you moved out."

"By the time the police left, it was awfully late." Emily clasped Fowler's hand in hers. "Besides, I wasn't alone last night."

"When Nikki phoned, she didn't mention that she'd stayed with you."

"Nikki didn't stay with me." Emily hesitated, fearing her uncle would overreact to the news that Ray Mitchell had spent the night with her. "Mitch stayed with me."

"My God, girl, you let that man stay here..." Fowler's face flushed. "He could have murdered you in your sleep. He could have—"

"You're getting upset over nothing." Emily squeezed Fowler's trembling hand. "Mitch is not the person who's been harassing me."

"I believe he is." Fowler turned, grasped Emily's shoulders and looked directly into her eyes. "There are things about that man you don't know."

"What things?" Emily asked.

"I've been making inquiries about this Ray Mitchell and—"

"Oh, Uncle Fowler, you had no right to do that."

Mitch jumped when the back door slammed shut. He turned his head. Nikki came up behind him.

"'Ray Mitchell' is an alias," Fowler said.

Every muscle in Mitch's body stiffened. His heartbeat accelerated, the drumming roar pounding inside his head. Fowler Jordan was going to tell Emily exactly who Ray Mitchell was and there wasn't a damn thing Mitch could do to stop him.

"What do you mean 'Ray Mitchell' is an alias?" Emily asked.

"The man you've been dating is not the man you think he is," Fowler told her.

Mitch's stomach knotted painfully. He knew what was going to happen. Nikki's small hand closed around Mitch's arm. Her nails bit into his flesh.

"This Mitch you're so smitten with is Mitchell Ray Hayden. M. R. Hayden of Styles and Hayden Construction Company." Fowler cleared his throat. "I'm so very sorry, my dear."

"What?" All the color drained from Emily's face. "What did you say?"

"I realize that this Hayden fellow didn't actually kill our Stuart, but—"

"Please, Emily...honey...please let me explain." Mitch stepped around the corner of the porch. Nikki followed close behind him.

Jerking her whole body around in one trembling move, Emily stared at Mitch. "You're M. R. Hayden?"

"Dammit! I didn't want you to find out this way." Mitch's eyes pleaded with her.

"You've changed a great deal, Hayden." Fowler Jordan focused his heated glare on Mitch. "I'm not sure I would have recognized you. Not at first, anyway. But the detective I hired to investigate you gave me irrevocable proof of your identity."

"You hired a detective to investigate Mitch?" Emily asked.

"My instincts told me that this new neighbor of yours couldn't be trusted, that he might well be your tormentor," Fowler said. "I think I've been proven correct. Mitchell Hayden set out to deliberately deceive you." Fowler grasped Emily's chin, forcing her to look at him. "I am so very sorry, dear child. I should have found a way to protect you from—"

"I didn't mean to deceive you!" Mitch said, knowing he had to defend himself before Emily's uncle convinced her that he was truly a monster. "I had intended to tell you when we first met, but I couldn't." Mitch took a tentative step toward Emily, then stopped when she backed away from him.

"Are you really M. R. Hayden?" The warmth in Emily's brown eyes died, turning her stare into a frozen glimmer.

"Yes, I'm Mitchell Ray Hayden. I was once co-owner of

Styles and Hayden Construction Company," Mitch admitted, and when he saw the look on Emily's face, he wished more fervently than he'd ever wished before that he could die on the spot.

Emily quivered from head to toe. She clutched the back of a nearby rocker.

"Emily," Mitch said.

"Em," Nikki said.

Emily closed her eyes. The pain was more than she could bear, but bear it she would. Just a little longer. "I trusted you. I believed I'd found someone I could love. You let me care about you. You let me lie in your arms all night and—"

"No, Emily, it can't be true. You didn't sleep with this man!" Fowler swayed on his feet. He reached out and grabbed the banister. "My God, Emily, how could you have—"

"Shut up!" Nikki screamed. "She doesn't need your censor. Not now. She needs our love and support."

Mitch wanted to take Emily into his arms and kiss away the pain he saw on her face. He wanted to comfort her. His sweet Emily. No, not his Emily. She would never be his Emily again.

Emily and Nikki and Mitch stood, unmoving, on the porch. No one said a word. Then Fowler reached for Emily. She shook her head. Fowler dropped his outstretched hand.

"You must come home with me, dear," Fowler said. "I'll take care of you and help you forget this ever happened."

Ignoring her uncle, Emily looked at Mitch. "Please leave."

"Emily, don't do this to me," Mitch begged. "Don't do this to us."

"There is no us," Emily said. "I fell in love with a man who doesn't exist. You're not my Mitch, the gentle, loving man who held me and comforted me last night." Emily choked back a sob. "You're more a stranger to me now than you were the day we met. Dear Lord, you're M. R. Hayden. You killed Stuart. You killed my baby!"

Emily balled her hands into fists. She hated M. R. Hayden, but she loved Mitch. No, no, no! It wasn't fair! With blind fury, Emily lunged at Mitch, pounding her fists into his solid chest.

Again and again. She screamed at him, saying over and over, "You killed Stuart. You killed my baby. You ruined my life."

Mitch stood there, allowing her to vent her torment, taking every blow without feeling anything, taking every word she spoke to heart, dying inch by inch as Emily destroyed his last hope of redemption.

Chapter 9

Mitch found Zed Banning alone in his Mobile condo. All the way there, he'd known what he was going to do. He was going to ask Zed Banning why the hell he'd ever bothered to bring him back to the Gulf, why he'd given a damn about saving him from self-destruction. He'd have been better off drinking himself to death than dying a thousand times over every time he remembered the look of loathing on Emily's face.

"So you and Emily Jordan finally got around to sharing past histories." Zed stepped back, swinging out his arm in an invitation to enter.

"Why, Zed? That's all I want to know. Why?" Mitch stared at the man who'd given him a chance to put his life back together, the man who had saved him from himself, the man who'd given him a job and a place to live when no one else in the country would give M. R. Hayden the time of day. "Why did I ever think she'd forgive me?"

"Come on in. I'll fix you a drink."

Zed turned and left Mitch standing in the doorway. He picked up the remote control to the television and switched off the sports channel he'd been watching. Then he walked behind the chrome, glass and leather bar at the far side of his living room, set up two glasses and lifted a bottle of ginger ale from the metal shelves beneath the bar. "Neat or on the rocks?"

"Neat." Slamming the door behind him, Mitch entered the room, walking slowly, taking his time.

Zed poured their drinks, picked up the glasses and rounded the side of the bar. "Sit down." He handed Mitch his ginger ale. "I don't think you need anything stronger."

Mitch sat down, took a sip, then frowned at Zed. "You knew all along what would happen. You tried to warn me, and once again I wouldn't listen."

"I wasn't a hundred percent sure what would happen," Zed said. "There was always a chance that the lady would see past her own hurt and loss and realize you weren't responsible for what your partner did."

"You didn't seem surprised to find me on your doorstep? You already knew what had happened with Emily? How?"

"I just got a call from Fowler Jordan, cursing a blue streak, demanding to know how I had the nerve to give a killer a job and allow him to move into a cottage next door to his niece." Zed huffed loudly. "It seems Jordan holds me responsible because I'm the man who brought you back to this area and gave you a job."

"Well, I don't suppose you could defend your actions, could you? After all, in a way, I am a killer."

"You didn't kill anyone!" Standing beside Mitch's chair, Zed took a sip of his drink. "You made some errors in judgment about your partner. You trusted the wrong people. If anyone is responsible for Stuart Jordan's death, it's Randy Styles."

"I was a fool. The biggest fool who ever lived. All I could see were dollar signs, big-time success and Loni Prentice in my bed every night." Mitch gulped down the remainder of the ginger ale, wishing with all his might it were whiskey. But Zed had been right not to serve him any hard liquor. Not today. It would be far too easy to drown his sorrows in the bottle. "Why couldn't I have discovered what Randy was doing before anyone had to die, before Emily lost her husband and child?"

"I assume Emily didn't take the news well when you told

her who you are." Zed sat down on the tan leather sofa across from Mitch's brown leather chair. "Give her time and she'll come around."

"Are you crazy?" Mitch glared at Zed, then looked down at his feet when he saw the pity and deep concern in his friend's eyes. "Yeah, you're crazy, but I'm crazier than you are. All you did was bring me back to the Gulf and give me a job. I'm the fool who moved next door to the widow of a man killed in the collapse of one of Styles and Hayden's buildings. I'm the one who asked her for a date.

"You didn't put Emily and me in the situation we're in now. You warned me to tell her who I was. I don't see how anyone could blame you for what happened."

"If I hadn't brought you back to Alabama, you'd probably be dead now. You know that, don't you?" Zed asked.

"Yeah, well, I'd probably be better off and so would Emily," Mitch said.

"If there's something real between you and Emily Jordan, you'll find a way to work through this."

"Do you honestly think that Emily will ever be able to forgive me for my part in the collapse of the Ocean Breeze Apartments?" Mitch set his empty glass down on the sleek, beige metal table beside his chair. "I was fooling myself when I thought she'd understand. I was living in a fantasy world."

"I'm sorry, Mitch. But you can't run away from Emily. Not now. Not after you've gotten this deeply involved with her. You owe it to her and to yourself to face the past and make peace with it. Even if she never forgives you, you have to find a way to forgive yourself."

"I guess you're right, except you didn't figure in the possibility that maybe Emily and I might...well, that we might..."

"Are you finally admitting that you're in love with her?"

"I'm admitting that I've never felt about another woman the way I do Emily. She made me happy, Zed. Happier than I've ever been in my life."

"And how does she feel about you?"

"Before or after she found out that I'm M. R. Hayden?"

Zed took another sip of his ginger ale, then set it down on

the glass-and-chrome coffee table in front of him. "Before?"
Zed asked.

"I think she was falling in love with me." Standing abruptly,
Mitch nearly knocked over the metal table at his side. Running
his fingers through his hair, he paced the floor. "I didn't get the
chance to tell her who I was. Hell, I should have told her I was
M. R. Hayden when we first met. She wouldn't be hurting so
bad if I'd been up front with her in the beginning."

"So why didn't you tell her yourself that you're M. R. Hayden?"

"That's a long, complicated story."

"I've got time to listen."

"I didn't get a chance to tell Emily I'm M. R. Hayden because last night when I took her home from our date, we discovered that someone had broken into her house and ransacked
her living room. Whoever did it left her a message."

"What sort of message?"

"'Don't ever see him again. He's the wrong man for you,'"
Mitch said. "The message was scrawled, in spray paint, across
the mirror in her living room. Somebody's been harassing her
for weeks—phone calls, letters and now the break-in. I'm just
afraid that now that my true identity has been revealed, her uncle
will convince her I was the one behind everything."

"But we know it wasn't you," Zed said. "So that means
whoever has been harassing Emily is still out there. She's still
in danger. She's going to need you."

"I'd do anything in this world to protect her, but how can I,
when she isn't going to let me get anywhere near her?"

Positioning himself on the edge of the sofa cushion, Zed
spread his legs apart and dropped his clasped hands between his
knees. "You want my advice, old buddy?"

"I have a feeling you're going to give it to me whether I
want it or not."

"If Emily means as much to you as you say she does, then
don't let her cut you out of her life. Make her understand what
happened five years ago. Tell her what kind of hell you've put
yourself through out of guilt. Give her the chance to understand
that you're innocent of every crime except poor judgment."

"Emily is a very loving person. I was counting on her understanding. I had hoped she'd find it in her heart to forgive me," Mitch said. "I think maybe if I'd been able to tell her the truth myself, she wouldn't have taken it so hard."

"While Fowler Jordan was ranting and raving during our telephone conversation this morning, he inadvertently told me something I think you should know."

"What did he say?"

"While he was damning me for putting the man who had killed Emily's husband in such proximity to her, he blabbed on and on about Emily's pain, her numerous surgeries, her pitifully scarred back."

"Her scarred back?" Mitch felt as if he'd been poleaxed in his stomach. "I thought the surgeries had removed the scars from her back."

"Sit down."

Mitch sat, staring intently at Zed, waiting to hear something his gut instincts told him he didn't want to know. "I knew that Emily was injured in the building collapse. She was the woman...the dark-haired woman the fireman saved." Mitch ripped his wallet from his back pocket, flipped it open and jerked out the frayed piece of pink satin. "I just didn't know how badly burned she was."

"Her uncle said she was scarred for life." Zed glanced down at the scrap of pink Mitch held between his thumb and forefinger, took a deep breath and looked directly into Mitch's bleary eyes.

Hot, salty bile rose in Mitch's throat. Emily had been injured, trapped and in pain. He never had been able to erase the image from his mind of her still body draped over the fireman's shoulder.

Mitch Hayden hadn't cried since he was a little boy. Men didn't cry. Certainly not tough guys like him. No matter how deeply hurt he was, he didn't cry.

Zed Banning looked away, as if he couldn't bear to see Mitch's face.

Agony consumed Mitch when he suddenly realized why Emily seemed to have reservations about a sexual relationship. The scars on her back! Dear God, she didn't want any man to see her scars.

Clutching the scrap of Emily's pink nightgown in his hand, Mitch stood up and walked toward the front door. Zed didn't follow him. Mitch closed the door softly behind him.

Outside, the sky was clear, the air crisp, the sun bright. After slipping the scrap of pink cloth back into his wallet, Mitch put on his helmet, swung his leg over his Harley and rode off down the road.

Tears blurred his vision. He opened his mouth on a silent scream and tasted his own tears as they streamed down his cheeks, down his nose and into his mouth. After running away from what had happened five years ago, he'd thought nothing could ever hurt him again, that he had sunk as low as a man could sink and still be alive. He'd been wrong. Nothing could have prepared him for the agony he felt now, as he realized that once again, he was responsible for Emily's suffering. His greed and stupidity had not only cost Emily her husband and unborn child, but had put her through ungodly physical and mental suffering. He had taken Emily's life away from her.

And he had been so damn sure he could find a way to redeem himself in her eyes, that he could make her understand that he, too, had been one of Randy Styles's victims.

But now he knew that there was no way she'd ever be able to forgive him, just as there was no way he'd ever be able to forgive himself.

Emily stood in the doorway of her bedroom, staring at the damask chaise longue where she had spent the night in Mitch's arms. No, not Mitch. M. R. Hayden. Mitchell Ray Hayden, the co-owner of Styles and Hayden Construction Company.

"Em?" Nikki walked up behind her and placed her hand on Emily's back. "What are you doing?"

"I lay there in his arms all night long, pouring out my heartfelt hopes and dreams. I told him all about my Hannah books, about my relationship with Grammy, about how I'd always longed to have a child." Emily choked on the tears lodged in her throat.

"Come on in the kitchen and let me make us something to eat. It's way past lunchtime."

"I'm not hungry." Emily stepped over the threshold into her bedroom. "When Uncle Fowler told you who he was last night, why didn't you call me?"

Nikki waited in the hallway. "I didn't know what to do. You were already falling in love with him. I hadn't seen you so happy since... Before Mitch called this morning and told me about the break-in, I'd decided to keep my mouth shut and let Fowler be the bearer of bad tidings. Please, Em, I'm sorry I didn't come over here and tell you last night. If I'd known what had happened and that Mitch would stay the night—"

"It's all right. It was my fault, not yours."

"No, it wasn't your fault. And it wasn't even Mitch Hayden's fault. If I blame anyone, I blame that awful Zed Banning. He's the one who brought Mitch back to the Gulf."

"Zed Banning had no way of controlling Mitch's actions. Mitch is the one who sought me out, rented a cottage next to mine and deliberately set out to gain my friendship."

Emily reached out, her hand hovering over the back of the chaise. Leaning down, she breathed in the smell of Mitch Hayden. A hard knot of pain formed in the pit of her stomach. She had never felt as safe and secure and cherished as she had last night.

She ran her hand over the raised surface of the material covering the chaise. Would she ever be able to forget the feel of Mitch's arms around her, of his lips against her neck, on her ear, in her hair? How long would she relive the pleasure and the pain of having fallen in love with the man whose construction firm was responsible for her husband's and child's deaths, and responsible for the scars that disfigured her back?

"Don't do this to yourself," Nikki said.

Emily sat down on the chaise. "I didn't think anything could ever hurt me so much again. Not after losing Stuart and our child. But this... Oh, God, Nikki, I'm in love with Mitchell Hayden." Covering her face with her hands, Emily sobbed quietly, her shoulders trembling.

Nikki ran across the room, dropped to her knees beside the

chaise and took Emily's hands into her own. "I think he loves you, too, you know."

Swallowing her tears, Emily wiped her face with her fingers and looked at Nikki. "He knew who I was. He did this to me intentionally."

"Oh, Em, I don't think Mitch is a terrible man. Not really. I have a feeling that he's paid dearly for his part in the collapse of the Ocean Breeze Apartments."

"No matter how much he's suffered, he can't change the past and neither can I. He can't bring Stuart back. Or the baby. And he can't erase the scars from my body."

"If he'd told you who he was that first day you met, what would you have done?" Nikki asked.

"I don't know. I suppose I would have talked to him, listened to what he had to say. But I never would have dated him. I never would have..."

"But you were attracted to him." Nikki squeezed Emily's hands. "You aren't a bitter person filled with hatred. You're too kind and forgiving. If Mitch Hayden had come to you and asked for your forgiveness and understanding, what would you have done?"

"I don't know! I told you, didn't I, that I read and reread the transcripts from the trial? I realize that M. R. Hayden wasn't directly involved in any of his partner's illegal dealings. I still hate Randall Styles. And sometimes I even hate M. R. Hayden, for not realizing sooner what his partner was doing. Soon enough to have saved Stuart and..."

"You don't hate Mitch," Nikki said. "If you hated him, you wouldn't be hurting this way."

"Maybe I don't really hate M. R. Hayden. Not anymore. But at this precise moment, I do hate Mitch as much as I love him. I hate him for destroying my hopes of knowing love again, of trusting a man enough to consider allowing him to see my scarred body."

"Oh, Em."

Nikki and Emily both jumped when they heard the loud knocking at the front door. Nikki bolted straight up. Emily sat erect on the chaise.

"What if it's Mitch?"

Nikki looked at Emily, questioning her.

"I can't see him. Not now."

"I'll find out who it is, and if it's Mitch, I'll tell him you're not ready to see him."

Emily bit down on her bottom lip. "And if Uncle Fowler has come back, let him in. Maybe I can make him understand why I don't want to move back to Mobile with him."

"He was terribly upset that you plan to stay on here at the cottage," Nikki said. "But when I told him I'd stay with you, he seemed to calm down a little."

Emily followed Nikki up the hallway, but stopped in the archway between the dining room and the living room. She watched while Nikki made her way through the rubble in the living-room floor and opened the front door.

"Who are you?" Nikki demanded.

"Zed Banning. Who are you?"

"I can't believe you've got the nerve to show your face around here, Zed Banning!"

"Now, just calm down, little she-cat," Zed said. "Retract your claws or I'll cut them off."

"You arrogant bastard! How dare you play God with Emily's and Mitch's lives. Do you have any idea how much harm you've done?"

Zed took a step inside, but found himself blocked by Nikki's petite body. "Who the hell are you, lady?"

"I'm Nikki Griffin. Emily Jordan's friend."

"Well, Nikki Griffin, move out of the way or I'll pick you up and put you on my hip."

"You and what army?" Pointing her finger in Zed's face, Nikki glared at him. "Emily's been through enough today without having to listen to your weak excuses about why you sent Mitch Hayden into her life."

"This isn't between you and me, Nikki Griffin. I want to speak with Ms. Jordan."

"Well, she doesn't want to speak to you."

"Is that right, Ms. Jordan? Don't you want to know why I

brought Mitch back to the Gulf? Why I gave him a job when no one else would? Why he rented a cottage next door to you?''

Emily stepped out from the shadows behind the archway. ''Let him in, Nikki.''

''Em, don't you listen to a word this—''

''Someone needs to muzzle you,'' Zed told Nikki.

''Come on back to the kitchen,'' Emily said. ''My living room isn't fit for company.''

Stepping around the debris on the floor, Zed followed Nikki through the living room, stopping to stare at the printed message on the mirror. *Don't ever see him again. He's the wrong man for you.*

''Someone got destructive,'' Zed said.

''Yes, they did.'' Nikki glared at him. ''But Emily isn't going to be alone here anymore. I'm moving in with her for a while, until the police find out who did this.''

''The only way you could protect her is if you carried a gun as big as you are.'' Zed made his way through the dining room, smiling at Nikki when she frowned at him.

Emily and Zed sat down at the kitchen table. Nikki hovered behind Emily.

''Sit down, she-cat, you don't have to protect Emily from me. I'm here as a friend, not an enemy.''

Emily nodded agreement. ''Yes, please sit down, Nikki, and quit giving Mr. Banning the evil eye.'' When Nikki sat down, Emily turned to Zed. ''I'm ready to listen.''

Zed laid his big hands on the table, rubbing the wooden surface with his fingertips. ''For the past five years, Mitch has been in as much pain as you must have been. Maybe more.''

''I find that hard to believe,'' Nikki said.

''Will you stay out of this!'' Zed slammed his fist down on the table. ''You aren't helping the situation.''

''You don't scare me with your macho huffing and puffing!'' Nikki defiantly tilted her chin upward.

''Stop it. Both of you,'' Emily said. ''Nikki be quiet. Go on, Mr. Banning.''

''Mitch isn't a bad man. He's a good man who used bad

judgment. He trusted the wrong man and he fell in love with the wrong woman.''

A stinging pang of jealousy hit Emily. Unexpected. Unwanted. Why did she care that Mitch had been in love with another woman?

"He was young and ambitious," Zed said. "Mitch had been dirt poor, and more than anything else, he wanted to make something of himself. He worked for me for several years after he got out of the marines. He was bright and hardworking. He'd probably be my partner by now if he hadn't met Loni Prentice and Randy Styles.''

"He became Randy Styles's partner instead of yours," Nikki said.

"That's right." Zed nodded agreement. "Loni persuaded Mitch to borrow as much money as he could, then add that to his life's savings and invest everything in a partnership with Randy Styles. Styles promised Mitch quick success and big money," Zed explained. "Styles came through with his promises. He just didn't bother telling Mitch that he was taking some shortcuts, using substandard supplies, buying off building inspectors and bedding Loni on the side.''

Zed leaned back in the kitchen chair, shoving it away from the table. "The buildings Mitch constructed were top-notch, but by the time he found out what Styles was doing, it was too late. Ocean Breeze collapsed, and it was all over.''

"He lost everything." Emily crossed her arms at her waist, gripping her elbows, hugging herself. She closed her eyes. "Mitch lost everything, too.''

"Randy Styles ran off with as much money as he could liquidate in a hurry, and Loni, who was Mitch's fiancée by that time, ran off with Styles. Then Mitch had to go to court and face the lawsuits and face the people who'd been injured when Ocean Breeze collapsed. After the trial, Styles and Hayden Construction Company was bankrupt and no one would give Mitch a job.''

Zed stood and rounded the table, then reached down and took Emily's hands. "Yeah, just like you, Mitch lost everything. And he's spent five years punishing himself for what happened. He

had become a homeless bum when I found him and persuaded
him to come back to the Gulf.''

One lone tear cascaded down Emily's face, falling onto Zed's
hand. He looked at her. She nodded her head.

''If you can ever find it in your heart to forgive him, he'll
finally be able to forgive himself.'' Zed released Emily's hands.
''Think about what I've told you.''

''Nikki will see you out,'' Emily said.

''No, I'll see myself out.''

Neither Emily nor Nikki said a word until they heard the front
door close, then Emily stood up and walked out onto the back
section of the porch. Nikki followed.

''What are you going to do?'' Nikki asked.

''I'm going to go on living, the way I have for the past five
years. One day at a time.''

''What about Mitch?''

''I'm not ready to see him or talk to him. Right now, it hurts
too much just to think about him. About us.''

At sunset, Mitch Hayden drove his Harley up the driveway
of his rented cottage. After dismounting and removing his helmet, he turned to stare at the house next door. More than anything he wanted to see Emily, to hold her in his arms and beg
her to forgive him. But he didn't dare go to her. After everything
he'd done to her, he had no right to ask for her forgiveness, let
alone for her friendship or her love.

ARTS
GAME

E!

YOURSELF IN...

Play "Luck

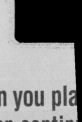

when you pla
...then contin
with a sweeth

1. Play Lucky Hearts as instruct

2. Send back this card and you'll
   books have a cover price of $

3. There's no catch. You're unde
   ZERO — for your first shipme
   of purchases — not even one

4. The fact is thousands of reade
   Reader Service™. They like the
   the best new novels BEFORE t
   discount prices!

5. We hope that after receiving y
   choice is yours — to continue
   invitation, with no risk of any k

The Silhouette Reader Service™ — Here's how it works:

Accepting free books places you under no obligation to buy anything. You may keep the books and gift and return the shipping statement marked "cancel." If you do not cancel, about a month later we'll send you 6 additional novels and bill you just $3.57 each plus 25¢ delivery per book and applicable sales tax, if any.* That's the complete price — and compared to cover prices of $4.25 each — quite a bargain! You may cancel at any time, but if you choose to continue, every month we'll send you 6 more books, which you may either purchase at the discount price... or return to us and cancel your subscription.

*Terms and prices subject to change without notice. Sales tax applicable in N.Y.

If offer card is missing write to: Silhouette Reader Service, 3010 Walden Ave., P.O. Box 1867, Buffalo, NY 14240-186

BUSINESS REPLY MAIL
FIRST-CLASS MAIL   PERMIT NO. 717   BUFFALO, NY

POSTAGE WILL BE PAID BY ADDRESSEE

SILHOUETTE READER SERVICE
3010 WALDEN AVE
PO BOX 1867
BUFFALO NY 14240-9952

NO POSTAGE
NECESSARY
IF MAILED
IN THE
UNITED STATES

Chapter 10

Mitch stood on the beach, not looking out at the bay, but at Emily Jordan sitting alone on her porch, a huge straw hat on her head and a sketch pad in her hand. They were back where they had started—as strangers, watching each other from afar. He wanted to go to her, to tell her how sorry he was for everything she had suffered, but he wasn't sure he had the courage. Days had passed, turning into a week, and still he waited.

Nikki was staying at the cottage with Emily. He saw the two of them coming home in the evenings together, saw them taking long walks on the beach and often sitting on the porch until dark.

He'd found out from Zed, who'd taken a personal interest in the situation, that Emily's secret admirer hadn't made any more phone calls or sent any more "love" letters. That could mean anything, couldn't it? Maybe Emily's admirer had gotten one of the things he'd wanted—for Emily to stop seeing Mitch Hayden. But the thing he wanted most, he still didn't have—Emily herself. So why no more phone calls, no more letters?

The police had questioned Mitch—twice. He was sure Fowler Jordan had implied that he was the man they sought. Maybe

Jordan truly believed he posed a threat to Emily. Mitch was afraid that if the police concentrated all their attention on him, the real stalker might remain free. Free to break into Emily's home again. Free to attack her.

Out there somewhere was the real culprit. Zed had warned Mitch to keep a close eye on Emily's cottage. Whoever was responsible for the break-in might try again, when Emily and Nikki were at home.

But Mitch needed more than to guard her at a distance. He needed to talk to Emily, even if she never forgave him. He needed to tell her his side of the story, to explain that he hadn't realized until it was too late what his business partner was doing. He wanted Emily to know that he had spent the last five years in a guilt-induced hell.

But would she talk to him? Would she even let him near her?

"He's coming this way," Nikki said, shading her eyes with her hand. "I'm going inside to fix some iced tea."

"No, Nikki, don't go. Don't leave me alone with him." Emily clutched the charcoal pencil in her hand.

"It's taken him a week to build up enough courage to come over and talk to you. You've been waiting for this. You want to hear what he has to say, and neither of you need me around when he says it."

"Yes, I know. It's just that I don't know if I have the courage to see him." Emily laid down her sketch pad and pencil on the wicker table, placed her hands in her lap and waited for Mitch. Nikki hurried along the porch toward the back of the house.

She sat quietly, listening to the waves roll into shore, listening to the soft wind blowing and to the sound of her own heartbeat drumming in her ears. What would he say to her? How would she respond? She had long since made her peace with the hatred she'd felt for the unknown man, M. R. Hayden, but there was no peace between her and Mitch. There never could be as long as they didn't talk to each other.

Mitch put his foot on the bottom step, looked up at Emily and waited for some sign from her. She stared at him, her brown eyes filled with sadness.

"May I—"

"Yes," she said.

He couldn't remember a time in his life when he'd been so nervous, so damned scared he'd say or do the wrong thing. This was his one and possibly only chance to make things right with Emily, to plead his case and beg her forgiveness.

Mitch took the steps two at a time, then halted abruptly at the edge of the porch. "How have you been? Zed told me that the letters and phone calls have stopped."

"For now," Emily said.

"I'm glad Nikki is staying with you."

"I know you've been keeping an eye on us, and that Mr. Banning is doing what he can to help, as a favor to you. He— he even offered to hire a bodyguard for me, but I think that's going a bit too far, don't you?" She couldn't bring herself to look directly at Mitch; instead she stared at his feet.

Mitch couldn't stop staring at Emily, at her downcast eyes, at her soft, pink lips, at the fall of dark hair curling out from underneath the straw hat. "If things escalate...if this guy becomes violent again...a bodyguard might not be a bad idea."

"If things worsen, I'll probably move back to Mobile." Emily wrung her hands. "I was always safe when I lived with Uncle Fowler. He protected me from the world. But I wanted to start living again, to get out on my own." She laughed, the sound a mockery of the real thing. "Just look what's happened to me."

Mitch hadn't been overly impressed with Fowler Jordan upon his brief meeting with him, but he didn't doubt the man's devotion to Emily. Stuart Jordan's uncle had devoted the past five years of his life to Emily. But maybe during those five years, he'd become too accustomed to running Emily's life.

"You still don't have any idea who is harassing you and why?" Mitch asked.

"Do you know that since last Sunday morning, all sorts of crazy thoughts have gone through my mind."

When Mitch took a tentative step toward Emily, she glanced away from him, turning her head slightly to gaze out at the bay.

"I've wondered if it's possible that Uncle Fowler is right about you. That you really are my tormentor."

"You can't honestly think I'd—"

"Yes, the thought did cross my mind."

"Emily, for crissakes, I would never do anything to hurt you. I would never—"

"No, you wouldn't do anything to hurt me. Nothing except kill my husband and child and..." Emily scooted her chair away from the wicker table, intending to stand up and run into the house. She couldn't do this. She couldn't have this conversation with Mitch. Despite what she'd thought, she wasn't ready. "I'm sorry. I know what happened with the Ocean Breeze Apartments wasn't your fault."

Mitch touched her. She froze to the spot. Reaching out, he grasped her shoulders in a gentle yet firm hold. "I'd lie down and die for you right here and now if it would change anything. If I could give you back your life, I'd do it."

Emily refused to look at him. She hung her head, avoiding any eye contact. "Please, let me go. I know...I understand that you were duped by your partner, that you were taken in by some woman."

Noting the jealousy in Emily's voice, Mitch rejoiced inwardly, realizing that Emily had to still care about him to be jealous. He willed himself not to smile about this one small reason to hope.

"Her name was Loni. She was blond and sexy and...and I didn't really love her. Not the right way. I was young and stupid and acted like a damned dog running around after a bitch in heat." Mitch gave Emily a gentle shake. "I made so many mistakes, honey, but I've paid dearly for them, and I'm still paying. Nothing has ever hurt me the way seeing you in so much pain does."

She swallowed her tears. She would not let him see her cry again. "I don't hate you, Mitch. I came to terms with what happened to Stuart and our baby a long time ago...but I can't forget. I'll never be able to forget." She pulled away from him. "You see, I have scars on my back that will be a reminder to me for as long as I live."

"Emily?" Mitch clasped her chin in his hand, tilting her head upward until she looked him directly in the eye. "I thought that if you could forgive me, it would be enough, but it's not. I want more. I want you to let me try to make things right. I don't know how, but I need to do something, anything to help you."

She saw the truth of his words in his ice-blue eyes, the sincerity of his plea. "Remember what you told me about pity? Well, I don't want your pity. Not now or ever."

"It's not pity, Emily. I care about you. I care so much it hurts. Please, help me find a way to—"

"Do you really want to do something for me?"

"Anything."

"Then go away, Mitch. Go away and leave me alone. There is no place for you in my life. I—I've decided that I...I'm probably going to start seeing Charles again. He's very fond of me...and..." When Mitch glared at her, anger glimmering in his eyes, Emily jerked her chin out of his grasp, turned quickly and walked away.

"Emily?"

She stopped just before rounding the corner of the porch, but she didn't look back at him. "Yes?"

"They don't matter to me, you know. The scars on your back. If you had allowed me to see them, I would have told you how beautiful you are. And you are beautiful to me. All of you."

"Goodbye, Mitch."

He stood on the porch for several minutes after she walked from the side porch to the back of the house and went into the kitchen. "This isn't goodbye, pretty lady," Mitch whispered. "I couldn't leave you now, even if I wanted to."

There wasn't a damned thing Mitch could do about Emily's decision to date Charles Tolbert again. Nothing except let the anger inside him fester, growing like a rotting sore. He couldn't help thinking of Emily as his. If that made him a fool, then he was a fool. If he believed Tolbert could make Emily happy, it might make letting her go a little easier. But as long as Emily wanted him, then she couldn't find happiness with anyone else. And he knew she wanted him.

So, for the time being Mitch had to stand by, doing what little he could. He watched Emily's house at night, listening for any signs of an intruder. Sometimes, in the early-morning hours, he'd stand outside her bedroom window, at a discreet distance, and remember when he'd held her in his arms all night long.

But since the night of the break-in at Emily's house, there had been no more letters or phone calls. Could that mean Tolbert had been her secret admirer, the one who had warned her to stop dating Mitch, and now he had what he wanted? Or was this mystery man simply playing a waiting game? Hopefully, Emily would be safe for the time being. Safe in another man's arms!

Seeking freedom from his pain, Mitch got on his Harley, accelerated quickly and raced up the highway. He'd come a long way down from the top of the world where he'd been five years ago. He'd sunk pretty low by the time Zed found him in Arkansas, but he'd worked hard the last few months to put his life back together. Emily had given him a reason to care again. She'd given him hope.

Some of the guys at the construction site had told him about a rough and rowdy nightspot where the music was loud, the beer cheap and the women available. He wasn't interested in another woman—only Emily. But he sure as hell could use a few beers and enough noisy distraction to dull his senses for a couple of hours.

Mitch parked his motorcycle in the parking lot, hung his helmet on the seat and headed toward the Blue Lagoon. By the sound of the upbeat country music he heard, once he got inside he wouldn't be able to hear himself think.

A smoky haze permeated the crowded room. A small band blasted out an instrumental hit. Mitch made his way to the bar, ordered a beer and ignored the blonde who was giving him the eye.

"Want some company, sweetie?" She sat down on the empty stool beside Mitch.

"No."

"What's the matter—your girl leave you for another guy?"

Mitch jerked around, staring at the woman as if she were a gypsy fortune teller.

Grinning, she ran the tips of her fingers up his arm. "I guessed right, huh?"

"Look, I'm not interested."

"Don't you like blondes?"

"I used to," he told her. "But my tastes have changed. I prefer brunettes now. One brunette in particular."

"Lucky lady." She leaned into Mitch's side, brushing her large breasts against his arm. "Last chance, sweetie. If you don't want what I'm offering, I'll find somebody who does."

"Then go find him, *sweetie,* and leave me the hell alone."

Ignoring the woman, Mitch ordered himself a second beer. Maybe he was stupid to refuse her. Maybe he should buy her a drink and find them a table somewhere. Within an hour he could have her laid out naked on a motel bed, with her legs spread and her arms open wide. God knew he needed a woman. Needed one bad. But just any woman wouldn't do. Not anymore.

A few months ago, he would have taken the blonde up on her offer of "companionship." But not tonight. He'd lost his taste for loose women. Mitch clutched his beer, waiting for the woman to leave.

"Hey, Kellie baby, come over here and meet some friends of mine," a loud masculine voice called out from across the room.

Lifting the beer to his mouth, Mitch took a deep swallow and looked over the edge of his glass, scanning the room. His stomach knotted tightly. For five years he had frequented places like this, places where he could pick up a woman, get drunk cheap and find a few hours of forgetfulness. But he had left that life behind him, and he wasn't going to sink that low again. Not ever.

Mitch paid for his beers and headed for the door. The refreshing night air hit him the moment he stepped outside.

Once he had thought that Emily Jordan's forgiveness would be enough. He'd been wrong. He needed more from her. He needed to find a way to make her happy, to give her the life she truly wanted. Somehow, someway, he was going to do just that.

Emily stood a discreet distance behind Rod while he worked on his most recent painting. She'd never known a student as talented as Rod; actually, his talent far exceeded hers. But he hadn't quite matured enough to come into his own. He was still searching for his unique style. She had told him that there was only one Monet, one Picasso and one Rod Simmons. Once he truly knew himself well enough to know he must paint for himself and himself alone, he would learn to takes risks—risks that could create his best work.

She inspected the still life he was creating, a study in contrasting textures and values. "This painting has been a real challenge to you, hasn't it?"

Rod stepped back a couple of feet, studying his work, then turned to Emily. "Trying to capture the light through those clear glass objects has been one of my most difficult projects. But I think using the series of glazes, each one in a different color, helped me achieve the effect I wanted."

"I'd like to display this piece in our window, once you've finished." Emily laid her hand on Rod's shoulder. He tensed instantly and she wondered why. She had often placed her hand on his back or shoulder and he'd never flinched at her touch the way he'd just done. Emily removed her hand.

Rod stepped away from her, closer to his painting. "All I lack now is the finish."

"Color lifting will soften a highlight edge," Emily commented, her mind wandering as she checked her watch. Charles was supposed to pick her up at six and it was five till now. They were going to meet Uncle Fowler for dinner and both men would be displeased that she hadn't taken time to run home and change. But this last class of the day had run over a few minutes and when Rod had asked if he could stay and speak privately to her, she'd agreed.

"I appreciate all the extra time you give me, Emily." Rod began gathering up his supplies. "You're really a wonderful person."

Rod's innocent compliment stirred a sense of uneasiness in Emily. Since the break-in, she'd been questioning every little comment others made, especially men. Even though nothing else had happened, not even a note or phone call, she didn't feel completely safe. Uncle Fowler had tried to convince the police that Mitch Hayden was behind Emily's harassment and the break-in, that he could have easily hired someone to ransack Emily's home while he wined and dined her. Nikki still thought Charles was the culprit, but then, Nikki didn't like Charles and made no secret of the fact she thought Emily was an idiot for dating him again. And now here Emily was suspecting Rod, simply because he'd told her she was a wonderful person.

"I'm more than glad to give a talented student a little extra help," Emily said. "Rod, I don't mean to rush you, but I do have a date tonight, so could you tell me why you needed to see me privately?"

"Is your date with that Mitch guy?" Rod peered at her with eyes narrowed to slits. A harsh frown marred his youthfully pretty face.

"No, it isn't, but I hardly think that's any of your business."

"I'm sorry. You're right." Rod proceeded with the cleanup job he'd started. "I asked you to stay over because...well, I...er..." Turning abruptly, he unbalanced his easel. Just as it began to topple, he reached out and grabbed it. With his back to Emily, he said, "I'm awfully sorry about what happened at your house. I think it's terrible that anyone would be that destructive."

"How did you know about—"

"The police questioned me." Rod turned around slowly and lifted his eyes to gaze directly into Emily's face. "I hope you know that I'd never break into your house and destroy your nice things. I'd never do anything to hurt you."

Rod was the second man in her life who had sworn he'd never do anything to hurt her. And she wanted to believe them both. "Rod, no one has accused you of anything. I'm sure the police are questioning many of the people I know. Probably all of my male art students, since my mystery caller is definitely male."

Rod's face turned crimson beneath his tan. "Well, there's a big difference in calling someone and sending them letters and in breaking into their house. I mean calls and letters aren't destructive. They don't hurt anyone. But breaking into a person's house is a different matter altogether.''

''You're right.'' Emily wished she didn't feel so nervous simply because she was alone with Rod in her upstairs studio. She was being silly. Of course Rod would never hurt her. Besides, Nikki was still downstairs. All she had to do was call out her name and she'd come running.

''I'd say that they're two different people, wouldn't you?''

''What?'' The more Rod talked, the more uneasy Emily became. A sudden sense to run almost overcame her. She backed slowly away from Rod.

He took several tentative steps toward her. ''Don't you think it's possible that whoever broke into your home is someone other than the man who's been calling you and sending you letters?''

''The police seem to think it's the same person,'' Emily said. ''They think we might be dealing with a stalker.''

''No, you aren't!'' Rod surveyed the room quickly, as if he were looking for an escape. ''What I mean is that whoever broke into your house might be a stalker, but not the other person.''

''Why do you think that?'' Emily checked her watch again. ''Rod, I'm sorry, but—''

''Emily,'' Nikki called out from the stairway.

''Yes,'' Emily replied. ''What is it?''

''Charles is here.''

''Tell him I'll be right down.'' Emily rushed to the stairs, halted momentarily and glanced back at Rod. He looked like a lost and frightened kid. Suddenly she felt very foolish for suspecting him. ''Thanks for trying to help me make sense of this mess, but why don't we leave all the theorizing to the police.''

''I suppose you're right. Goodbye, Emily. Have a nice time tonight.''

''See you day after tomorrow.''

Emily rushed downstairs. When she reached the bottom, Nikki pulled her aside, into the storeroom.

''Nikki, what are you doing?'' Planting her hands firmly on her hips, Emily glared at her friend.

''You're making a major mistake dating Charles Tolbert.''

"Stay out of this. Whom I choose to date is my business."

"The only reason you're dating Charles is because of what happened with Mitch." Nikki pointed her index finger in Emily's face. "You're doing just what Charles and your uncle wanted you to do. You're falling back into the safe life Fowler Jordan planned for you."

"Right now, a safe life doesn't seem so bad," Emily said. "Not after what happened with Mitch. I took a chance on love and see what it got me." Emily opened her hands, palms up, in an exasperated gesture. "My God, Nikki, I fell in love with a man whose construction firm was responsible for Stuart's death!"

"Mitch Hayden didn't kill Stuart or your baby. He isn't responsible for the scars on your back."

Emily dropped her hands to her sides and nervously rubbed them against her hips. "I can't discuss this right now. I don't want to talk about Mitch. I don't want to think about Mitch. All I want to do is forget him."

Emily ran from the storeroom, slowing her pace when she saw Charles waiting by the counter, a concerned look on his face.

"Is everything all right?" he asked.

"Yes, of course. Everything's fine." She walked behind the counter. "Just let me get my purse and I'll be ready to go."

"Are you sure you're all right? Nothing has happened, has it?" Charles asked. "You haven't had any more calls or letters, have you?"

"No, I haven't. Nothing is wrong. I'm just running behind a little this evening." Emily picked up her purse, came out from behind the counter and smiled at Charles. "I'm sorry I didn't get a chance to go home and change."

"Your slacks are a bit casual, but you look lovely." Charles took her arm and draped it over his.

"Nikki," Emily called out. "Don't wait up for me tonight. I don't know what time I'll be home."

Nikki appeared in the storeroom doorway. "Stay out as late as you'd like, and have fun."

Nikki's smile was pure devilment, and Emily knew what her

friend was thinking. She might as well have said it aloud. *Have fun. If you can have any fun with someone as boring as Charles.*

"I'm sure we'll have a delightful time," Emily said, then walked out the door with her date.

She might not have fun with Charles Tolbert, but she would be safe. Uncle Fowler had kept her safe for five years, but as soon as she'd left his protection, her life began to unravel. Letters and phone calls from a secret admirer. Her house broken into and her living room ransacked. But worst of all, she had opened herself up for love again and had been destroyed by a truth she still didn't want to face.

Chapter 11

Emily and Nikki had felt somewhat obligated to attend Zed Banning's annual big bash since Zed had tried in every way possible to help Emily after the devastating truth about Mitch came out. And he *had* hand-delivered their invitation to this gala affair.

Emily had invited Charles to be her escort, which had pleased not only Charles, but Uncle Fowler, as well. Now that she was no longer seeing Mitch Hayden, her life seemed to be back on track. The same old safe but boring track it had been on before she'd moved out of Uncle Fowler's home. Her uncle was already talking about her wedding to Charles. And no matter how many times she told him that she wasn't going to marry his young protégé, he didn't listen.

Zed held his black-tie party at the Neptune Room of the Ocean Side Hotel. It was reported that Zed owned the hotel, which his construction company had built on the Gulf about seven years ago.

Emily wasn't overly fond of loud music and huge crowds, but she agreed with Nikki that good manners dictated that they at least put in an appearance. Emily just wished that Nikki had chosen a different date. "I feel sorry for Rod, mooning around over you all the time. I just think he needs to realize you aren't the only woman in the world. It'll be good for him, and for you, too." How could Emily argue against such reasoning?

The moment the four of them entered the room, Emily wished they hadn't come. The lounge was packed with people dressed to the nines. Beautiful women and wealthy men. Zed's friends, acquaintances and business associates.

She had been raised with money and social position, but her family hadn't been wealthy enough to expose her to the upper echelon of high society, where multimillionaires and billionaires rubbed elbows with movie stars and world leaders. And even though Uncle Fowler's inherited wealth did give him entrance to this world, he seldom ventured into it.

"Some shindig, huh?" Puckering her lips, Nikki sucked in her cheeks. "Reminds me of the parties Mother and Warner used to give."

"Let's make a pact tonight," Emily whispered. "Neither of us is going to talk about or even think about the past."

"I promise," Nikki agreed.

"I suppose, if one is as wealthy as Mr. Banning, one can afford to throw away good money on these frivolous affairs." With his long, thin nose turned up in a snobbish manner, Charles Tolbert glanced around the room. "A vulgar display of wealth." He tsk-tsked loudly.

Emily frowned at him. "If you'd rather not have come with me tonight, I would have understood." She patted his arm with a mock show of concern. "I know how you dislike attending parties when you don't know anyone."

She wasn't fond of large social gatherings, either, preferring smaller more intimate parties with friends. But Zed Banning had been more than kind to her in recent weeks. Not accepting his hand-delivered invitation would have shown a lack of good manners. Besides, she needed some sort of distraction to get her mind off Mitch Hayden. It seemed no matter how busy she kept herself or how often she saw Charles, she couldn't stop thinking about Mitch, who she assumed, due to his lack of social standing in South Alabama, wouldn't attend tonight's gala affair. Three weeks had passed since she had discovered his true identity. Time enough to have accepted that he could never be a part of her life. But her heart yearned for him. And her body ached with wanting.

"Come on, let's find something to drink. But not too much, or you'll be dancing naked on the tables before midnight," Emily told Nikki, then glanced around, looking for a waiter. "Not that you need to dance on the tables to get attention. Not in that outfit."

A waiter carrying a tray of champagne stopped. Nikki, Emily and Rod retrieved glasses of the bubbly. Charles declined the offer of liquor.

"What's wrong with my outfit?" Nikki asked.

"Nothing, if your purpose in wearing it is to attract male attention," Charles said.

Emily inspected the neat, tailored, black suit Nikki wore. The straight skirt hit Nikki midthigh, and her slender legs were encased in black silk stockings. The draped collar suit was stunning, the jacket tapering at the waist, where three gold-and-pearl buttons held it together. Nikki wore nothing under the jacket, which plunged to a provocative V in front, revealing the high, round swell of her small, firm breasts.

"Well, that *was* my intention." Nikki sipped her champagne. "I'm attracting your attention, aren't I, Rod?"

Rod choked on the sip of champagne in his mouth, coughed several times, then recovered his composure. "You look gorgeous, Nikki. You and Emily are the two prettiest women here."

"Now, that's what a girl likes to hear," Nikki said. "A man who proclaims you the fairest in the land before he even checks out the competition."

"I see that Banning has had a feast set up." Charles nodded toward the buffet tables.

"Good idea, Charlie. Why don't we fix ourselves a plate and mingle?" Nikki suggested.

Emily followed Nikki's lead, as did Rod and Charles, and the foursome made their way along the buffet tables. Nikki loaded her plate with a wide variety of edible delights, while Emily chose only cheese and grapes.

"Are you ladies enjoying yourselves?" Zed Banning placed his hand on Emily's back, but he stared directly at Nikki, then looked down at her plate. "Haven't eaten all day, Nikki?"

"As a matter of fact, I had pancakes for breakfast and then Emily and I ordered pizza for lunch." Nikki put on her best fake smile for Zed. "I'm just glad I'm not one of your simpering lady friends who nibbles on carrot sticks and lettuce and worries constantly whether or not she'll impress you with her gorgeous body."

"Well, Nikki, you don't ever have to worry about being one of my lady friends and impressing me with your body." Zed winked at Emily, who almost choked on a grape when she heard his remark.

"Thank God for big favors." Nikki released an exaggerated sigh.

"All right, you two," Emily said. "Take off the boxing gloves for one night."

"For you, Emily, anything." Zed turned his attention to the two men flanking Emily and held out his hand. "I'm Zed Banning, your host."

"Oh, forgive me," Emily said. "Zed, this is Charles Tolbert, a dear friend and my escort for the evening." The two men exchanged a brief handshake. "And this is Rod Simmons, one of my art students, and Nikki's escort." The two shook hands.

"Well, welcome to my little shindig, boys. Eat, drink, mingle and enjoy yourselves." Zed pulled Emily from her sandwiched position between the other two men. He placed his arm around her, then reached out and encircled Nikki's shoulders with his other arm. "You gentlemen don't mind if I steal the ladies for a few minutes, do you?"

"Sure, it's fine with me," Rod said.

"I'm not sure about—" Charles said.

"There's a gentleman here from Republic Books," Zed explained. "I'd like Emily to meet him."

"How did you know..." Emily let her question die midsentence. She'd been about to ask Zed how he knew she had written a children's book and meeting the publisher of a house that specialized in children's books would be a dream come true for her. Mitch must have told Zed. Had Zed asked the man here tonight for the sole purpose of introducing him to her?

"Well, you can introduce me to someone old and rich, with one foot in the grave and another on a banana peel," Nikki said. "A rich, old codger who has a thing for sweet, young innocents."

Glancing at Nikki's cleavage, Zed laughed heartily. "Sweet and innocent would rule you out immediately."

"Why would you want Emily—" Charles asked.

"That's great, Emily," Rod said at the same moment Charles spoke. "You can tell this guy from Republic Books about your Hannah book."

Charles's lips formed a soft oval, as realization dawned on him. "Oh, yes, of course, your little book. By all means, go meet this man."

"You'll excuse us, won't you?" Zed took the ladies away.

Nikki kept her phony smile plastered to her face while Zed led her and Emily through the crowd, briefly introducing them to various men and women.

Zed stopped abruptly. "Hardy, I'd like for you to meet someone."

The dignified gentleman in his early sixties turned around and smiled. Emily thought he resembled the Colonel Sanders image, with his mane of white hair, mustache and beard.

"Emily, may I introduce Mr. Hardy Winston. Hardy, this is Ms. Emily Jordan. Emily is the young woman I told you about."

"I am enchanted," Hardy said.

"I hope you don't mind that I mentioned to Hardy that you've written a book he might be interested in," Zed said.

Emily smiled sweetly. "No, I don't mind at all."

Nikki cleared her throat.

"Oh, sorry." Zed pulled Nikki from his side and positioned her in front of him, her head just reaching his chest. "This is Emily's friend and business partner, Nikki Griffin. And I think it's my duty to warn you that she does bite."

Chuckling softly, Hardy inspected Nikki from head to toe. "Delighted to meet you."

"Nikki, why don't you and I dance and give Hardy and Emily a chance to talk," Zed suggested.

Nikki frowned, but accepted Zed's arm and followed him onto the dance floor.

"Would you care to dance, Miss Emily?" Hardy asked, in his thick Southern drawl. "It would give an old man great pleasure to dance with such a lovely young woman. While we're dancing, you can tell me about this book of yours. Zed seems to think I'll want to publish it."

"I... Yes, I'd like to dance." Emily wondered where Charles was and if he was terribly annoyed with her for inviting him to this party and then deserting him shortly after arriving. When this dance ended, she'd have to find him and make amends.

Hardy escorted Emily onto the dance floor. The band was playing a Kenny G. hit called "Morning." Hardy took Emily into his arms, his movements practiced and precise. She smiled at him when he told her what a marvelous dancer she was.

Across the room, on the edge of the dance floor, Mitch Hayden, wearing a tux he'd borrowed from Zed, stood watching Emily in another man's arms. It took every ounce of his willpower not to storm across the dance floor and take her away from the other man. Jealousy ate away at his insides as he saw her smiling at and laughing with someone else, even if the guy was old enough to be her father.

He hadn't wanted to attend Zed's party. But when Zed told him that Emily would be there, he had accepted. He would gladly face the demons of hell for a chance to see her, to talk to her.

She looked more beautiful tonight than ever before. So soft and delicate. So utterly, completely feminine. The cinnamon-colored silk dress she wore skimmed her ankles, sweeping around her legs as she swayed to the music. The waist was fitted, showing off how small she was there, and the shirred bustline enhanced her round, full breasts. Hannah McLain's gold locket dangled from the gold chain around her neck.

"There's no point in eating your heart out over Emily dancing with someone else." Nikki Griffin slipped her arm through Mitch's.

Mitch tensed at Nikki's touch, but he didn't pull away from her. "Where'd you come from?"

"From Zed Banning's evil clutches," Nikki said. "He asked me to dance with him, but once we were where Emily couldn't hear, I told him I'd rather dance with King Kong."

"I'm sure Zed was crushed."

"Yeah. You couldn't put a dent in that guy's ego with a guided missile." Nikki tugged on Mitch's arm and smiled. "Come on, Mitch. Dance with me."

"I'm surprised you'd even speak to me," Mitch said. "Considering who I am and what happened between Emily and me, I thought you'd hate me."

"How can I hate you when you're the man who brought Emily back to life?" Nikki led Mitch onto the dance floor. "She may be hurt and confused right now, but sooner or later she's going to realize that you can offer her something she desperately needs."

"And what do you think I can offer Emily?"

"Love and acceptance."

Mitch took Nikki into his arms. "I'm afraid I don't understand."

"Hang around for the long haul and you'll figure it out."

Mitch eyed Emily across the room and he knew he had to dance with her. He needed to hold her in his arms again, if only for a few stolen moments.

"Are you interested in changing partners for a third time?" he asked.

"What?"

Mitch nodded toward Emily and her dance partner.

Nikki grinned. "Sure, come on."

Mitch maneuvered Nikki across the dance floor, leading her closer and closer to his objective. Whirling Nikki around, Mitch released her, then tapped Emily's dance partner on the shoulder.

"Change partners," Mitch said. And before anyone had a chance to agree or protest, Mitch stole Emily out of the other man's arms, leaving him little choice but to accept Nikki or make an embarrassing scene.

"How dare you!" Emily tried to pull out of Mitch's arms, but he held fast.

"I dare," he said. "Dance with me, Emily. People are looking at us, wondering why we aren't dancing."

"I don't care."

"One dance."

She didn't verbally agree, but she allowed him to lead her into the dance. When the music stopped, she turned from him. Mitch caught her by the wrist and tugged her back into his arms. She went, reluctantly at first, but finally accepting the fact that she wanted to be in his arms. The band played another Kenny G. hit, the utterly romantic "Forever in Love."

Mitch didn't say a word; neither did Emily.

To simply hold her was enough.

To be in his arms was enough.

The music wrapped its bluesy sweetness around them, cocooning them in its warm, dreamy depths as he held her close, her head on his chest, his lips pressed against her hair.

If only the past didn't exist. If only there were no yesterdays, just tonight. Emily tried not to think, simply to feel, to enjoy these precious moments when her thoughts alone could destroy the pleasure.

"I miss you." Mitch whispered so softly he wasn't sure she'd heard him. He didn't want to say or do anything to make her run away.

She willed herself to stay calm, not to overreact to what he'd said. Was she prepared to be honest with Mitch? With herself? "I've missed you, too."

He hugged her closer, one hand tightening at her waist, the other caressing her neck. Slowly moving his fingers into her hair, he grasped the back of her head. Emily closed her eyes, experiencing the sheer ecstasy of feeling Mitch's blatant desire for her. How could she still want this man? How could she still love him?

Don't think! Don't remember! The plea was his as well as hers.

"I came here tonight because Zed told me you'd be here."

Mitch led her across the dance floor and through the crowd toward the balcony.

She went with him, powerless to stop herself. The half-full moon shined like a bright, partially formed ball of cream in the darkness.

"It's been more than three weeks since you found out who I am, nearly two weeks since we last spoke." Mitch held her around the waist, fastening his hands just above her hips. "Has anything changed? Have you reconsidered giving us another chance?"

"I've tried not to think about us, about what I'd hoped..." Emily pulled away from him. He let her go.

"I haven't been able to think about anything else but you. I'm worried about your safety. I want to be there for you, Emily. I want to take care of you. Protect you."

Turning her back to him, she gazed out over the long stretch of beach and the dark, pulsating ocean.

"I can't allow you to come back into my life because you think I need a bodyguard."

"I want back in your life under any circumstances." Mitch walked up behind her, only inches separating their bodies.

"It would be too easy to say yes, please come back, please take care of me, please love me." Emily gasped when Mitch draped his arms around her, pulling her back against his chest, her hips against his erection. "But I can't. I'm too confused about my feelings, and I think you're confused, too. What you're feeling for me now is pity."

"I know what I feel, and it isn't pity."

"Then it's guilt," she said, resisting the urge to lean against him, to accept whatever he was offering.

"Dammit, Emily, it's not guilt and it's not pity." He whirled her around in his arms, forcing her to face him. "Yes, I feel guilty as hell. I'll always carry around a heavy burden of guilt. And yes, I'm consumed with regret about what happened to you. But, pretty lady, what I feel for you is desire. It's pure old-fashioned lust. I want you more than I've ever wanted anything or anyone in my life."

Emily bit her bottom lip in an effort to keep from crying. She wanted to believe him. "Oh, Mitch, please. The situation between us is so complicated."

"It could be simple. We could make it simple. You and I and a night alone together."

He drew her into his arms, lowering his head as she gazed up at him, transfixed by his demanding stare, hypnotized by the depth of emotion she saw in his eyes.

His lips took hers with sweet, tender fury. Demanding, pleading and yet so very careful not to take more than she was willing to give.

Emily responded, surrendering herself to the kiss, to the way Mitch made her feel. She slipped her arms around his neck, drawing him closer.

He thrust his tongue inside her mouth. She returned the urgency of his invasion. The kiss deepened, growing hotter and more intense, until they had to break apart, gasping for air.

"Dear God, Emily, give me another chance. Just tell me what I have to do."

Emily's chest rose and fell with her labored breaths. She wanted to reach out, to touch his face, to tell him that she loved him and that nothing else mattered. Stuart didn't matter. The baby didn't matter. Her scarred back didn't matter. But she couldn't. Because Stuart and their child and the scars on her back did matter.

"I can't." She took a deep breath. "I want to, but I can't."

She ran from him. Left the balcony. Into Neptune's lounge. Mitch walked over to the edge of the balcony and looked down. Any other man might jump and put an end to his misery, but not Mitch Hayden. Whatever agony he experienced, he deserved. Maybe he hadn't paid dearly enough for his sins yet. But how could he ever make atonement to Emily if she was too afraid of her own feelings to name his penance?

Emily didn't see Charles Tolbert until she bumped into him. He grasped her by the shoulders.

"Is something wrong, Emily? Are you running from someone?" Charles asked.

Taking a deep breath, she straightened her hair. "Just running from myself."

"Well, I was hoping I could talk you into a dance."

"I'd like that."

Charles could be sweet, even charming, at times. And he was always available. Being with him tonight might help her keep Mitch at bay. She didn't dare risk being alone with Mitch again.

Emily danced several times with Charles as well as Rod and Zed. She and Charles shared a dessert plate and she even persuaded him to taste some champagne. And Hardy Winston sought her out again, to remind her that he expected her to send her Hannah book directly to him and he'd see the right editor took a look at it.

From time to time, she would feel someone's eyes on her and catch a glimpse of Mitch across the crowded room. He was watching her—wanting her—needing her. She couldn't—wouldn't—allow herself to succumb to the hunger she saw in his eyes or the desire she felt as intensely as he did.

Mitch had watched her from afar all night while she danced with, ate with and smiled at Charles Tolbert. Little by little the jealousy gnawed away at him until he didn't think he could bear the sick anger that welled up inside him. And then just when he'd decided to leave, he had seen Emily, Nikki and Rod enter the elevator with Tolbert. He'd caught up with them on the main floor, and stood silently by while the foursome got in Tolbert's Mercedes and drove away.

And now Mitch stood on the beach, as close to Emily's cottage as he could get without being on her porch. He could make out two silhouettes in Emily's open front door. When Tolbert kissed Emily, Mitch thought he'd die. It didn't matter to him that it had been a quick kiss, not much more than a brushing of lips. Emily was his. He didn't want any other man touching her.

"Thank you for escorting me to Zed's party," Emily said.

"You're quite welcome. I always enjoy being with you," Charles told her. "I'd like to take you out again very soon. It would please me very much. Perhaps we could invite Fowler to join us for the symphony.''

''Yes, that would be nice.''

''I'll call you tomorrow, then.'' He lifted her hand to his lips. ''I believe we could be very happy together, Emily. We have so much in common. Similar backgrounds and upbringings.''

''Good night, Charles.'' Emily eased her hand out of his.

''Good night, my dearest. 'Parting is such sweet sorrow.' ''

Emily tensed when Charles quoted Shakespeare to her. She shouldn't have been surprised; she knew that he had a fondness for classical literature. But she couldn't help thinking about how her mystery man had quoted poetry to her. Was Charles the person who had sent the letters and made the phone calls? Had he been the one who had cautioned her against Mitch? Was he capable of breaking into her home and wreaking such havoc?

Alone in the shadows, Mitch waited for Charles Tolbert to back his Mercedes out of Emily's driveway. Then he bounded up on the porch, knocked at the front door and waited, wondering if Emily would talk to him or slam the door in his face.

She opened the door. Her eyes widened. Her mouth rounded into a silent gasp.

''Don't get involved with Tolbert just to spite me.''

''I am not getting involved with Charles to spite you.'' Stiffening her spine, Emily squared her shoulders and glared at Mitch. ''You must think I'm a total fool just because of what happened with you.''

''Emily, I don't think you're—''

''I'm going to continue seeing Charles and my reasons have nothing to do with you,'' Emily lied.

''I don't believe you,'' Mitch said.

Emily gripped the doorknob, preparing to close the door. ''Go away, Mitch. Please, leave me alone.''

When she tried to close the door, Mitch blocked her move with his shoulder, insinuating himself a couple of inches over the threshold. ''Be careful, honey. I'm not sure you can trust Charles Tolbert. He might be—''

"If I can't trust Charles, then who can I trust? Uncle Fowler? Nikki? Maybe Zed Banning?"

"You can trust me."

Emily stared incredulously at him. "How can you say that, after what happened between us? You lied to me. You hid your true identity from me."

He was so close, too close. Releasing the doorknob, Emily took a step backward. She needed to put some space between her body and Mitch's.

He reached out and touched a stray tendril of her dark hair. Their eyes met and held, ice blue pleading with warm cinnamon.

"You can trust me with your life," he said, curling her hair around his finger. "There are no lies between us now, no more secrets. I've told you that I'd do anything for you, but you have to believe me. Believe me enough to trust me, to give me a chance to prove myself."

She wanted to believe him, wanted to trust him. In her heart of hearts, Emily knew that she loved Mitch Hayden, despite his past, despite everything that stood between them. "I believe you mean what you say."

He took a step closer to her. Her heart beat rapidly, as a warm flush spread over her body. Releasing her hair, he skimmed the side of her face with the back of his hand.

"I'm only a phone call away," he said. "If you need me, for anything, all you have to do is ask."

He didn't want to leave her, but he knew he must. She wasn't ready for anything else, not even a good-night kiss. If he kissed her, he wouldn't be able to leave, and it would be wrong to take advantage of Emily when she was still so uncertain about her feelings.

"Good night, pretty lady."

Before he could change his mind and beg her to come home with him, Mitch turned and walked away, feeling so alone, yet keeping close to his heart the fact that Emily had said she believed him. Surely there was a way to prove himself to her, to show her that he'd do anything to make her happy.

Chapter 12

Emily stood on the porch watching the sunset, breathing in the unique aroma of the sea, absorbing the beauty of the red sky, the glistening ivory sand and the blue-gray waters of the bay at day's end.

She had just come home from an early dinner date with Charles, their fifth in the three weeks since the night of Zed's party. She cared too much for Charles, as a friend, to let their relationship go any further. She didn't love him and she never would. She had decided that after tonight, she wouldn't see him again. He'd made it abundantly clear that he loved her and wanted to marry her. And they both knew their union would please Uncle Fowler.

But it had been unfair of her to continue seeing Charles, leading him on, when she was in love with another man. The man next door. The man she hadn't spoken to in twenty-one days. Was he out there somewhere, on the beach? Inside his cottage? Was he watching her?

She glanced back inside her open front door at Charles, who was deep in conversation on the telephone. He had apologized to her for having to make a business call, and she had assured him it was quite all right.

Emily sat down in one of the big wicker rockers, leaned her head backward and closed her eyes. What was she going to do about her life? She couldn't allow things to continue the way they were now. She felt positive about her decision to explain to Charles why there was no point in their seeing each other again.

Deciding what to do about Mitch Hayden wasn't so easy. Could she ever forget the past? Was there any way she could look at Mitch and not remember that he was M. R. Hayden?

Mitch had made some big mistakes in his life. The biggest had been trusting the wrong people. Even though Mitch hadn't done anything illegal or underhanded himself, he'd been duped into allowing his partner to construct unsafe buildings. Emily could understand Mitch's desire to get rich quick. He'd come from the depths of poverty and scratched his way to the top. Unfortunately, he hadn't paid close enough attention to what was going on around him.

She didn't doubt that Mitch had suffered greatly in the past five years. Losing his business, his reputation and his fiancée in one fell swoop had nearly destroyed him. But it had been in the years since the trial, since Styles and Hayden Construction had gone into bankruptcy, that Mitch had paid for his sins.

Zed had told her how Mitch had become little more than a bum on the streets, drinking too much, getting into too many fistfights in seedy dives, daring God to strike him dead with every action he took.

And Emily didn't doubt Mitch's sincerity when he had said he'd do anything in the world for her.

So what did she want from Mitch Hayden? She wanted him to love her the way she loved him. She wanted him to marry her and give her a child. She wanted him to make love to her and not see the scars on her back.

She was sure that if she asked all this of him, he would give it to her. But she could never ask. She would never know if his actions came from real love or only from his own guilt and a deep sense of pity.

"Sorry that took so long." Charles came outside onto the porch and sat down beside Emily in a matching wicker rocker. "You look very pensive, dear. Is something wrong?"

"Yes and no." She turned to him and smiled. "I've enjoyed our dating again..."

"I hear a 'but' coming." Reaching across the arms of their chairs, he took her hand in his. "Have I said or done something wrong?"

"No." She shook her head. "You've been a perfect gentleman, and perhaps, under different circumstances..." Emily pulled her hand out of his grasp. "I can't see you again, Charles. I'm sorry, but I've been wrong to let you think that there could ever be more than friendship between us."

"I see." Leaning back in the rocker, Charles bent his knee, crossing one leg over the other.

"Would this decision to end our relationship have anything to do with Mitchell Hayden?"

"I really don't think that's any of your business."

Charles uncrossed his legs and stood, tall and elegant in his tailored suit, linen shirt and silk tie. "Hayden's a bit rough around the edges for a lady like you, Emily. According to Fowler, money and success didn't turn him into a gentleman when he was at the top of his game, and now that he's nothing more than a construction worker, he's even cruder than ever."

"I don't want to discuss Mitch with you."

Charles gazed down at Emily, then shook his head. "You'd be a fool to trust that man after all he's done to you. My God, woman, his construction firm was responsible for your husband's death."

"You warn me not to trust Mitch. He warns me not to trust you." Emily stood, facing Charles. "I'm very fond of you, but I don't love you. All we can ever be is friends."

"Yes, well, I had hoped for more. You're an incredibly lovely lady. One who would do credit to any man." Slumping his shoulders like a defeated soldier, Charles bent his head. "Fowler will be terribly disappointed that things didn't work out for us. He has his heart set on our marrying and moving into his home."

Emily touched Charles's arm, wishing she'd never met Mitch Hayden, wishing her heart were free so that she might have eventually accepted Charles as her life's mate. But now that she'd known what real passion felt like, she could never settle for anything less. Even if it meant spending the rest of her life alone.

"I'm sorry. I wish I could do what Uncle Fowler wants, but I can't."

"You're in love with Hayden, aren't you?"

She couldn't answer Charles. She simply stood there staring at him until he leaned over, kissed her on the cheek and walked down the front steps and out to his Mercedes.

Curled up on the damask chaise longue in her bedroom, Emily held a glass of peach-flavored sparkling water in her hand. A thin volume of Elizabeth Barrett Browning's poetry lay in her lap. Closing her eyes as she leaned her head back, she listened to the steady beat of the rain, which had started nearly an hour ago. The spring rain had begun slowly, a soft peppering on the roof, but had turned into a heavy downpour within fifteen minutes.

Carl Reinecke's Harp Concerto permeated the room with the tender sweetness of a music that brought to mind moonlight and roses, good wine and warm smiles. Emily felt at peace for the first time in weeks. She had made a decision tonight. She couldn't go on lying to herself, pretending that she didn't want Mitch Hayden in her life. She accepted the fact that nothing could change the past. Hers or Mitch's.

Perhaps she and Mitch had no future together, but tomorrow, she would talk to him, be as honest with him as she could be and still maintain some semblance of her pride. Others might call her a fool. Perhaps she was.

Suddenly the room went pitch black. Emily screamed. Dear Lord, what had happened? Had the spring rain turned into a storm without her notice? When Emily jumped up, the book of poetry dropped to the floor. She gripped the glass in her hand.

Stay calm. Don't panic. Look out the window. Search for light.

But there was no light. The moon and stars were obscured by thick cloud cover and heavy rain. Then, unexpectedly, off in the distance, she saw a pale glimmer of illumination. A flashlight? Or her imagination?

She felt her way across the room and set the glass of water down on her dressing table. Listening for the sound of thunder, she heard only the pounding of the heavy rain. No thunder. No lightning. No storm. Why had the electricity gone off?

Light the kerosene lamp on the dresser, she told herself. The matches are in the top drawer.

Darkness, thick and heavy, surrounded her, bearing down on her like an enormous weight. She could feel the nervous pumping of her heart as she took slow, tentative steps in the direction of the dresser. Bumping into the dresser's edge, she grasped the side, then reached out, feeling for the lamp. Finding it, she kept one hand draped around the base while she opened the top drawer and searched inside for the box of matches. After retrieving the matches, she released the lamp momentarily.

On the first try, she couldn't seem to light the match. Nor on the second try. Her hands trembled. *Light the damn match!*

A flicker of pale orange burned at the tip of the third match. Carefully lifting the glass chimney, Emily lit the lamp. The soft, warm glow illuminated the room with its dim light.

Emily breathed a sigh of relief. Some of the fear drained from her. More light. She needed more light. She kept a supply of candles and a kerosene lamp for every room. The electricity didn't go off all that often, except in stormy weather, but when it did, Emily was always prepared. She would never find herself alone in the dark if she could help it.

Holding the lamp high in her hand, she walked out into the hallway, but stopped dead still when she heard the shattering of glass in her kitchen and the murmur of two male voices.

Walking backward, Emily eased into her bedroom and closed the door, locking it behind her. Someone was breaking into her house. Two men, who'd been whispering to each other.

She had to get help. Immediately. She set the lamp on the table and picked up the phone. Without giving any thought to what she was doing, she dialed the number as she clutched the phone fiercely in her hand.

"Hello," the deep masculine voice said.

"Mitch! Help me! Someone's breaking into my house!"

"I'll be right there! Do you hear me, honey?"

"Yes, Mitch, please—" The line went dead. Emily dropped the telephone. Whoever had severed her electrical lines must have suddenly remembered that he hadn't cut the phone line, as well.

Emily never had owned a gun. She didn't believe in guns. But dear Lord, she wished she had one now.

Was there anything in her bedroom she could use as a weapon? If they broke down the door, how would she defend herself, one woman against two men?

Open the window and go out onto the porch, she told herself. But it was dark outside. Pitch-black.

She heard the sound of footsteps inside the cottage. She covered her mouth with her hand, sucking in her breath, resisting the urge to scream.

Stay calm. Mitch is on his way over here. But what if the men were armed? What if they shot Mitch? Dammit, why hadn't she called 911 instead of Mitch? If anything happened to him, she would never forgive herself.

And why had she insisted that Nikki return to her home, assuring her best friend that she didn't need a baby-sitter? Why hadn't she done as Mitch and Zed suggested and had a security system installed? She'd been stupid to think she was safe now, to think that the harassment was over, that there would be no more trouble. She had been wrong. Dead wrong.

The footsteps came down the hallway. The door to the bedroom beside hers opened and closed. With her eyes glued to her own bedroom door, Emily waited. The footsteps came closer. Her doorknob turned. A man's voice called out.

"Are you hiding, Emily?"

She didn't recognize the voice, had no idea who he was. She didn't move and barely breathed.

"Be a good girl and keep Mitch Hayden out of your life and we'll leave you alone," another male voice said.

"Now you're all alone in the dark and the boogeymen are going to get you."

On tiptoe, Emily crept toward the window, reached up and unlatched the lock. The doorknob rattled again. Emily eased the window upward. The wind blew the rain across the porch and through the open window, hitting her in the face. She peered outside into the deep, empty darkness.

She had two choices. Stay in the lit room and face her attackers. Or crawl out the window and run for safety in the darkness. The killing darkness. The darkness that had encompassed her that day five years ago. The darkness from which she had awakened to find her husband and child dead.

"If you promise to be a good little girl and stay away from Mitch Hayden, we won't hurt you." The doorknob rattled again.

"Sooner or later, we'll get you. Unless you cut Mitch Hayden out of your life for good," the other masculine voice said.

Emily lifted her leg up and over, bending her back as she slipped out the window. One foot and then the next landed on the porch. The blowing rain covered her, dousing her with its cool wetness. She shivered, as much from fear as from the damp chill.

On the porch, braced against the outside wall, she heard the two men's voices coming through her locked bedroom door. Get away! she warned herself. Run! Now!

She turned to face the night and froze on the spot. She couldn't see anything, not even her own hand in front of her face. Glancing back at the open window, she saw the faint light coming from the kerosene lamp.

She couldn't stay here, cowering like a fool. She had to do something.

Mitch phoned for help before he stormed out of the house. He had no gun, no real weapon other than a baseball bat a former tenant had left in the hall closet. He had no idea what he would encounter when he got to Emily's house. All he knew was that if anyone had hurt her, he'd kill them! With his bare hands, if necessary.

He fought the cool, drenching rain that seeped into his jeans and shirt, pelting his face, slicking his hair against his head.

Clutching the flashlight in one hand, waiting to turn it on, waiting until he needed it, he gripped the baseball bat in his other hand. He rounded the side of the cottage. Making his way onto the porch and to the back door, he stepped on shards of something that crunched under his feet. Flipping on the flashlight, he saw that he'd stepped on glass—glass broken out of Emily's back door. Just like last time, he thought. Shining the flashlight, Mitch ran the beam up to the electrical service entrance and saw the line dangling in the branch of a nearby bush. The severed telephone wire lay on the ground.

Dammit, why had Emily been so stubborn about refusing to have a security system installed? Of course, even a security system couldn't stop the most determined culprit. Whoever was inside Emily's house could kill her before the police arrived. But he wasn't going to let that happen.

Turning off the flashlight, Mitch walked through the open back door and into the kitchen. He heard the crash of wood breaking. He ran through the house, down the hallway and toward Emily's bedroom. His heartbeat roared in his ears. The door hung precariously on the brass hinges. A soft pool of light spread across Emily's room. In front of an open window, their backs to Mitch, stood two dark-haired figures, shrouded in rain slickers. Neither man appeared to be more than five-eight or nine, and despite the bulkiness of their slickers, both appeared to be slender.

Could he take them both? Maybe. Possibly. But if they were armed, he was a dead man.

Glancing around the room, he couldn't find Emily. Had she slipped out the window? God, he hoped so.

A surprise attack would be his best bet. With the sleek, silent movements of a panther, Mitch crept up on the two dark figures, one bent over, his head out the window.

"We scared her good."

The guy laughed, and Mitch wanted to break him in half.

"This was easy, huh? Five hundred bucks just to scare some woman who's afraid of the dark."

"Yeah, and more money than last time," the other man said, pulling himself out of the window. He started to turn around.

Neither man knew what hit him. Mitch strategically aimed the baseball bat and knocked first one and then the other to his knees. Then Mitch kicked one man in the groin, and while he fell onto the floor, yelping in pain, Mitch dropped the baseball bat and landed a hard right cross to the other man's jaw. He reeled from the blow, then lunged at Mitch. Mitch rammed his fist into the guy's belly. He fell to the floor, his head thumping loudly when it made contact with the hard wood. With both men lying in crumpled heaps on the floor, their legs and arms crisscrossing, Mitch glanced down and saw that the men were actually only teenage boys.

"Dammit! What the hell!" Mitch kicked the baseball bat across the floor. The sight of the boys, one moaning loudly, the other not even moving, urged Mitch into action.

Leaning down, he felt for a pulse in the silent boy. They were both still alive, although the one Mitch had knocked out was still unconscious.

Quickly Mitch rummaged around in Emily's dresser, finding the drawer where she kept her panty hose and stockings. Using the panty hose, he hog-tied the assailants' hands and feet together and left them lying on the floor.

Rushing back outside, he turned on the flashlight and began his search for Emily. She had to be out here somewhere. Wet, cold, alone and probably scared half to death in the darkness.

He circled the house, searching the porch and the shrubbery in the yard, then he made his way toward the beach. He called her name, but it was lost on the wind. He called again and again, hoping she might hear him.

His feet caught in the wet sand, slowing his movements. "Emily. Where are you, honey?"

"Mitch!"

He scanned the area with his flashlight and saw her there in the sand, on her knees, halfway between her cottage and his.

He ran to her, dropping the flashlight as he fell to his knees and drew her into his arms. "It's all right, honey. You're safe. I'm here now."

"Two men...in my house...threatening..." She gulped the words, breathless, her body quivering.

"They're not going to hurt you. I took care of them. And the police are on their way here." Mitch held her, stroking her wet hair, kissing her forehead, the side of her face, her ear.

"I crawled out the window." She clung to him, her fingers biting into his arms. "I was so scared, but I knew I didn't have any choice. The darkness! Oh, Lord, Mitch, the blackness was like the day Stuart died, the day I—"

"You were very brave, Emily. You faced your worst fear. You saved yourself."

The rain poured down over them, but neither cared. Mitch held her there, both of them on their knees in the sand. He knew he'd die for this woman, and felt certain Emily knew it, too.

"Come on, honey, let me get you back to my place, where you'll be dry and warm."

"Those men... My house..."

"The police will take care of them."

"When the police get here, I want to go back to my house. I want to see those men. I want to know who they are."

"There's no need for you to do that. I'll take care of it."

"No! I have to find out for myself who they are. They warned me to never see you again. They said if I didn't get you out of my life, they'd come back and get me."

The two teenagers, who'd finally given their names as Tony Grissom and Paulie Beall, told the police, Mitch and Emily that a man had offered them two hundred dollars to break into Emily's house the first time and scrawl a specific message on her mirror. Ransacking the living room had been their idea. Then the same guy had offered them another five hundred dollars to come to the cottage and scare the hell out of Emily tonight. He had instructed them on how to cut the electrical and phone wires and exactly what to say to Emily. He'd also told them not to harm her in any way.

"We were just supposed to scare her and warn her to stay away from some guy named Mitch Hayden," Tony explained.

They swore they didn't know the man who had hired them,

that a friend of a friend had told them this guy was looking for somebody to do a job for him.

"Honest to God, we never met the guy. We just talked to him on the phone," Paulie said. "He mailed us half the money before the job and the rest afterward. This deal was the same as the first time."

Understanding the ordeal Emily had been through, the police said it would be all right for her to come down to the station the next day. Mitch never released his hold on her, not even when she tried to pull away from him after the ambulance carried away the two badly bruised boys. One of the attendants said Tony Grissom had a mild concussion and Paulie Beall a few broken bones.

Finally alone, Mitch suggested Emily pack an overnight bag and come home with him. She adamantly refused. No one was going to keep her from staying in her own home.

Shaking his head, both amused and irritated by her stubbornness and pride, Mitch lifted her in his arms and carried her down the hallway. After sitting her on the edge of her bed, he began unbuttoning her wet blouse. She slapped at his hands.

"What do you think you're doing?" she asked.

"I'm helping you get out of these wet clothes. You need a warm bath and some hot coffee."

"I can undress myself, thank you very much."

Tugging on her arm, he pulled her to her feet, then reached out and picked up the kerosene lamp. "I'll walk you to the bathroom, and while you're taking a bath, I'll light a few more lamps. But I don't guess I'll fix you any coffee, though, with the electricity off."

"I have some brandy in the kitchen. The shelf above the sink."

"I'll get us some in a few minutes."

Emily walked with Mitch down the hallway and allowed him to set the lamp on the side of the bathroom sink. Then she ushered him out. He made his way back down the dark hallway with the aid of his flashlight, halting momentarily when he heard the sound of running water in the shower.

She showered quickly, savoring the warm water as it cleansed her body. Then she toweled herself dry, wrapped her hair turban-style and slipped into her robe that hung on the back of the bathroom door. The robe had been a Christmas present from Nikki, a silk-lined, damask robe in a soft taupe, designed in a subtle jacquard similar to fine European linen. She tied the belt securely, making sure her body was completely covered from shoulders to below knee level.

She couldn't allow herself to think about what had happened tonight. If she did, she might fall apart, and no matter what happened in her life, she never intended to lose her sanity. She'd been through too much, suffered too greatly, to allow recent events to bring her down.

But the one thing she couldn't stop thinking about was the fact that she'd called Mitch when she needed help. Not the police, but Mitch. Of course, he lived next door. He'd been close. But she admitted to herself that no matter where Mitch lived, she would have called him first. In that one moment of sheer desperation, when she'd needed someone she could count on, she'd wanted Mitch.

Opening the bathroom door, Emily immediately noticed the light coming from her bedroom. Not the pale, distant glimmer of one lone kerosene lamp, but the intensity of a blazing forest fire. She eased her way down the hall, stopping on the threshold of her bedroom. She gazed inside and was awed by the incredible sight she beheld. She gasped, then sighed.

Two kerosene lamps burned brightly on each side of the bed. Candles, dozens of white and beige and pink and blue and lavender candles, had been placed on every table, on the dresser, on the chest of drawers. Their flickering lights illuminated the room with an ethereal, misty glow, bathing everything in a muted gold wash.

And there in the middle of her bedroom stood Mitch Hayden. Big and tall and naked, except for the green-and-tan plaid cotton-knit throw he'd wrapped around his waist, which hit him midthigh, giving him the look of a Highland warrior.

Chapter 13

Emily couldn't take her eyes off Mitch. His blond hair and hard, muscled body appeared as golden as everything else in the room. The thick, curly hair covering his arms and legs and chest glistened as if it had been dusted with burnished gilt.

Gazing at her with those incredible, ice-blue eyes, he held out a snifter of brandy, it, too, a topaz-tinted brown in the antique crystal glass.

She couldn't move. She couldn't speak. She could only stare at him, her heart beating wildly, her breasts tightening to diamond points, her body moistening and softening.

"Come on in, Emily, and sit down." He nodded at the damask chaise longue where he'd held her in his arms all night, on that night so many weeks ago. "I found the brandy."

Taking a deep breath, Emily moved one tentative step forward. Then another. And another. Until she stood directly in front of Mitch. With trembling fingers, she reached out and accepted the brandy, grasping the snifter, clutching it in her hand.

"Sit down. Drink your brandy. It'll warm you," Mitch said, taking a sip of his own drink, then setting his glass on a nearby table.

Emily obeyed. She sat down on the chaise, lifted the snifter to her lips and sipped the brandy. Mitch walked around behind her, unwrapped the towel from her hair and dropped it to the floor. He threaded his big fingers through the damp strands, then reached over and picked up a comb from Emily's dressing table.

"You have beautiful hair." He lifted her hair in his hand, running the comb through from scalp to the ends, where her hair rested against her shoulder blades.

Emily swallowed hard. "Did you light every candle you could find in the house?" She glanced around the room.

"Yeah, I guess I did." He laid down the comb on the dressing table. "I wanted you to have plenty of light. I wanted you to feel safe and secure." He took her shoulders in his huge hands, kneading her through her robe. "I don't want you ever to be afraid again."

Emily shivered. "Thank you."

"Finish off your brandy."

She lifted the snifter to her lips. He sat down beside her on the chaise, his makeshift kilt spreading apart over his muscular legs.

She smiled, then looked up into his grinning face and laughed. "Was that the only thing you could find to put on?"

"Yeah. I'm afraid all your clothes are way too small, even your other robes."

"It's very becoming," Emily said. "Makes you look a bit like a Scotsman in a kilt." She didn't tell him that the very sight of him conjured up images of an ancient warrior. Strong. Invincible. Come home from battle to claim his woman. Emily shivered again.

"Are you cold?"

"No. I..." She took another sip of her brandy. "I'm fine. The shower and the brandy warmed me." And the nearness of Mitch Hayden.

"I'll go with you in the morning, to the police station. We'll see this thing through together." He touched her gently, placing his knuckles under her chin and lifting her face. "I'm not going to leave you. Not tonight. Not until we've put a stop to the person who's doing this to you. After that, I'll go whenever you ask." He dropped his hand from her face, letting it skim the side of her neck and across her shoulder, grasping a handful of her robe as he clamped his fingers around her upper arm.

Emily ran her tongue over her upper lip, then closed her mouth and stared at Mitch. What should she tell him? That he couldn't stay? That they could never have a relationship? That the past would always stand between them?

"Tonight, let me hold you, the way I did once before. Let me be here for you. Comfort you. Please, Emily, don't try to send me away. I won't go."

She finished off her brandy, set the glass on the nearby dressing table and turned to him, nodding in agreement. "You'll stay with me, help me resolve our problems, help me find out who hired those boys to break into my home? You'll do all that and ask nothing in return?"

"Yes, I'll do all that. I owe you even more. Let me do this for you."

"Because you feel guilty? Because you feel sorry for me?"

"Dammit, Emily, there's a lot more to the way I feel than guilt and pity!" He squeezed her arm, jerking her toward him.

"Is there, Mitch? Is there really?"

"If you only knew. If I could show you how I feel, I'd scare the hell out of you. I lie awake at night, hurting because I want you so much. Don't you know the difference between desire and pity?"

She eased away from him, leaning her body against the back of the chaise. Did she dare believe him? The look in his eyes told her that he wanted her. The tension on his face, in his body, so very visible, assured her that he wasn't lying. But it didn't matter if what he felt for her right now was desire because, once he saw her scars, the desire would vanish and be replaced by pity and disgust.

"I don't want to care about you," she said, her voice barely a whisper. "I should hate you, and I think, for a just a little while, I did hate you. You were guilty of greed and pride and perhaps stupidity, but you weren't guilty of murder. I know you didn't intentionally do anything to harm other people."

"Are you saying that you've truly forgiven me?" He reached down and took both of her hands into his.

"Yes, you already know that I've forgiven you, and I...I..."

"You what?" He brought her hands to his chest, laying them there against his thick, curly hair, against his hard muscles, against his loudly beating heart.

"I care... I—I fell in love with you before I knew about your past." She spread out her hands on his chest and felt the heat of his body.

"And now? How do you feel about me now?" He covered her hands with his.

She quivered. "I don't want to love you, but I do."

He couldn't bear the look of fear he saw in her eyes. Dear God in heaven, why was she afraid of him? Didn't she know, hadn't he told her, that he'd die for her?

He lifted one of her hands off his chest and brought it to his mouth, kissing her open palm. "I don't deserve your love. I don't deserve anyone as loving and kind and generous as you. But I want you, Emily. I want you more than anything."

She tried to smile, but the tears lodged in her throat acted as a deterrent, keeping her from expressing the pleasure his words gave her. She touched his face, allowing her fingertips to linger, to savor the sheer masculine strength of his features. Swallowing her tears, she sighed.

"There hasn't been anyone since Stuart, and I was a virgin when we married."

Mitch held his breath, praying with all his might that he could be the man Emily needed tonight. "I'd want you if there'd been a hundred men."

"I never thought I'd have the courage..." She stood up and walked across the room, stopping in front of her bed. "I was severely injured the day Stuart died. Burning debris fell across my back. I've gone through numerous operations, and the doctors did all they could do."

"Emily, you don't have to—"

"Yes, I do have to!"

"But it must be so painful for you to remember, to relive that day, those operations."

"I can never forget, Mitch. Don't you see? I live, every day, with a reminder of what happened to me. A horrible, ugly reminder."

With more courage than she knew she possessed, Emily loosened her robe and dropped it to the floor.

She stood there in front of Mitch, like a precious offering before a pagan god. He had never seen anything as beautiful, as irresistible, as Emily Jordan, naked in the candlelight, her long, dark, damp hair falling over her shoulder, touching the top of one perfect breast.

"You're so beautiful." His breathing ragged, his pulse pounding at breakneck speed, he stood and opened his arms to her.

"No, I'm not beautiful." She turned slowly, her shoulders shaking as she exposed her scarred back to the man she loved.

From a thick line of scarred flesh just between her shoulder blades to a narrow line of heavy scar tissue across the top of her buttocks, the back side of Emily's body bore the evidence of her pain and suffering—a visual testimony of her agony.

"My God!" He'd done this to her. He and Randy Styles. And Loni. They were responsible for those scars, for every moment of anguish she'd known because of them.

Reaching down to the floor, she picked up her robe and started to put it on, but before she could slip into it, Mitch grabbed her, knocking the robe from her hand. She stared up at him, her eyes dry, her expression one of resignation, as if she had long ago accepted her fate.

"Don't cover yourself." He pulled her into his arms, then ran his hands up and down her arms. "You *are* beautiful, Emily. Your scars don't diminish your beauty. If anything, they enhance it."

She tried to pull away from him. "Don't lie to me, dammit! You were appalled when you saw my back. Admit it!"

"I was shocked," he said. "And I hated myself, and Randy Styles and Loni. We destroyed your life."

"Please let me put on my robe." She tried again to free herself from his hold, but he held fast. "You can stay the night. In the other bedroom. I accept your offer of help."

"No." He lifted her into his arms. She struggled briefly, then simply tensed her body and stared at him as he carried her across the room and laid her down, on her side, atop the crochet-lace bedspread. He removed the plaid shawl from around his waist, tossing it on the floor.

"Mitch, what—"

He lifted her hair, dividing it in two and draping it on each side of her shoulders. He kissed the back of her neck. She trembled from head to toe.

"Don't. Please don't," she said.

He paid no heed to her. He caressed her shoulders, her arms; then touched her back, smoothing his fingers over the scars that covered her body. Turning her so that she could watch what he was doing to her in the dressing-table mirror, Mitch worshipped her body. Lowering his head, he kissed, licked, then kissed again, every inch of flesh that had been ravaged by the fire.

Tears welled up in her eyes. She batted them away with her fingers. She couldn't bear this. She couldn't lie here and allow him to touch her this way. But dear Lord, she couldn't move. She couldn't make herself put a stop to the pleasure of the moment. Never had she been touched with such sweetness, such tenderness—with such love.

She felt his breath on the hollow at the base of her spine. He kissed the scars on her buttocks, then planted a garden of tiny nipping caresses up and down the back of her thighs and calves.

"Mitch." She moaned his name, the heat in her rising, a hot passion consuming her.

"If only I could kiss away the pain you endured." He licked a trail up her spine, halting at her neck. "Don't ever think I find your body ugly. To me it's beautiful. Every inch of you is beautiful." He traced the scars with his fingertips. "If anything, these scars make you more beautiful to me. Your scars are a part of you, a part of who you are, a part of what makes you such a special lady."

He slipped his arm beneath her, turning her ever so slowly so that their naked bodies touched. Firm, round breasts to hard, muscled chest. Sleek, slender thighs to strong, hairy legs. Femininity to masculinity.

She looked at him, all golden man there in the candlelight, his ice-blue eyes filled with desire. She couldn't speak. She couldn't think. She could barely breathe.

He gazed down into her warm brown eyes and knew that no power on earth could stop him from making love to this woman. Emily needed and wanted him as much as he did her. Tonight, he would make her his completely. He would keep her safe. He would ease her pain.

"I want you," he said, lowering his head, taking her lips in a kiss that said all that was in his heart and more.

Emily raised her arms, circling his neck, threading her fingers through his hair as he deepened the kiss. She had dreamed of this, but had never dared to hope it could happen. Mitch had seen her scars. He had called them beautiful—beautiful because they were a part of her. And now he was making love to her.

Lifting her body up to his, she caressed his hardness with her softness, pleading, enticing, inviting.

He touched her with the upmost gentleness, as if she were a fragile flower or a delicate piece of porcelain that he dare not handle too roughly for fear of damaging it. Bracing his body with his elbow, he rose over her, gazing down into her eyes, smiling that wonderfully seductive smile that said more than words could ever say. Her heart soared, taking flight at the sheer joy of lying beneath Mitch, of knowing and yet not knowing what was to come.

With the fingertips of one hand, he traced the outline of her face, never taking his eyes off her. "Let me love you, Emily. Tell me that it's all right."

Swallowing, she nodded affirmatively and smiled at him. "It's all right. I want you to make love to me, Mitch."

Neither the past nor the future existed. Only the present. Only this glorious moment, here, now, with Mitch, on the brink of ecstasy.

Never had she felt about anyone the way she felt about Mitch. Just looking at him was a pleasure. Touching him and having him touch her took Emily's breath away, so intense was her reaction. She had fantasized about lying naked in his arms, about knowing the power of his complete possession.

Mitch kissed her shoulder. A soft, tender kiss. He skimmed his hand down her arm, across her breasts, over her stomach. A whispery touch. Light. Almost indiscernible. Emily shivered with the need coursing through her. Why didn't he touch her, really touch her? As he moved his hand over the tops of her thighs, she spread her legs involuntarily, then realizing what she'd done, clamped them together.

Mitch inserted his hand between her clenched thighs, forcing them apart. "Don't think about what you're doing, honey. Just react to the way you feel. To the way I make you feel."

Relaxing, Emily accepted his caresses. One of his hands covered her breast, kneading, pinching gently. She sighed, loving the way his thumb and fingers stroked her mound, leisurely spreading the folds of her femininity and entering the warmth of her body. She arched up against him.

"Easy, honey. Easy." Lowering his head, he took one begging nipple into his mouth, laving it with his tongue, then suckling greedily.

"Mitch!"

With the progressive attention to her breasts and her feminine core, Mitch brought Emily closer and closer to the brink of fulfillment. All the while whispering her name, telling her she was beautiful.

She exploded into a million tiny particles of satisfaction, moaning as Mitch took her mouth and moved his body up and over hers. He entered her with a hard, driving plunge while the last waves of completion claimed her. She cried out at the sensation of having him buried deep inside her, a joy she could not begin to describe.

She clung to him, her nails biting into his buttocks as she wrapped her legs around him and moved to the rhythm he set with the steady, arousing dips in and out of her body. He groaned crude, exciting words of praise and intent while he took her higher and higher, his mouth hot on her flesh, his lips at her breasts, his teeth nipping her neck and shoulder, his hands grasping, clasping, clutching.

Nothing existed except the two of them and the intensity of their emotions, their bodies sharing the most basic of pleasures.

Only the sound of their breathing, their moans and Mitch's occasional heated phrases blended with the constant, cascading beat of the falling rain outside the cottage.

She tensed beneath him, her body on the edge, wavering on the precipice of fulfillment. Mitch took her mouth, thrusting his tongue inside at the exact moment he rammed into her with a force that ignited the fire of completion. She cried out, trembling convulsively. Accelerating his lunges, Mitch found his own release, pouring himself into her as he climaxed.

Burrowing his head into her shoulder, he shuddered and groaned as Emily held him to her. He eased off her damp body to lie beside her, his arm draped across her stomach. Emily snuggled against him.

They fell asleep in each other's arms, their bodies replete with satisfaction, their minds dulled by the contentment that comes after making love.

Emily awoke in the early-morning hours before dawn, finding herself lying spoon fashion, Mitch's chest against her back, his breath warm on her neck. Glancing around the room, she noted that the candles had burned down, but most of them still glowed softly, keeping the room bathed in golden light. She eased out of Mitch's arms and made her way down the hallway to the bathroom, not giving her robe a second thought.

When she returned to her bedroom moments later, she found Mitch propped up on one elbow and the covers thrown back to reveal his naked body. He had a semi-erection, and Emily couldn't take her eyes off that particular part of his anatomy. She forced herself to look up at his face. He grinned.

"Do you have any idea how beautiful you look standing there in the doorway like a framed picture highlighted by golden light?" He slipped out of bed, but didn't make a move toward her.

Emily stood there, one foot in the bedroom, one in the hall. She stared at Mitch Hayden, all six feet three inches of him, and was overcome by the irresistible urge to touch him, to caress those broad shoulders, that wide, muscular chest, those powerful legs. Her fingers itched to curl themselves in his chest hair, to nip at his tiny nipples, to dance down his belly and wrap themselves around him.

She took a tentative step forward. Mitch waited, unmoving beside the bed, his chest rising and falling rapidly. When she stood a foot away from him, she reached out and touched his shoulder. Mitch jerked her into his arms and kissed her forcefully. She responded, returning the fierceness of his kiss.

"I don't think I'll ever get enough of you, pretty lady." Bending his knees lower and lower as he made his way down the front of her body, he forged a trail of damp heat from her neck to the apex between her thighs, his tongue darting in and out, flicking her intimately as she clung to his shoulders, her legs weakening.

On his knees in front of her, Mitch backed her trembling body to the edge of the bed and eased her down, her legs dangling off the side. Parting her legs, he situated himself between them and lowered his head to reach his goal.

Emily squirmed, burrowing her hips into the mattress, trying to escape his marauding mouth and at the same time reveling in the sensation of his tongue against her femininity. Reaching up, Mitch caressed her nipples.

Everything inside her tightened painfully, and then released, shock waves of fulfillment washing over her. Mitch lifted her legs high, draping them around his neck, resting them on his shoulders. Grasping her hips, he pulled her forward, positioning her on the edge of the bed. With her body still quivering with spasms of release, he entered her, hard and fast. She cried out, loving the feel of him inside her.

Embedding himself deeper and deeper, Mitch took her in a frenzy of desperate need, every male instinct within him urging him on.

Emily felt herself soaring again, her body reaching for that ultimate high. "Yes," she cried out. "Harder!"

As he obeyed her command, accelerating and strengthening his thrusts, the powerful shots of release rocketed through him.

Emily tightened around him, clutching him as she found her own satisfaction only moments afterward.

"I love you. Oh, Mitch, I love you so!"

Mitch fell forward, resting his head between her breasts, his mouth seeking and finding one tempting bud. She jerked away, crying out, her body overly sensitive to a mere touch.

He laughed. She laughed. After endless moments draped together on the edge of Emily's bed, they scurried up and under the covers. Mitch pulled her into his arms. They lay there, sated bliss spreading over them like ocean waves across the beach. Within minutes they both slept, the peaceful, exhausted sleep of lovers.

Chapter 14

Emily awoke alone in the bed. Finding her robe lying on the floor, she slipped into it and went out into the hallway, searching for Mitch. She found him, wearing nothing but his partially dry jeans, standing on the back of the wraparound porch.

She watched him, his hip resting on the banisters as he gazed out at the beach. What was he thinking? she wondered. Was he thinking about her? Remembering their night together? Was he regretting what had happened?

Emily backed up against the edge of the kitchen counter. She couldn't just go rushing outside and throw herself into his arms. Last night had been beyond reasoning—she had ceased to think. But in the bright light of day, she knew only too well that she had to face reality.

Mitch Hayden had made love to her and she had found heaven in his arms. Never had she known such passion, such utter and complete fulfillment.

She had told him that she loved him. Dear Lord, she had cried out her love in the throes of passion. But not once had Mitch told her he loved her. And why should he? Emily asked herself. Despite how much he'd wanted her, how completely he had satisfied her, Mitch Hayden pitied her and their loving night had been born out of that pity and out of his overwhelming sense of guilt.

He had tried to convince her that he found her completely beautiful, despite the hideous scars on her back. He had kissed and caressed those scars without showing any signs of revulsion. Had he looked at her disfigured flesh and felt responsible? Of course he had. Mitch Hayden was an honorable man. Time and circumstances had matured him into the man Emily loved.

It would be so easy to accept what he was offering, and she had no doubt that he would offer her whatever her heart desired. If she wanted him to marry her, he would. If she wanted him to father her children, he would. Hadn't he told her that he'd do anything for her, even die for her?

Swinging open the back door, Emily walked out onto the porch. Turning around when she approached, Mitch reached out, tugged on her hands and pulled her up against him. She laid her head on his naked chest, her nose tickled by his hair. She smelled the unique aroma that was Mitch, and also the undeniable scent of her own body embedded in his skin.

He threaded his fingers through the long, tangled mane of her dark hair. "Sleep well?"

"Yes. Did you?" Tilting her head, she looked up at him.

"I can't remember the last time I slept so soundly." He kissed the tip of her nose.

"I'm afraid I can't offer you breakfast, unless you want some cereal," she said. "I suppose the milk in the refrigerator is still good."

"I have a better idea. Go get dressed, pack a bag and come stay at my place. I'll fix you breakfast. I can whip up a mean batch of scrambled eggs and toast, or I can make my famous western omelette."

Easing a few inches away from him, but allowing him to keep his arms around her, Emily laid her hand on his chest. "You want me to stay with you? Move over to your cottage?"

Mitch caressed her arms from shoulders to wrists, then took her hands into his, holding them securely between their bodies. "It's the perfect solution for both of us."

"How's that?" she asked.

"I'm not going to let you be alone for one minute until we find out who's behind the break-ins and the threats," he said. "I could stay here with you, but right now you don't have any power, and no phone, and the glass panes in your back door are broken."

"So you're inviting me to stay with you until my power and phone are restored and my back door is repaired because you're determined to play bodyguard?"

"I want to be more than your bodyguard, pretty lady." He lifted her arms and placed them around his neck.

Emily's stomach flip-flopped. "What do you want to be?"

"Your bodyguard, your friend, but most of all, I want to be your lover. Tonight. Tomorrow night. All the nights for the rest—"

Leaving one hand around his neck, she reached out and covered his lips with the tip of her index finger. "I'll go get dressed and pack enough for tonight. I won't argue with you, Mitch. I need you. But, when this business about the break-ins and the threats is over, you and I have some important things to settle between us."

"I thought we did that last night." He kissed her finger that hovered over his lips.

"Last night was special. I'll never forget it."

"Hey, you make it sound as if it'll never happen again, and I'm here to tell you that—" he jerked her back into his arms, pressing her against his aroused body "—last night was just the beginning for us."

Twenty minutes later after phoning Nikki to tell her about the break-in last night and that she'd be late for work, Emily stood at the kitchen counter in Mitch's beachfront cottage. She'd convinced Mitch to leave the cooking to her. Deftly mixing together the ingredients for pancakes, she began preparations for their breakfast while Mitch showered and shaved.

She wasn't a fool. She knew only too well that she and Mitch didn't have a future together. But she also knew that by allowing Mitch to stay in her life, now, when she truly needed someone for support and caring and protection, she could help ease his guilty conscience. He so desperately wanted to do something for her. This way, he could.

Once the police caught the person responsible for the break-ins, she and Mitch would have to face the truth about their relationship.

The ringing phone jarred Emily from her private thoughts. Leaving the wooden spoon resting in the pancake batter, she wiped her hands off on the dishcloth she'd laid over her shoulder and reached out for the wall phone near the back door.

"Hello."

"I knew it! I told myself you weren't foolish enough to trust that man, but there you are at his house," the agitated masculine voice said. "You could have called me yourself and told me what happened instead of having Nikki call. But then, I suppose you knew how upset I'd be. When Nikki told me that you were staying with Mitchell Hayden, I couldn't believe it. Emily, have you lost your mind?"

"Good morning to you, Uncle Fowler. And yes, I'm just fine. Thanks for asking."

"Don't be sarcastic with me, young lady. I don't think this situation is at all amusing. I find it terribly disturbing!"

"I agree, Uncle Fowler. Those two hoodlums who broke into my house last night disturbed me. As a matter of fact, they scared the living daylights out of me!"

Fowler cleared his throat several times. "Well, yes, I suppose they did, and I'm so very sorry that you had to go through that, my dear. But the facts remain the same. Mitchell Hayden cannot be trusted, and I believe you're being unwise to stay with him when you could come home to me. Or you could stay with Nikki. That man will only hurt you again."

"Uncle Fowler, I wish I could make you understand how I feel about Mitch and why I trust him." Emily paused when she heard Fowler's groaning huff. "He rescued me from those boys who broke into my house. He doesn't want to hurt me. Don't you see? He saved me."

"He could have hired those boys just so he could play hero," Fowler said. "I warn you, Emily, don't trust the man!"

"What's happened to change you so? Up until recently,

you've been my biggest supporter. You've always believed in me and encouraged me—''

"You're the one who has changed—since you became infatuated with your husband's murderer!'' Fowler's voice trembled with emotion.

Emily clutched the phone with white-knuckled tension. Willing herself to stay calm, she took a deep breath. "Mitch didn't kill Stuart. He made some mistakes. He believed in the wrong people. But Mitch has paid dearly for what happened."

"I can't believe I'm hearing you correctly. What sort of spell has that man cast on you?" Fowler asked.

"As long as you're being this unreasonable, I'm not going to discuss Mitch Hayden with you."

"Don't you realize that I have your best interest at heart? I can't bear the thought of your wasting yourself on a man like that. The man is using you to regain respectability. If Stuart's widow can forgive him, then—''

"Please, don't do this to me. You know how much you mean to me. Don't make me choose between you and Mitch."

Mitch, freshly shaved and showered and neatly dressed in clean jeans and cotton shirt, walked into the kitchen. He halted behind Emily when he realized she was on the phone.

"He really has you fooled, doesn't he?" Fowler's voice rose to one octave below a scream. "Whatever's happened to make you trust this man so? My God, Emily, you haven't slept with him, have you?"

"That's none of your business."

"You have!" Fowler said, his voice loud enough to hurt Emily's ears. "He's brainwashed you. I beg you not to trust that man. Run from him. Get away, before he harms you. Please, let me come and get you. Let me take care of you. Keep you safe."

Emily shook her head, not knowing whether to feel sorry for her uncle or to be angry with him. "Nothing you say or do is going to convince me that Mitch is a threat to my safety."

Mitch reached around her and grabbed the phone out of her hand. Gasping, Emily jumped out of the way and stared at him with round eyes, startled by his actions.

"Jordan, this is Mitch Hayden. I just thought you should

know that if anyone wants to get to Emily, they'll have to come through me first."

Mitch slammed down the telephone receiver, then turned to Emily. "Want me to help you with the pancakes?"

"What?"

"Pancakes. Breakfast. Remember, you didn't want scrambled eggs or an omelette."

"Oh. Right." Mitch's words to her uncle kept ringing in her ears. Over and over again she heard him saying, *To get to Emily, they'll have to come through me first.* "You—you get the coffee ready. I'll make the pancakes."

He kissed her on the cheek, then swatted her on the behind. She gazed at him as if seeing him for the first time. When he smiled at her, her heartbeat accelerated. She smiled back at him.

"So the police don't have a clue who hired those boys to break into your house, huh?" Handing Emily a glass of iced tea, Nikki Griffin sat down beside her on the tan-and-blue striped sofa.

"Not a clue." Emily sighed. "But I...well, there's something that I haven't told anyone. Not the police. Not even Mitch."

Nikki sipped on her tea, then set her glass on the cocktail table in front of her. "What's going on? Why are you keeping secrets from the police?"

"It may be nothing. Really. Just a silly suspicion."

"So tell me!"

Emily scooted to the edge of her seat, moving closer, then glanced around the room as if checking for eavesdroppers. "Last evening, I had a date with Charles, and when he brought me home, I told him that I wasn't going to see him again, that I'd made a mistake leading him on."

Nikki whistled long and low. "I'll bet he wasn't pleased to hear that."

"He asked me if I was in love with Mitch and I told him that it was none of his business."

"I see. You're wondering if Charles is behind the letters and phone calls and break-ins, aren't you?"

"Isn't he the one with the most reason to want Mitch out of

the way? Charles wants me to marry him. I think he loves me, in his own way, but part of wanting to be my husband is his desire to please Uncle Fowler and move into Stuart's place as the Jordan heir.''

''But Charles thought he was getting somewhere with you,'' Nikki said. ''Why would he have hired those boys days ago to break into your house again last night?''

''I'm not sure, but I think Charles sensed that things weren't right between us, that I still had feelings for Mitch. Maybe he hired those boys hoping I'd turn to him for help and stay away from Mitch.''

''Anyone could have hired those young thugs.'' Nikki reached out and took Emily's hands into hers, giving her a reassuring squeeze. ''You said both of them are only seventeen and the police told you they're the kind of kids who are always in trouble, the kind who'd do just about anything for money.

''I know I've thought Charles was the bad guy in all this, but I'm not one hundred percent sure anymore.''

''Do you suspect someone else?'' Emily asked.

''Rod Simmons has been acting strange lately. Strange even for an artistic, moody, intellectual guy like him.'' Nikki released Emily's hands. ''I can't explain how I feel. It's just...well, Rod's been acting like he's guilty of something. Maybe I'm nuts. Maybe I'm just imagining things.''

''No, you're not nuts, and if you're imagining things, so am I,'' Emily said. ''I've noticed a change in Rod's behavior lately. I couldn't put my finger on it, but now that you mention it, he has been acting guilty. I think he's been trying to tell me something, but I've been putting him off, afraid of what he might say or do.''

''So, the suspects haven't changed since day one, have they?'' Nikki shifted uncomfortably in her seat, then stared directly at Emily.''

''What is it?''

''There are two more obvious suspects, you know.''

''Not Mitch.''

''Yeah, Mitch. Even though I don't think it's him. I'm sure

the police still have him at the top of their list, thanks to Fowler. And he's another name that should be on the list.''

"Uncle Fowler? You're joking." Emily's eyes widened in disbelief. "Nikki, if there's anyone on earth I can trust to never hurt me, to always do what he thinks is best for me, that person is Uncle Fowler.''

"Maybe he thinks scaring you into moving back to Mobile with him and into putting Mitch out of your life is what's best for you.''

"Uncle Fowler would never... No, it can't be him. The phone calls and letters were from someone who wanted to be my lover. Uncle Fowler doesn't feel that way about me. He loves me like a daughter or a little sister.''

"I thought so, too. But maybe we were wrong.''

"It has to be Rod or Charles or... It isn't Mitch and it isn't Uncle Fowler. Oh, Lord, Nikki, if only the police could discover the man's identity and put an end to this insanity. I don't know how much more I can take.''

"I can imagine how you must have felt last night. All alone in the dark, with two guys breaking into your home.''

Emily lifted the moist glass to her lips and tasted the cool tea. "I was scared to death, but at the same time, I was so angry. Angry with the men breaking into my house...but—but most of all, I was angry with myself because of my irrational fear of the dark.''

"I wouldn't call your fear of the dark irrational," Nikki said. "Didn't your psychiatrist tell you that fear of the dark was a common problem for people who'd lived through fires after being trapped in all that pitch-black darkness caused by the smoke?''

Emily set down her tea beside Nikki's on the table. She ran her fingers up and down the frosted surface, making streaks on the glass. "I faced the darkness outside when I went through my window. I was afraid, but I knew I didn't have any choice. Mitch said that I'd been very brave.''

"Mitch is right. It took a lot of courage for you to leave your only source of light.''

"I don't know what I'd have done without Mitch. He came

charging to my rescue the minute I called him." Releasing her tea glass, Emily leaned back on the sofa and faced Nikki. "I shudder to think what might have happened if those boys had cut the phone wires a minute sooner."

"You'd have made it to Mitch."

"Yes, I think I would have. I knew that if only I could get to Mitch, everything would be all right." Emily wiped her hands across the top of her thighs, then bunched up the soft lavender cotton material of her slacks, playing nervously with its softness between her thumb and forefinger. "I've tried to be strong. All these years since... I had to be strong. Uncle Fowler kept telling me to be strong. And I was. For Uncle Fowler's sake at first, and then for my own sake. I had to be strong to survive."

Nikki placed her hand on Emily's shoulder. "What are you trying to say?"

"I suppose I'm asking you if it's all right for me not to be so strong right now, if it's all right for me to lean on Mitch, to be thankful for his protection."

"Oh, dammit, Em, I'm the wrong person to ask about leaning on a man, about being thankful to some man for protecting you."

"Put aside your liberal feminist thinking for just one minute and answer me truthfully. If you were in my position, would you want a man like Mitch Hayden to take care of you?"

Nikki frowned, crinkling her freckled, slightly sunburned nose. "The question isn't fair."

"Confess," Emily said. "Not for your sake, but for mine."

"Okay. But if what I'm about to say ever leaves this room, I'll deny every word."

Emily laughed. "I'll never tell a living soul."

"If I were in your situation, yes, I'd want a man just like Mitch Hayden to take care of me. I'd want to know that he'd put his life on the line for me, that he'd stand between me and whoever was threatening my life." Glancing around the room, Nikki tapped her fingers on her knees. "That doesn't mean I wouldn't be trying to take care of myself, and if it came to a showdown, I'd be right there, fighting for myself. It's just that

I think it would be kind of nice to know I wasn't facing the big, bad world all alone.''

"Mitch told Uncle Fowler that if anyone came after me, they'd have to go through him first.''

"I'd say the guy's in love with you.''

"I wish I could believe that.'' Emily sighed, afraid that her doubts and fears would keep Mitch and her apart.

Was that what the future held for them? Doubt and uncertainty? Even if Mitch told her he loved her, could she believe him? He'd do anything to make her happy, wouldn't he? Even lie to her.

Mitch waited in the foyer while the housekeeper went to inform Mr. Jordan that he had a visitor.

So this was where Emily had spent the past five years, surrounded by wealth and a proud heritage. He couldn't begin to imagine what it would be like belonging to a prestigious family such as the Mobile McLains or Jordans. He'd been one of those Hayden kids who lived in a shack and wore hand-me-down clothes. He could well remember folks in Sutra, Mississippi, looking down their noses at Johnny Ray and Judy Hayden's passel of kids. Pity and charity. God, how he hated both.

And Emily thought all he felt for her was pity, that his feelings for her were born out of guilt. Hell, she was right, up to a point. He did feel guilty about the part he'd played in destroying her life; he'd probably always feel guilty. And maybe there was an element of pity in his feelings, a deep heartfelt sympathy for what she'd endured. But there was so much more to his feelings than pity and guilt. He cared for Emily Jordan in a way he'd never cared for another human being. And last night, he had wanted her more than he'd ever wanted another woman.

But would she believe him if he told her? Even if he swore on a stack of Bibles as high as Fowler Jordan's two-story house?

He knew he didn't deserve her, knew that she was far too good for him, but that didn't change the way he felt about her. He didn't have much to offer a woman, but he could and would offer Emily all that he had. And if she accepted him, he'd find a way to give her everything she wanted.

"Mr. Jordan will see you now," the short, plump, middle-aged housekeeper said. "This way, please."

She led Mitch into what he assumed was the front parlor, a room filled with priceless antiques.

"What are you doing here, Hayden?" Fowler Jordan, looking every minute of his fifty-six years, rested one hand on the back of a Chippendale chair and the other in the pocket of his silk robe. "You must know that you aren't welcome in this house."

"I'm here because I think you and I should join forces to protect Emily. The last thing she needs right now is to have to choose between you and me." Staring directly at Fowler Jordan, Mitch saw the bitter hatred etched on the man's face.

"You may have convinced my niece that you're innocent of any wrongdoing, that you had no part in my nephew's death, but you won't convince me. I know your type. Money-hungry trash who will do anything, use anyone, to get what he wants. A man with any conscience at all would never insinuate himself into the life of the widow of the man he'd murdered!"

"Look, Jordan, I've spent the past five years wallowing in guilt. You can't say anything to me that I haven't said to myself. But the bottom line is that I didn't murder anyone. I made some stupid mistakes. Mistakes I'll have to live with for the rest of my life. But Emily has forgiven me. She understands that I—"

"She isn't thinking straight." Fowler glared menacingly at Mitch. "The girl's a romantic. Always has been. Her grandmother raised her to want a husband and children. That's what Emily wants and needs. You can't offer her marriage and children. Charles Tolbert can."

"What makes you think I can't offer Emily marriage and children?"

Fowler's eyes bulged, making them look even larger through the bifocal lenses of his glasses. "I forbid it! Don't even think about the possibility. Believe me, Hayden, I'll find a way to stop you."

"I had hoped you and I could reach a compromise. For Emily's sake." Mitch shook his head, almost feeling sorry for Fowler Jordan. The poor man was as obsessed with Emily as he himself had been for the past five years. Only, Jordan's obsession was the controlling kind. Obviously, he thought he had the right to plan the rest of Emily's life.

"If you actually care about Emily, stay away from her." Fowler spoke quickly, his voice loud and quivering. "She would never marry someone I couldn't accept. And believe me, I could never accept you!"

"I'm sorry you feel that way."

Mitch turned and walked out of the parlor, knowing he hadn't heard the last from Stuart Jordan's uncle.

Chapter 15

The picnic had been Mitch's idea. He'd even prepared the pimento cheese sandwiches and carrot sticks himself. The apple juice and Vivaldi had been Emily's suggestions. They'd spread an old quilt out on the beach in the late afternoon, positioning Emily's huge beach umbrella to protect them from the warm June sunshine.

Mitch had thrown on a pair of cutoff jeans and cotton T-shirt, while Emily had dressed in baggy red shorts and a matching red-and-white striped top. They'd both opted to go barefoot, loving the feel of the damp, coarse sand under their feet.

Mitch lifted the juice bottle to his lips, sipping the cool liquid as he watched Emily working away busily on the charcoal sketch she had begun before they'd eaten. The blaring of trumpets and the forceful rush of violins blended with the call of seagulls and the song of the bay waters.

Lowering the juice bottle from his mouth, Mitch nodded toward the tape player beside the picnic basket. "What's that playing now? I must not have any taste for the finer things, because I'm afraid it sounds like a lot of racket to me."

Glancing over the top of her sketch pad, Emily smiled at Mitch. "Vivaldi's Concerto for Two Trumpets in C—"

"Sorry I asked." He shook his head. "I should have brought along one of my tapes."

Reaching out to the tape player, Emily switched off the music. "There, is that better? I'm afraid I think hard rock is a lot of noise, but we can probably compromise on cool jazz."

"We were raised in two different worlds, weren't we?" Mitch knew their individual tastes in music weren't the only differences stemming from their totally opposite backgrounds.

"What was it like growing up in Sutra, Mississippi?" Emily watched Mitch carefully, then she looked down as she continued sketching his handsome face. She didn't think he'd realized he was her subject.

"If I hadn't been the son of a lazy gambler who tried to make a living farming and a mother burdened with five kids, I might have enjoyed growing up in Sutra." Mitch picked up a carrot stick from a paper plate sitting in front of him. "We were what folks called white trash. I never owned a new pair of pants or a decent shirt until I went into the marines."

"Is that why getting rich was so important to you?" Emily studied the proportions of Mitch's nose and cheekbones. He had such a strong face, his features undeniably masculine.

"Being poor is a great incentive to get rich." He tapped the end of the carrot against his bottom teeth, then broke the stick in half. "I was hungry for money, and I desperately wanted to escape my childhood. I hated taking charity, and I swore that once I got away from home, I'd never allow anyone to pity me again."

"Tell me about Randy Styles and Loni." If she and Mitch were ever going to come to terms with the past, they'd have to face it—all of it.

"You don't want to know about them." The last thing on earth he wanted to discuss with Emily was his former partner and his ex-fiancée.

Emily shaded in the hollows of Mitch's face and neck, then closed her eight-by-six-inch sketchbook and laid her charcoal pencil on top. "Yes, I do. It will help me understand the person you were then, and the person you are now."

Mitch jumped up from the quilt, knocking over his empty juice bottle. Stretching, he gazed up at the clear blue sky. "Hey, I thought we came on this picnic to relax and enjoy ourselves, to get away from our problems."

"That's the reason you said we should have a picnic." Emily stood up beside Mitch and reached out to touch his back. "Did you love Loni a great deal?"

Mitch looked out at the bay, the blue-gray waters, the soft, rippling tide. "I thought I was in love with her. I was twenty-seven when we met. I wasn't a kid. I'd known a few women before her. But I wasn't mature enough to see through her act."

"How do you feel about her now?" Dropping her hand from Mitch's back, Emily stepped away from him, her gaze riveted to the bay.

"I don't feel much of anything. Regret that I didn't realize she was using me, and that's about it." He kicked the sand with the tips of his toes.

Relief spread through Emily, starting slowly in her chest and extending outward, upward and downward. She hadn't wanted to be jealous of Mitch's past relationship with Loni, but she had been.

"How do you feel about your husband? About Stuart?" Mitch asked, keeping his gaze focused on the bay.

An involuntary shiver rippled over her. How did she feel about Stuart? She had loved him. She had married him. And she had carried his child. "I loved Stuart dearly. He was a wonderful man. But Stuart's gone. He hasn't been a part of my life, except in my memories, for over five years."

"If I could change things..." Mitch left the sentence unfinished. He'd already said all there was to say.

Emily turned to him then, nodding, telling him silently that she knew what he meant, that she understood his regrets.

"Why don't we take a walk?" Emily held out her hand.

Mitch accepted, clasping her hand in his. They walked together up the beach, past Mitch's rental cottage, then turned around and walked in the opposite direction until they returned to where their quilt and picnic leftovers lay. They didn't talk during their walk, only held hands and occasionally exchanged a smile or a knowing glance.

"Come on. Sit back down." Emily dropped to her knees. "I want to finish my sketch while there's still some light."

"There's plenty of time for that." Mitch grabbed her arms, pulling her onto her feet. He had to do something to change the somber mood, to bring a smile to Emily's face. The past stood between them. Maybe it always would. But discussing it didn't do anything but make them both sad. And they'd both had enough sadness to last a lifetime. "Let's go for a swim."

"No!" Emily squealed as she tried to escape from Mitch, but when she did, he lifted her into his arms. Disregarding her giggling protests and flapping limbs, he carried her into the water.

The soft waves washed over them as Mitch lowered her to her feet, the water reaching her at hip level.

Emily struck a light, playful blow to Mitch's chest. "You don't listen very well, do you?"

"What's the matter? Didn't you want to play in the water with me?"

"I wanted to finish my sketch before the sun sets."

She started to place her hands on her hips for emphasis, but when a wave almost toppled her, she caught Mitch by the shoulders, then slipped her arms around his neck. His big body supported her as he gripped her waist, pulling her close enough to feel his erection.

Nuzzling her wet neck with his nose, Mitch nipped her earlobe. "What are you drawing that's so important?"

"Come back to the quilt and I'll show you."

"Later." He ran his hands downward, cupping her buttocks as his lips covered hers in a devouring kiss.

She clung to him as he deepened the kiss. The waves beat against them, until a fairly large one finally toppled them over and into the water.

Still holding Emily, Mitch brought them to the surface quickly. Gulping in air and then coughing, she hit the water with her hand, sending a shower up into Mitch's face. He lifted her, then tossed her into the surf. Swimming beneath the water, Emily caught Mitch by the ankles and pulled him under.

They played together like a couple of kids until they were both tired and breathless. Dragging themselves out of the ocean, they fell onto the quilt, drenching it as the water dripped off their wet bodies.

Laughing and panting from their exertion, they lay down, side by side, staring at each other, smiling.

The sun rested low on the western horizon, like a flaming red ball, shooting out orange and purple sparks across the slate-blue sky of approaching twilight.

Raising himself on his elbow, Mitch looked down into Emily's damp face. Her hair lay plastered to her neck and shoulders. Thick dark strands of coffee-brown silk. When he lowered his head to kiss her, she rolled over onto her stomach. He kissed the top of her head, relishing the sound of her giggling laughter.

"Behave yourself," she told him. "I might be able to finish my sketch if you'll cooperate." Emily dried her hands and arms off on the quilt.

"What do you want me to do?"

"Just lie still and be quiet."

Sitting up, Emily crossed her legs, then lifted her sketch pad and pencil. She studied Mitch for a couple of minutes, then began drawing furiously.

"You promised to show me what you're drawing," he said.

"I promised to show you if you'd come out of the water and back to the quilt with me."

"We're out of the water and back on the quilt."

"Now we are. But you didn't come back when I asked you to."

Mitch snatched the pad out of her hands. She gasped, then swatted at his hands. When he held up the sketch in the fading evening light, she tried to grab it away from him. Reaching out, he pulled her down and into his arms, her back to his chest, her hips resting in the vee between his legs. He held the pad in front of their bodies.

"It's me. You're sketching me." He stared at the picture, noting the way Emily had drawn him, his face strong, yet smiling and filled with warmth. Was this the way she saw him? Dear God, he hoped so. He looked like a happy man, a man not eaten alive with guilt and regret.

"Is this the way you see me?" he asked.

"It's just a rough sketch."

She grabbed the pad. He released it. She turned the pages over and laid the pad on the sand beside the damp quilt. She still sat in the curve of his legs, her buttocks positioned against him intimately. He took her shoulders in his big, strong hands, his grasp infinitely gentle.

"I don't have the right to love you, Emily."

His voice was low, the words almost lost on the wind, on the warm bay breeze that chilled her moist body. What was he saying? What was he trying to tell her? That he loved her? Or that he could never love her?

She tensed beneath his touch, every muscle in her body tightening, preparing her, protecting her. How did she respond to his statement? What did he want her to say?

Mitch felt the heavy tension between them and heard Emily breathing, deep and labored as if she were trying to calm herself. He squeezed her shoulders, then lowered his head to hers, brushing the side of his face against hers, resting his chin in the curve of her neck and shoulder.

"Since the first day we met, I've wanted you." He eased his hands downward, caressing her arms. "I knew that you were too good for the likes of me, but I wanted you all the same."

"Mitch?" She tried to turn to face him, but he slipped his arms around her, trapping her back against his chest, her hips against his groin.

He kissed her damp hair that clung to the side of her face. "You're everything a man could want. But I don't deserve you."

She trembled in his arms, tears forming a knot in her throat, a heavy weight in her chest. Didn't he know how much she loved him? That he was the only man in the world she wanted, needed?

"Mitch, the past is behind us," she said, her voice a strained whisper as she tried valiantly not to cry. "Neither of us will ever forget what happened, but you're going to have to forgive yourself for getting involved with Randy Styles and for not discovering the truth about him sooner.''

"I'm working on that. On forgiving myself. It may take the rest of my life. But having your forgiveness makes it easier.'' Clasping his hands at her waist, he lifted her slightly, turning her so that he could look into her eyes, those warm, cinnamon-brown eyes that told him how much she loved him.

"You know how I feel about you.'' She leaned into him, her expression begging him for a kiss.

"Do you know how I feel about you?'' he asked.

His question took her by surprise. She hadn't expected him to be so blunt, to come right out and ask her if she understood his feelings for her. The pity. The guilt.

"I think so. You've admitted that you feel guilty, feel partially responsible for what happened to my life five years ago. And I know you feel a certain amount of sympathy, even pity.'' Emily glanced down, unable to bear another moment of his heated stare. "You care about me, too, but—''

"That's my problem. Our problem. You don't know how I feel about you, and I'm afraid you'd never believe me if I told you, would you, Emily?''

She pulled away from him. He didn't try to stop her when she scooted off the quilt and stood, her back to him. "You're confusing love with guilt and pity. You think that it's your duty to make me happy, to give me back my life. I don't want you out of a sense of obligation. I couldn't bear it. I couldn't....''

She broke into a run, the sand flying about her feet as she raced down the beach. If he told her he loved her, would she believe him? Did she dare? How could she ever be certain?

Mitch jumped to his feet. "Emily!'' When she didn't reply, didn't turn, didn't slow down, he followed her, running to catch up with her.

She felt him behind her, knew he would overtake her, but she couldn't stop. She had to get away—away from Mitch and the possibility he'd tell her he loved her, away from herself and the way he made her feel every time he touched her.

Mitch caught her by the shoulders. She fought him as if he

were an attacker. Placing his leg between her knees, he toppled her to the ground, their bodies plummeting onto the sand. She struggled against his superior strength until he finally grabbed her hands, manacling her wrists and planting them firmly on the ground above her head.

"It won't work, honey. You can't escape this." His mouth came down on hers with a wild fury, more aggressive and commanding than he had intended. But dammit all, she was his. It was time she admitted the truth. No matter what had come before, no matter how many doubts she had about the sincerity of his feelings, nothing could change their hunger, their passion, their desperate need for each other.

Emily tried not to respond, but knew it was hopeless. Whether Mitch loved her or not, he wanted her. And heaven help her, she wanted him.

This was what she'd feared. This was what she'd run from—this uncontrollable desire.

The evening breeze stirred around them, creating chills and shivers at the same time their kiss ignited a blazing fire inside them. Tongues danced, teeth nipped, lips mated. Emily tore at Mitch's shirt. He pulled it over his head and tossed it on the beach, then hastily unbuttoned Emily's blouse, baring her damp, satin bra.

His hands skimmed over her body, halting briefly to unsnap the front hook of her bra, then delving between her thighs to cup her intimately. Emily moaned. Her body tightened around his hand and she lifted herself up to meet the sensation.

Mitch rose above Emily, lifted her in his arms and carried her back to the damp quilt. Knocking aside the tape player and the picnic basket, he laid her on the quilt and came down over her, covering her body with his own.

After fumbling with the snap and zipper on her shorts, Mitch managed to take off her shorts and panties at the same time. He undid his shorts and rearranged his briefs, freeing himself from their confinement.

Emily clung to him, stringing kisses across his shoulder, over his chest, teasing his tiny male nipples. Rising above her, resting on his knees, Mitch looked down at Emily, then took her breasts in his hands. He surrounded one tight nipple with his mouth, suckling her fiercely while his fingers delved into the waiting warmth of her body.

Her breathing quickened. He attacked her with hot passion, positioning himself between her legs and taking her in one swift, hard thrust. Lifting her hips off the quilt, she rose to meet him, clamping her legs about his buttocks, bringing their bodies closer, intensifying the friction. Her nails bit into his muscled back as he deepened his lunges.

Everything blended into one timeless moment of ecstasy. The smell of Gulf waters and sand. The heady, womanly scent of Emily. The sound of the surf lapping against the shore. The cry of seagulls overhead. The beating of two hearts in unison.

Emily closed her eyes, giving herself over to pure sensation, to the feel of completion rocketing through her. Capturing her and then releasing her. Flinging her into a vortex of pleasure that went on and on and on.

Mitch cried out, a male animal in the throes of fulfillment.

They clung to each other, their bodies quivering with the aftershocks of release, their fingertips seeking and finding contact with each other's bodies. She petted his hairy chest, fingering the curls. He stroked her hip, cupping her buttock in his hand.

He pulled her into his arms. They lay together on the private stretch of beach as the evening sun made a glorious exit, leaving only colorful fragments of light. With Emily naked and Mitch partially unclothed, they soon felt the chill of approaching night.

Together they rose from the quilt and dressed hurriedly; then gathered up their belongings and, hand in hand, walked back to Mitch's cottage. Without saying a word, they deposited the quilt, tape player, sketch pad and picnic basket on the kitchen floor, and Mitch led Emily into the shower. She didn't hesitate for one second, never giving the scars on her back a thought.

When daybreak came, Emily lay in Mitch's arms, somewhere between sleeping and awakening, Mitch's lips at her breast, arousing her senses, beckoning her to respond. Her eyelids fluttered open and then shut again as she lifted one hand to touch his face. Releasing her nipple, Mitch looked down at her, smiling when she opened her eyes.

"Good morning, pretty lady." He kissed her on the mouth, quickly, passionately.

Emily stretched, shoving back the light sheet and blanket that covered her lower body. Closing her eyes, she sighed as Mitch's tongue painted a damp trail from her lips to her breast.

"I'd like every morning for the rest of my life to begin this way," he said, then took her nipple between his teeth, playing with it, teasing her.

Emily squirmed against him, feeling his arousal against the side of her hip. "You're insatiable." She gasped when he flung his leg over her, mounting her.

"Are you complaining?" he asked.

Circling his neck with her arms, she brought his mouth down to hers and whispered against his lips, "I have no complaints."

They made love slowly, as if they had all the time in the world, exploring each other's bodies at leisure, tossing and turning on the bed, exchanging the dominant position again and again.

When Emily climaxed, she cried out her pleasure, clinging to Mitch as her body shuddered convulsively. Mitch's fulfillment followed, his body jerking with release as he groaned out his satisfaction.

Endless moments later, Mitch braced himself on one elbow and leaned over Emily. She gazed up into the face of the man she loved, his ice-blue eyes telling her that he adored her. But the smile faded from her lips when she noticed his solemn expression.

"What's wrong?" She stroked his cheek with her fingertips.

He grasped her hand, taking it to his mouth, nibbling on her fingers. "We need to talk. We have to face what you weren't ready or willing to face last night."

She shook her head. "Not now. Not when everything is so perfect."

"Everything isn't perfect, Emily. Not as long as your distrust stands in our way."

"My distrust?" Drawing away from him, she sat up in bed,

resting her back against the headboard as she pulled the sheet up to cover her nakedness. "I trust you, Mitch. My Lord, I love you. I've forgiven you for the past. I've begged you to forgive yourself. I'd put my life in your hands."

Sitting up beside her, Mitch lifted a lock of dark hair away from her face, draping it behind her ear. His fingers lingered on her neck, caressing her tenderly. "We have to talk about it. The problem is not going to go away."

"Not now, Mitch. Later, after we know who's been harassing me and he's behind bars. I can't deal with so much all at once."

"Yes now. Not later. We can't put off facing the truth. We're going to discuss it now, while we're alone with nothing separating us, not even our clothes. Now, right after we've just made love, when we're both vulnerable and all our defenses are lowered."

"Please—"

"I love you, Emily. I love you and I want to spend the rest of my life with you. I know that I don't have a lot to offer. Not right now. But I can give you all my love."

No, don't say it! Please, don't tell me that you love me! She wanted to scream at him, but it was too late. He'd already spoken the words, made the declaration—and she didn't dare let herself believe him.

The desire to run away overcame her, but she knew it would be useless. Mitch was right. Sooner or later they'd have to deal with her doubts. She only wished it could be later.

"Emily?"

Nodding, she clutched the sheet in her hand, wadding it into a knot at her throat. "You know..." She gulped in air, her breath catching on a sob. "You understand why I... How can I ever be certain that you really love me?"

"If you trusted me, you'd believe me." He let his hand drift down her neck to her shoulder, to rest there in a gentle grasp.

"I do trust you. It's just that...that..."

"You don't trust me. You think I'd lie to you. After what we've been through, you think I'd sacrifice myself to make you happy. That's what it all comes down to, isn't it?"

"I know you care about me, that you'd do anything to make

me happy, to atone for the past." Emily bit back the tears. She wouldn't cry, dammit! Not now! "Tell me how I could ever be sure you truly loved me."

"There's only one way." He pulled her into his arms. The sheet separating them dropped away, leaving their naked bodies touching, her breasts against his chest. "You have to take me on faith. You have to believe what I say is true, believe that I'd never lie to you."

Tears burned her throat, the pain in her chest threatening to cut off her breath. *Take him on faith. Believe that he'd never lie to you.*

Mitch sprang out of bed and hurried around the room until he found his jeans. Delving inside the back pocket, he dug out his wallet and held it up in the air like a trophy.

"I want to show you something," he said.

Emily stared at him, her heart racing, her mind a jumble of wild, confusing thoughts.

He flipped open his wallet, reached inside and pulled out a dingy piece of pink material. Emily gazed at the dirty scrap of silk he held between his thumb and forefinger. He walked back to the bed and sat down beside her, his hip bumping hers.

He grabbed her wrist. She balled her hand into a tight fist. Forcing her palm open, Mitch laid the tiny, grungy fragment in the middle of her hand. "See this?" he asked her. She nodded. "I've been carrying this little piece of pink satin gown around with me for over five years."

Every nerve in Emily's body zinged with anxious anticipation. Her breath lodged in her chest.

"When I heard what had happened at the Ocean Breeze Apartments that morning, I rushed over." Mitch's hands trembled.

Emily stared down at the scrap of pink lying in her palm, and knew on some instinctive level exactly what he was going to say.

"I was too late, of course, to do anything but watch," he said. "Moments after I arrived, a fireman brought out a woman wearing a pink nightgown. I didn't get a good look at her face, but I'll never forget her dark, singed hair hanging over the fireman's shoulder. And the memory of that pink gown seared into her back has haunted my dreams all these years.''

Tears welled up in Emily's eyes. Oh, dear Lord in heaven, she didn't think she could bear for him to tell her more.

''I picked up a piece of her nightgown off the sidewalk.'' He bent her fingers, closing them over the tattered silk square she held in her hand. ''Do I feel guilty? Do I blame myself? Would I do anything to make it up to you if I could?''

''Mitch, don't.''

''Don't what? Don't admit that I owe you, that the collapse of a building my construction firm erected took your life away from you and now I want to give you a new life to replace the old?''

''Out of guilt and regret, not out of love.''

''That's where you're wrong. That's where you're going to have to take me on faith. That—'' he nodded at her clutched fist ''—is the last secret between us. Now you know everything, have all the evidence against me.''

Pressing her fist against her cheek, Emily closed her eyes and took a deep breath. ''I'm going to throw this away. It's part of the past. You don't need it anymore.''

Mitch grabbed her. Her eyelids flew open. She stared at him, trembling, tears trickling down her face.

''I love you, Emily. More than I ever thought it was possible to love anyone. But I can't make you believe me.''

''I want to believe you.'' She tried to smile through her tears. Her lips trembled with the useless effort. ''Please believe me.''

''I do, honey. My believing you isn't our problem.''

''Will you give me time, Mitch?''

''If I thought time would change the way you feel, I'd give you all the time in the world. But if you can't take me on faith now, do you honestly think a week or a month or even a year will make a difference?''

Tell him you believe him! Take him on faith. You know you want to. He's offering you your heart's desire.

''Are you...I mean, do you want to marry me?'' she asked.

''Hell, yes, I want to marry you. What do you think I'm talking about here? I want to be your husband. I want to give you those children you've always wanted. Be my wife, Emily, and I'll spend the rest of my life doing everything I can to make you happy.''

"Please, Mitch. Right now isn't the right time to make such a monumental decision. I can't think clearly with you so close to me, so soon after...after... I need some time away from you to think.''

"All right. Take some time. But please, pretty lady, don't break both our hearts.'' He kissed her. Softly. Sweetly. Pleadingly. "Don't you think that we've both suffered enough?''

Chapter 16

"Rod's upstairs waiting for you." Nikki walked into the storage room.

"He's early, isn't he? Or have I lost track of time?" Emily laid the knife she'd been using to open boxes on top of the battered old wooden desk, dusted off her hands on her jeans and checked her watch.

"He's early," Nikki said. "And something's wrong. When he asked if you were here, he couldn't even look me in the eye."

"Maybe I should go on up and talk to him. See what's wrong."

When Emily moved past her, Nikki grabbed Emily's arm. "I know you'd like to credit Rod's strange behavior lately to his artistic temperament, but you know as well as I do that there's a good chance he's the person who's been harassing you. And if he's the one who hired those boys to break into your house, then he's lost it. I mean *really* lost it. He could be dangerous."

"Just let me go upstairs and talk to him." Emily smiled reassuringly, hoping she could convey a sense of calm that she really wasn't feeling. She knew as well as anyone that Rod might be responsible for the harassment, but her instincts told her that he wasn't dangerous. Despite her convictions, she felt a sudden unease settle in the pit of her stomach.

"Scream if you need me. I have a gun in my purse."

Emily gave Nikki a disapproving glare, shook her head and uttered several tsk-tsks. Nikki shrugged, the look on her face one of pure innocence.

"All right, all right." Nikki waved her hands expressively. "So I agree with you. I can't see Rod as some dangerous stalker, either."

Sighing, Emily nodded, then headed upstairs. Rod stood alone in the middle of the studio, his gaze riveted to the new painting he'd just begun. Already a departure from his earlier, safer works, this abstract held the potential of being his best ever, Emily thought.

"Nikki seems to think you have a problem of some kind," Emily said, trying to convey both understanding and strength in her voice.

Rod turned around slowly and looked directly at Emily, his eyes bloodshot and swollen. A dark stubble covered his face. Apparently he hadn't shaved since the last time she'd seen him. His clothes were wrinkled, looking as though he'd slept in them. Normally Rod was neat, clean shaven and filled with energy.

"I—I won't be able to take any more lessons." His voice trembled every so slightly. "I'll probably be going away for a while."

"Why, Rod? Has something happened?" Emily approached him, but when he started backing away from her, she stopped several feet from him.

"I'm going to turn myself in to the police today," he said.

"Why are you going to do that? What did you do?" Please, dear Lord, don't let him tell me that he's the one who's been harassing me. Emily's stomach knotted painfully.

Slumping his shoulders in defeat, Rod bowed his head. He looked so pathetic. Like a lost and frightened child. It was all she could do not to rush over and caress his dark curls and whisper soothing words to him.

"I didn't have anything to do with either of those break-ins at your house. I swear I didn't.'' Lifting his eyes just a little, he peered shyly at Emily through his long, black eyelashes. ''I wrote the letters and made the phone calls. I didn't have the courage to tell you face-to-face how I felt about you. I thought if I could be romantic, be your secret admirer for a while, then… But just as soon as somebody broke into your house and painted that warning on your mirror, I never sent another letter or made another phone call.''

''You're the one who wrote the letters and made the phone calls, but you weren't responsible for the break-ins or the threats. Is that right?''

Emily wondered if she'd be a fool to believe him. Maybe so. But her instincts told her that Rod wasn't lying. There was no reason for him to confess to anything. The police had no proof of any kind against him. Only Rod's own sense of guilt had prompted this poignant confession. She supposed she should be angry with him, but she couldn't find it in her heart to chastise him when she felt only sympathy for him.

''I'm sorry that I ever did something so stupid, writing the letters and making the phone calls.'' Rod lifted his head just a fraction, his gaze dancing nervously around the room, not focusing on anything. ''I didn't mean to harass you. The last thing I wanted to do was frighten you. I love you, Emily. I…I'm sorry. I'm going straight to the police and tell them what I did.''

''Oh, Rod.'' Emily rubbed her forehead in frustration. ''Do you want me to go with you and tell them that I believe you?''

''Do you, Emily? Do you really believe me?'' Lifting his head completely, he looked directly at her. The tears that filled his eyes began to spill down his cheeks. ''I would never threaten you. I'd cut off my right arm before I'd hurt you. I hope you know that.''

''I believe you.'' She held out her hand to him. ''Now, let's go clear things up with the police.''

''You don't have to go with me. There's no need for you to put yourself through any more than you've already been through. I can do this alone.'' He walked toward the landing, hesitating before taking the first step down. ''If—if I need you, I'll call you. Will that be all right?''

"Of course it'll be all right."

"Can you ever forgive me?" Not waiting for an answer, he bolted down the stairs.

Emily slumped against the wall, feeling as though the wind had been knocked out of her. Poor Rod. He'd courted her in a shroud of secrecy, with sweet, poetry-filled letters and breathy, lovesick phone calls. But he swore he hadn't been responsible for the break-ins. That he hadn't been the one who had threatened her, warned her to stay away from Mitch. And she believed him. But if it hadn't been Rod, then who? The only other person she could think of was Charles. But it couldn't possibly be Charles, could it? He was so...so...so normal. And normal people didn't have the house of someone they professed to love vandalized, did they?

"I cannot believe you're doing this," Mitch Hayden said. "The boy harassed you for weeks on end. And just because he says he wasn't behind the break-ins doesn't mean he wasn't."

"Look, if you don't want to go in with me, then you don't have to," Emily said. "I can do this by myself."

Mitch grabbed her arm, stopping her from opening the door to the Fairhope police station. "You can't post bond for him until after he's sent to Bay Minette. You might as well wait until they've made the transfer. If you insist on helping him, I'll drive you up there in the morning."

"I can't believe they arrested him. I'm not going to press charges."

"They're holding him on suspicion of breaking and entering, for the first time your house was vandalized and for—"

"Rod didn't break into my house," Emily said adamantly. "And he didn't hire those teenage boys. Stop and think. Where would Rod get an extra five hundred dollars to pay those young hoodlums? Every spare dime he has he spends on his painting supplies."

Mitch released her arm. "All right. We'll talk to Detective Kenyon, but I'm telling you—"

"Are you coming in with me or not?" She hesitated momentarily, then when Mitch didn't reply, she opened the door and marched in.

Mitch followed her, cursing softly under his breath. He tended to agree with her assessment of Rod Simmons. Why would the guy confess to having made the phone calls and written the letters if he'd been responsible for breaking into her home, knowing he could do some hard time for the latter crime? All he'd had to do was keep his mouth shut. There was no way anyone could prove he'd been Emily's secret admirer. No, Mitch figured the young guy had gotten a bad case of guilty conscience and probably had become scared after the second break-in.

"I want to see Detective Kenyon," Emily demanded.

"Ms. Jordan, Detective Kenyon has left for the day. May I help you?" the young policeman behind the desk asked.

"I want Rod Simmons released immediately. I'm not pressing charges against him."

"Yes, ma'am. You made that perfectly clear to Detective Kenyon when you called. But I'm afraid we can't release him. He's being sent over to Bay Minette in the morning. The only way Rod Simmons is going to be set free is if somebody posts his bail tomorrow."

"Then if I can't help get him released this evening, may I please see him?"

"Emily, what's the point in that?" Mitch shook his head, knowing he wouldn't be able to prevent her seeing Rod if the police agreed.

"Ma'am, why can't you just wait and see him tomorrow?"

"I want to speak to him tonight. Please." Emily looked at the young officer with soft eyes and presented him with her most sincere smile. "I need to assure him that he hasn't anything to worry about."

"All right. But just for a couple of minutes."

Mitch walked Emily up North Section Street, away from the police station, past the Welcome Center and toward the Paint Box.

"Well, are you satisfied now?" he asked, stepping briskly to keep up with her hurried stride. "You saw Rod and reassured him that you'd post his bail tomorrow."

"I think it's ridiculous that they arrested him. He's so obviously innocent." Emily waved at an elderly gentleman sitting on the Renaissance Café balcony.

"Okay," Mitch said. "If Rod is obviously innocent, then who is obviously guilty?"

Emily stopped abruptly on the corner. She swallowed hard, then turned and looked up at Mitch. "I'm not sure anyone is obviously guilty, but... I suppose Charles is the most likely suspect. It's just that I don't think he's the type to take such drastic measures."

Mitch grasped Emily's shoulders with gentle force. "Charles Tolbert is in love with you. And believe me I know what drastic measures I'd be willing to take if I thought I could make you mine forever."

"You wouldn't threaten me or try to frighten me the way..." Emily's heartbeat skipped a beat. She reached out and caressed his cheek. "No, you would never harm me in any way. I do believe that."

She pulled away from him and continued her trek up the street. Mitch followed at her side. The minute she opened the door to the Paint Box, she heard Fowler Jordan's authoritarian voice.

"You can't mean to tell me that Emily intends to bail that young hooligan out of jail!"

"She believed him when he said he wasn't behind the break-ins at her house." Nikki glanced toward the door and sighed visibly when she saw Emily and Mitch. She glanced at Fowler and frowned, then she nodded in Charles Tolbert's direction.

"I shall have a talk with Emily and we'll just see—"

"What do you want to talk to me about?" Emily cut her uncle short when she walked into the shop and slammed the door behind her.

Both Charles and Fowler turned sharply, concern on their faces when they looked at Emily. Then simultaneously, they glared at Mitch.

Fowler opened his arms and walked toward Emily. "Nikki

tells me that Rod Simmons has been arrested, that he's the one who has been harassing you all these weeks.''

Emily went into her uncle's arms, allowing him to hug her. She returned the gesture, then pulled free. Charles hovered nearby. Mitch stayed by the door.

"Rod confessed to having made the phone calls and to having written the letters, but that's all."

"After all he's done, you aren't seriously thinking about paying that boy's bail, are you?" Charles asked.

"It's none of your business what I do," Emily told him. "But if you must know, then yes, I am."

"My dear Emily." Fowler shook his head sadly.

"What are you two doing here anyway?" Emily looked pointedly at her uncle, then focused her stare on his young protégé.

"Well, Charles and I decided this would be a perfect evening to take the *Black Pearl* out for a trip down to the Gulf," Fowler explained. "And I'd hoped you might join us. I had Mrs. McMurphy pack us a picnic dinner before she left this evening."

"You should have called first," Emily said as she glanced over her shoulder at a glowering Mitch. "I have other plans."

"With Hayden?" Charles demanded.

"Yes," Emily said.

"Then bring Mr. Hayden along, my dear." The corners of Fowler's mouth curved into an almost smile.

"Fowler, you can't mean—" Charles said.

"If you're determined to see Mr. Hayden, despite my reservations, then I see no alternative but for me to try to make the best of it." Fowler forced his lips into a wider smile.

"Don't do me any favors, Jordan," Mitch said.

"Mitch, if Uncle Fowler is willing to try, then—"

Mitch opened the door and walked out so quickly that the door slammed shut before Emily realized what had happened.

"I'm sorry. I can't go sailing with you and Charles this evening," Emily said. "It was a lovely idea, but I don't think Mitch wants to go. Besides, I heard it might rain."

Without looking back, Emily rushed out the door and down

the sidewalk. She caught up with Mitch half a block away, in front of the Fairhope Single Tax Corporation offices.

"Wait, Mitch, please." She grabbed his arm.

He halted, but didn't turn around. "Why aren't you getting ready to go sailing on your uncle's yacht?"

"Because you and I had plans to spend the evening together, and you made it perfectly clear that you didn't want to share me with Uncle Fowler and Charles."

Mitch turned, slowly, hesitantly, and slipped his hand around Emily's neck, drawing her toward him. "I'm sorry I acted the way I did. I had no right to—"

Emily placed her index finger over his lips. "Shhh. You don't have to say another word. I understand that you think Charles might be behind the break-ins and I realize you know Uncle Fowler hates you. I wasn't thinking when I said what I did. I simply reacted to Uncle Fowler's overture."

Mitch tightened his hold on Emily, bringing her closer and closer. He lowered his head; she lifted hers. And their lips met in a hot, ravenous kiss.

Raising his head, Mitch smiled. "Let's get off the street. If we don't, we're going to make a public spectacle of ourselves."

"Let's go home," she said breathlessly, her heart drumming loudly in her ears. "To my house. The repairs are finished and the security system was put in today. We can have a late supper and then sit out on the porch and watch the stars."

There was nothing Mitch wanted more than to "go home" with Emily. Go home with her and stay forever. But unless he could convince her that his feelings for her were real, the kind that lasted a lifetime, there would be no forever for them.

The rain came in windy torrents, drenching Emily and Mitch when they made a mad dash from her car to the house. He had driven like a maniac down Mobile Street, past the Grand Hotel and onto Scenic Highway 98. The heat inside him rose higher and higher with each glance in Emily's direction. All he could think about was making love to her, to laying claim to her body and making her his. But she wasn't his. She might never really belong to him.

Emily punched in the security code, then waited for Mitch to unlock the door. The rain had soaked her pale-pink cotton dress, making it almost transparent. He could see the outline of her body through the sheer material. The curve of her hips. The ripe swell of her breasts, her aureoles visible through her bra, their tips pebble hard. And the dark V at the junction between her legs that beckoned him to explore the hidden riches inside.

Mitch grabbed Emily around the waist, turning her into his arms. She tried to wriggle away from him, but he pulled her close, their wet bodies pressing together.

She looked up into his face and smiled. Mitch eased her back against the wall, nudging his knee between her legs.

Before she could speak, he nibbled at her lips. Sighing, she flung her head back to expose her neck. He kissed the soft, smooth flesh, then licked a zigzag pattern from her chin to the top button on her dress. Emily shivered.

Mitch undid the first button. Emily laid her hands on his chest. He undid the second button. She unbuckled his belt. He undid the third button. She unzipped his jeans. He undid the fourth button. She slid her hand inside his jeans and searched for the opening in his briefs. He unsnapped the front closure of her bra, exposing her breasts to his hungry mouth.

He feasted on her breasts, taking his time with each one. Emily writhed against him. When her hand covered his sex, he moaned deep in his throat, then thrust his hand up and under her dress. She moved her hand back and forth, eliciting another moan from Mitch, as his arousal grew harder and larger.

He jerked her panties down over her legs. When they dropped to her ankles, she kicked them aside. While she caressed him, he eased two fingers up inside her and thought he'd explode on the spot when he found her dripping with need.

The rain blew onto the porch, misting their heated bodies. Mitch lifted Emily, bracing her against the wall, then drove into her, embedding himself fully.

Emily clung to him, whimpering, pleading softly for him to end the torment and give her release. Cupping her hips in his big hands, he set the rhythm for their bodies as they mated on the front porch of Emily's cottage. At twilight. In the middle of a summer rainstorm.

Fast and furious, with a scorching passion, Mitch took her with savage pleasure. In those moments of pure, animalistic sex, she was his, completely. There was no past, no future, only the present.

She cried out her fulfillment. He captured the cry with a tongue-thrusting kiss. And her release triggered his, erupting inside him with earth-shattering spasms.

They clung to each other for several minutes, their breathing labored, their bodies overly sensitive, as fragmented shudders rippled inside them.

"I couldn't wait," he said in a husky voice, a voice still controlled by a desire only momentarily sated. "I didn't mean to take you out here on the porch like this." He pulled her bra together and fumbled with the hook.

Emily grabbed his hands, lifted them to her lips and kissed him. "No one could see us. And don't apologize. Couldn't you tell how badly I wanted you?"

"I could tell. These feelings between us are pretty strong, aren't they? Stronger than anything I've ever known."

She put her arms around him and laid her head on his chest. "I've never felt such a powerful desire."

"More than desire, Emily. Much more than desire."

He detected the slight frown forming on her lips and knew she was wondering if she could believe him. What the hell was it going to take to convince her?

"Now I'm the one who's sorry," she said. "I ruined the moment, didn't I? You knew what I was thinking."

"You didn't ruin anything, pretty lady." He kissed the top of her head. "You can't help the way you feel. I understand. It's just that there's nothing I can do to make you believe me... Nothing I can do to make things right between us."

Chapter 17

Sweat trickled off Mitch's forehead, ran down his face and dripped off his chin. Perspiration dampened his white T-shirt, sticking it to his chest like a soggy glue. He removed his yellow safety helmet, ran his fingers through his wet hair and stood there wishing he had a cold beer.

He had missed half a day's work yesterday taking Emily to Bay Minette to get Rod Simmons out of jail on bond. He'd never known anyone with a heart as big as Emily's. She was the type of woman who would go out of her way to help a stranger. For her friends, she'd do just about anything. And despite what Rod had done, Emily still considered him a friend.

And what would Emily do for the man she loved? For starters, she had forgiven him. She had mended his broken life, given him a reason to live and taught him the true meaning of love. But the one thing she couldn't do for him was believe him when he told her he loved her.

"Hey, Mitchell," Earl Tatum, Mitch's foreman, called out to him.

"Yeah?"

"A guy named Rod Simmons left a message for you. He

wants you to stop by his apartment when you get off from work—'' Tatum scanned a ripped piece of notepaper he held in his hand ''—number A-7, Greenbriar Apartments.''

''Did he say anything else?''

''Yeah. That's why I'm delivering the message myself instead of sending it by one of the men,'' Tatum told Mitch. ''This Simmons guy said to tell you that he's found out who was behind the break-ins at Emily Jordan's house and he thinks you two ought to talk.''

Mitch mumbled a crude curse. Simmons had found out who had hired the teenagers to break into Emily's house? How the hell had he found out? Unless he'd been the one responsible. Maybe that was it. Maybe Simmons wanted to confess.

''Thanks, Earl.''

Mitch checked his wristwatch. Four o'clock. He wondered what Earl Tatum would think if he asked to get off early today after taking off all of yesterday morning. He needed to talk to Rod Simmons as soon as possible and get to the bottom of this new development. Could it be that Simmons actually wanted to confess to him? Or had someone else made the call? If that was the case, then this could be a setup.

''Hey, Earl, what's the chance of my leaving early?'' Mitch asked.

Earl Tatum frowned, wrinkling his weathered forehead and deepening the lines around his eyes. ''Go on. Get out of here.''

Grinning at his foreman, Mitch waved goodbye. Before going to Simmons's apartment, he had to make one small detour. He needed a weapon. Just in case. And he knew just where to get a gun.

Emily left Nikki in charge of the Paint Box, as she customarily did when she taught classes away from the store. Teaching a watercolor class for kids, ages eight to fifteen, at the Fine Arts Museum of the South in Langan Park in Mobile, was a work of love for Emily. Hannah McLain had been a benefactor of the museum, donating a thousand dollars annually, and Emily herself was an associate, donating two hundred and fifty each year. The children were set up with their Pentel watercolor kits, their medium-sized brushes and real watercolor paper. Emily insisted no substitutes be used. The class consisted of twelve boys and girls of various ages.

She had seen genuine potential in two of the students, especially a thirteen-year-old girl named Kristy Springer.

Emily stood beside Kristy's easel, watching while the young girl studied the painting she'd begun in class two weeks ago.

"You're trying too hard to capture every detail," Emily said. "Remember what I told you during the first lesson about choosing the particular qualities that you're most interested in."

"I love the colors, Ms. Jordan." Kristy frowned at her creation, then glanced up at Emily. "I want to capture all those bright, glowing colors."

"Then forget detail. Work the subject broadly. You started out well by working wet-in-wet. Now add crisp definition where it's needed. That way you'll have a combination of soft and hard edges."

A hand went up across the room, near the entrance doorway. Nodding to the student, Emily noticed the door opening and wondered who would be interrupting her class.

"I'll check back with you in a few minutes," Emily told Kristy. "Keith needs my immediate attention."

When Emily glanced over at Keith, she saw Brenda Harden, one of the museum's secretaries, motion to her. Emily walked between the rows of easels and eager students, making her way as quickly as possible to Brenda.

"Is something wrong?" Emily asked.

"You have a phone call," Brenda said. "I wouldn't have disturbed you, but he said it was an emergency."

"I'll be right there." Emily turned back to her class. "Y'all continue working. I'll be back in just a few minutes."

She rushed out of the classroom, down the hall and into Brenda's office. She lifted the receiver off the desk and put it to her ear.

"Yes, hello. This is Emily Jordan." She took several deep breaths, praying this wasn't bad news.

"Emily." She didn't recognize the voice, but it had the same muffled quality as the voice of her secret admirer. But that wasn't possible. Rod would never make another "mystery" call to her again.

"Yes." Her heartbeat accelerated.

"Rod Simmons has confessed to hiring those boys to break into your house. He called Mitchell Hayden and admitted it to him. Now Hayden is on his way to Simmons's apartment."

A slight hesitation. An odd little snicker.

"If I were you, I'd stop Hayden before he harms Simmons. You wouldn't want to see your lover in prison for murder, would you?"

"Who is this?" Emily demanded. "How do you know—"

The dial tone hummed in Emily's ear.

"Emily, what's wrong?" Brenda asked.

"I need to make a phone call and check on something" was Emily's only reply.

With tense fingers, she quickly punched the numbers.

"Banning Construction," the man answered.

"I need to speak to Mitch Hay—to Ray Mitchell, immediately. It's an emergency."

"I'm sorry, lady, but Mitch isn't here. He had to take off early this afternoon on some personal business."

Emily's heart caught in her throat. "Do you...do you know where he went?"

"No, ma'am, can't say that I do."

"Thank you." Emily hung up the phone. There was only one thing she could do. She had to find Mitch—find him and stop him before he saw Rod.

Mitch dismounted, hung his helmet on the Harley and scanned the first-floor apartment doors. Opening one saddlebag, he removed the 9 mm he had "borrowed" from Zed's apartment. It had been fairly simple to get in, using the key Zed had given him when he'd stayed there the first couple of weeks he'd been in the Gulf area. He had no intention of using the weapon he'd taken from Zed's gun collection, but he wasn't fool enough to walk in unarmed on a man who claimed he knew who was responsible for the break-ins at Emily's house. The same man who had confessed that he'd been Emily's secret admirer. For all Mitch knew, this could be a setup. Maybe Rod Simmons was behind everything. Maybe he'd asked to see Mitch, intending to eliminate his competition. Mitch shoved the handgun's muzzle under the waistband of his jeans, the grip resting against his side.

The late-afternoon sunshine hit the west side of the Greenbriar Apartments' pastel-pink exterior wall. Heat waves shimmered near the surface. A black-lettered sign hung from the metal hinges outside the manager's office. This was a no-frills building, but it seemed neat and clean.

Glancing around, checking things out, Mitch marched along down the sidewalk in front of the ground-level apartments, then stopped outside the door of number A-7. The curtains were drawn. Cursing under his breath, he held his shaky hands out in front of him.

His gut instincts warned him to be careful. Something didn't feel right about this. But what could happen? A kid like Rod Simmons was no match for him, even if the boy had a weapon.

Clenching his teeth so tightly his jaws ached, Mitch drew in a deep breath, then released it slowly. He grasped the knob with one hand and knocked on the door with his other. He swung the door open a few inches.

"Simmons?" Mitch glanced inside the dark room. The sunlight spread a streak of illumination across the living-room floor. "Simmons? You here?"

Mitch took a tentative step inside. Hell, where was Simmons? Mitch checked the small kitchen. Empty. Then he entered the bedroom. No one was there. But from the rumpled bedsheets, scattered beer bottles and clutter of open books on the floor, Mitch surmised that someone had been there earlier.

He walked farther inside the room, flipped on a lamp and glanced around, taking note of everything from floor to ceiling. Smoke spiraled up from a cigarette lying in the ashtray. A bumping thud hit the bathroom door.

"Simmons, is that you?"

A tight knot formed in Mitch's stomach. Slowly, cautiously, he walked silently toward the closed bathroom door. Easing the

9 mm from the waistband of his jeans, he grabbed the doorknob and flung open the bathroom door.

Rod Simmons lay on the floor, bound and gagged with thick, gray duct tape. Thrashing about on the floor and groaning, he stared up at Mitch with pleading eyes.

What the hell! Suddenly Mitch heard a sound at his back. He half turned, then felt the weight of something heavy crash down on his head.

Emily slammed on her brakes, rocking her LeSabre to a screeching halt. She jumped out, left the door open and ran into the Paint Box. Breathless, her hands trembling, her heart racing, she visually searched the shop.

Nikki stood on a stepladder, placing a wooden carving done by a local artisan on a shelf with several other sculptures. With his arms crossed over his chest, Zed Banning leaned against the wall a few feet away, watching Nikki.

Emily sighed. Relief flooded through her. She didn't know what Zed was doing here, but thank God he was. He could help her stop Mitch from beating the living daylights out of Rod. And Emily had no doubt that if he got his hands on the boy, that's exactly what Mitch would do.

"Em?" Smiling, Nikki glanced over her shoulder. "You're back early."

Emily dashed across the shop and grabbed Zed's arm. "Please, help me. We've got to stop Mitch. I don't know how much of a head start he has, but if we don't hurry, it'll be too late."

Zed followed Emily into her office. Standing in the doorway, he watched while she flipped through her address book.

"Come on. I've got his address now." Emily paused beside Zed, her gaze meeting his.

Zed clutched Emily's shoulders. "Tell me what's wrong."

"I just told you. We've got to stop Mitch!" Emily dropped her tightly balled fists to Zed's chest. "Someone called me while I was in the middle of my class at the art museum. They said that Rod had confessed to the break-ins and that Mitch was on his way to Rod's apartment to—'' Emily gulped in large swallows of air. "Come on. Hurry. Please, Zed. Let's go. Now!''

"Em, you're hysterical." Nikki backed down off the ladder. "Who called you?''

"We're wasting time with all these questions." Emily pulled on Zed's arm. "I don't want Mitch to hurt Rod, no matter what Rod's done. And I certainly don't want Mitch to get into trouble.''

Zed shook her gently. "Calm down. I'll go with you.''

Nikki grasped Emily's arm, halting her mad rush out the door. "Mitch isn't going to do anything stupid. He probably just wants to confront Rod. Besides, if you don't know who called you, then how can you be sure what they said is true?''

"I *don't* know for sure," Emily admitted. "But if it is true, Mitch might tear Rod apart. You know how protective he is of me.''

"Where's Rod's apartment?'' Zed asked.

"Greenbriar Apartments on Wayland Street," Emily said.

"Come on, we'll take my car," Zed told her.

Two police cars blocked the entrance to the Greenbriar Apartments. Emily clutched Nikki's hand as she stared at the flashing lights atop the vehicles. Her breath caught in her throat; her chest constricted painfully.

"Something's wrong," she said.

Emily glanced at Zed, who swerved his Jeep Grand Cherokee up on the sidewalk and into the parking area to the left of the police cars. A young officer strutted toward Zed, hollering at him to move his Jeep.

"Stay put," Zed told Nikki and Emily. "I'll find out what's going on." He got out and met the young policeman. "What's wrong here, Officer?''

"Mister, you'll have to move your Jeep. We've got a homicide here. We don't want anybody interfering with our investigation.''

Emily stuck her head out the Jeep window and called to Zed. "Who's been killed? Ask him about—''

"Look, Officer—'' Zed noted the youth's name badge. "Officer Monroe, we have a…an acquaintance who lives here and the ladies are understandably worried. Could you just tell me the victim's name?''

''I'm sorry, sir, but I'm not at liberty to release any information at this time.''

Emily clutched her hands together in an effort to keep them from trembling. *A homicide. Someone had been murdered.* The victim couldn't be Rod Simmons. Mitch might have beaten him up, but he never would have killed him!

With siren blaring, an ambulance pulled up behind the police cars. Officer Monroe hopped in one of the vehicles and pulled it out of the way, allowing the ambulance to drive into the rectangular-shaped parking area in front of the apartment building. Zed slipped around the other police car and walked toward the manager's office.

Emily opened the door. Nikki grabbed her by the arm.

''Zed told us to stay put,'' Nikki said.

''I can't stay here not knowing what's happened and if Mitch is somehow involved.'' Emily got out; Nikki quickly followed her.

Zed motioned to them, warning them to stay back, but Emily disregarded his caution. Officer Monroe spotted the two women and stopped them before they could reach Zed.

''Ladies, I'll have to ask y'all to leave,'' Monroe said.

''Please.'' Emily gave the officer her most soulful expression and lowered her voice to an irresistible feminine sweetness. ''If you could just reassure us that our friend isn't the victim, I promise we'll be on our way.''

''I wish I could help you, ma'am, but—''

At that precise moment a man in a dark suit and a uniformed policeman led a handcuffed Mitch out of a ground-level apartment and into the parking area. Nikki gripped Emily's hand. Zed dashed down the sidewalk, headed in Mitch's direction.

''Mitch!'' Emily screamed his name.

Mitch inclined his head, looking in all directions. ''Emily!''

Emily jerked away from Nikki and shoved past Officer Monroe. Paying no heed to Nikki's cries or the young policeman's commands, she rushed straight toward the man she loved. All that mattered to her was getting to Mitch.

When Emily neared Mitch, Zed Banning grabbed her. "He's being arrested. They're not going to let you see him. Not now."

"Zed," Mitch called out. "Take care of her, will you? And get me a lawyer." He nodded at the men holding him prisoner. "They're taking me to the police station. They think I killed Rod Simmons."

"No," Emily cried. "Please, no."

"Pull yourself together," Zed whispered softly to Emily. "We'll find out what the hell's going on. I'll get Mitch a lawyer. Trust me. I'll handle things." Zed pulled Emily to his side and slipped his arm around her waist. "I'll take care of everything," Zed told Mitch.

The police placed Mitch in the back of the patrol car. Emily and Zed stood and watched them leave, then Zed led Emily away from the scene just as the attendants brought out a body bag and placed it in the ambulance. Nikki rushed over to Emily.

"Come on, Em. Let's get out of here." Nikki held tightly to Emily's hands, while Zed kept his arm draped around her waist.

"I can't believe this," Emily said. "Mitch wouldn't kill Rod. He wouldn't kill anybody."

"Only in self-defense," Zed assured her.

Emily allowed Zed and Nikki to help her to the Jeep. Nikki crawled in the back seat with her, but Emily pulled away when her friend reached out for her.

"I'm all right," Emily said. "We have to help Mitch. He'll need a lawyer."

"I'll call Jason Wilbanks, my lawyer, and he can get hold of the best criminal lawyer in these parts." Zed started the Jeep, backed up and headed toward downtown Fairhope.

Emily sat quietly, a slow, deadly numbness spreading through her. Doubts and uncertainties waged a silent war with love and trust.

Rod was dead. Shy, sweet, talented Rod. But how was that possible? Mitch wouldn't have killed him. He couldn't have. Could he? She wanted to believe that Mitch was innocent, that he was not capable of murder.

She had to see him, talk to him, hear him say that he hadn't killed Rod Simmons.

His head hurt like hell! Mitch squirmed in the wooden chair, his mind only now clearing enough for him to fully realize exactly what had happened to him. He'd been set up. But by whom? And why? Because of his relationship with Emily? That had to be it. Nothing else made any sense.

"Want to tell me what happened?" the heavyset man in a tailored, three-piece suit asked.

Mitch glanced over at the lawyer Zed Banning had hired for him. His old friend had wasted no time in getting the man to the Fairhope police station. The police were still waiting to question Mitch; he had adamantly refused to give them any answers without his lawyer present.

"What's your name?" Mitch asked.

"Gerald Hightower. Are you sure you're all right, Mr. Hayden? Sure you don't need a doctor? I told you my name when I walked in here less than two minutes ago."

"Sorry." Mitch rubbed the knot on his head. "I'm okay. Just a bit fuzzy. Whoever hit me gave me more than one lick. I feel like I've been run over by a Mack truck."

Mitch surveyed the lawyer from his neatly styled brown hair to the tips of his Italian leather shoes. The man looked successful. Hell, the guy looked rich.

"I want you to tell me everything that happened. And I mean everything," Gerald Hightower said. "I guess you realize you're in a lot of trouble, Mr. Hayden. You were found at the scene, with the murder weapon in your hand."

"Yeah, I know it looks bad. But I swear I didn't kill Rod Simmons. I had no reason to kill the boy."

Mitch wondered why Emily and Zed and Nikki had shown up at the Greenbriar Apartments just when he was being arrested. Maybe whoever had set him up had wanted to make sure Emily saw the police take him away.

"Why did you take a weapon to Rod Simmons's apartment?" Hightower asked.

"For self-defense," Mitch said. "But it didn't help me much, did it? I got coldcocked from behind, and the killer used my gun.''

''You didn't see who hit you?''

''Nope.''

''Well, the killer did more than use your gun, Mr. Hayden. He used your hand to pull the trigger.''

Mitch groaned. He'd been set up royally. The real killer had set a trap and he'd walked right into it, so sure he could handle the situation. But he thought he was dealing with Rod Simmons. Poor guy. Someone was willing to murder Simmons and let him hang for the crime in order to clear a path to Emily. Who? He could think of only one person. Charles Tolbert. Hell, he'd never figured the guy had the guts for it. But there was no one else, was there? Unless Fowler Jordan...

''Do you have any idea who'd want to frame you for murder, Mr. Hayden?''

''Sit down, Counselor.'' Mitch pointed to the chair on the other side of the table. ''I have a long, sordid little story to tell you.''

Chapter 18

Emily couldn't believe that it had come to this. Today was Mitch's preliminary hearing. The past two days had been a living hell for her. The police weren't interested in another suspect, weren't interested in listening to anyone's theories about what might have happened the afternoon Rod Simmons was murdered. As far as they were concerned, they had their man.

Mitch had been transferred from the Fairhope jail to the Baldwin County jail in Bay Minette yesterday morning. At this point all they could hope for was that the judge would release Mitch on bail. Mr. Hightower had said the evidence against Mitch was so strong that there was no doubt he would have to stand trial.

For the first time since her marriage to Stuart, Emily hadn't been able to turn to Fowler Jordan for help. When she had suggested that Charles might be Rod's murderer, her uncle had gone into a rage.

"I can't believe that you're still defending Mitchell Hayden!" Fowler had said. "Despite everything he's done—killing Stuart and your baby and now Rod Simmons—you still think you're in love with him."

She had wanted to confront Charles, but realized that she

should heed Nikki's warning to stay away from him. After all, he would hardly confess to murder. And if he really was unbalanced, who was to say what he might do?

"I'm going to take a shower," Nikki called out from her bedroom. "Zed's not due here to pick us up for another hour, is he?"

Emily checked the wall clock. "Fifty minutes. You've got plenty of time."

The telephone rang. Emily jumped. She'd been a nervous wreck for the past two days. She picked up the receiver. "Hello, Nikki Griffin's residence."

"Emily, my dear, I must see you immediately. Your very life could depend upon it."

"Uncle Fowler?"

"Yes, dear. Please, come to Mobile, to my house, as quickly as you can."

"What's wrong? What do you mean my life could depend on it?" Emily's stomach flip-flopped.

"Are you alone, my dear? Is there someone else listening to our conversation?"

"Nikki's taking a shower. I'm alone in her living room. We're waiting for Zed to pick us up for Mitch's preliminary hearing. What's going on, Uncle Fowler? You're scaring me."

"You have every right to be scared, after what I've just learned."

"What have you just learned?"

"I've discovered the truth, a horrible, ugly truth, about Charles." Fowler's voice quivered.

"What have you found out about Charles?"

"Charles has been behind everything. He confessed to me. He...he...oh, dear God, Emily, how could I have been so blind?"

"You have to call the police, Uncle Fowler. Now. Tell them what you know."

"No, Emily, I—I'm not certain I can do that." Fowler's voice lowered to a mere whisper. "I need to see you...to talk to you...before I turn Charles over to the police. I want to do the right thing. But...Charles has been like a son to me. I need to talk to you, for you to help me do what I must. Please, Emily.''

"Are you at home now, Uncle Fowler?" Emily asked.

"Yes, I'm at home. Charles just left. He went on in to work as if...as if nothing had happened. He thinks I see things his way. That I approve of what he did."

"Stay right there. I'll call the police and have them meet me at your house."

"No, please, Emily. Please, come and talk to me first, then...then I promise I'll go with you to the police."

"Uncle Fowler, I don't understand why you want to wait, why you—"

"Please, come to me as quickly as you can. And please, don't mention this to anyone. Not even Nikki. I simply can't believe that Charles would... He actually killed Rod Simmons and framed Mitch Hayden."

Emily debated her options. Poor Uncle Fowler was distraught. He wasn't thinking clearly. It was up to her to stay sane and rational, but it was also up to her to keep her uncle calm and willing to turn his beloved protégé over to the police.

"I'll leave right now and be at your house shortly," she told him.

"You won't call the police? You'll come here and talk to me, and then we'll go to the station together?"

"I won't call the police. I'll be there in a little while, and I'll stand by you and help you get through this nightmare. I promise."

"You're such a dear girl. I do love you so, Emily."

"Just sit tight until I get there, and if Charles returns before—"

"He won't. Remember, he thinks I'm on his side. That I actually approve of what he did." Fowler sighed deeply. "Please hurry."

"I'm on my way." Emily replaced the receiver, breathed in deeply, then released her breath slowly.

Her instincts told her to call the police, but if she did and they showed up on her uncle's doorstep, he might panic. Once he saw that she was there to give him all the support he needed, he would do the right thing. Knowing how her uncle felt about Charles, and his obvious emotional dilemma over having to turn him in to the authorities, Emily didn't want to do anything that might cause him any more grief.

But if she didn't show up at Mitch's hearing, he would worry and wonder what had happened to her. And if she just left without leaving any kind of message, Nikki would go ballistic.

Checking her watch, she realized court would convene soon. If she could persuade her uncle to go to the police immediately, Mitch would be a free man today.

She had to hurry. She scribbled a quick note for Nikki, telling her that she'd meet her and Zed at the Bay Minette courthouse, that she wanted to leave early so she could see Mitch before the hearing. Just a little white lie so Nikki wouldn't worry too much.

But she needed to let someone know where she was going, so that if she was delayed, Mitch wouldn't worry. She decided the best thing to do was leave a message with Zed Banning's secretary.

Emily jerked up the phone, hurriedly punched the numbers for Zed's office and waited. "This is Emily Jordan. I need for you to get a message to Mr. Banning at the courthouse later this morning."

"You can reach him on his cellular phone," Sandra Whitten said. "You have that number, don't you, Ms. Jordan?"

"No, I don't want to call Zed and disturb him right now. Please, just make sure he receives my message when he arrives at the courthouse."

"All right, Ms. Jordan. What message would you like for me to relay?"

"Please write this down and get every word," Emily said. "Tell Zed that I am meeting my Uncle Fowler at his house, and that I'll bring my uncle with me to Bay Minette. He has discovered that Charles Tolbert killed Rod Simmons."

"Is that the complete message?" Sandra asked.

"Yes. Thank you."

Fowler met Emily at the door and pulled her into an embrace, hugging her fiercely. "Thank God, you're all right. Did you park in the garage, the way I asked?''

She slipped her arm around his thin waist and led him from the foyer into the front parlor. "Of course I'm all right. And yes, I parked my car in the garage, but I don't understand why—''

"I'm heartsick, my dear, simply heartsick. To think that I trusted him, loved him like a son, wanted you to marry him.''

"Come on and sit down, Uncle Fowler. We need to decide how you want to handle this situation.''

He glared at her, his mouth trembling as he spoke. "You didn't call the police, did you?''

"I promised you that I wouldn't,'' she told him. "And you promised me that you would—''

"Yes. Yes, I will. I will. I'll do what I must do. But first, I need time to think, to try to make sense of what has happened, to understand why Charles would do such a thing.''

"Don't torture yourself this way. It breaks my heart to see you so upset.''

Fowler allowed Emily to help him onto the sofa. When she sat down beside him, he clasped her hands. "You're so very sweet. You know that all I've ever wanted for you was your happiness.''

"We have to contact the police and tell them that they've arrested the wrong man—an innocent man—for Rod Simmons's murder.''

"You love Mitch Hayden very much, don't you?''

"Yes, I do. I love him with all my heart.''

"I had so hoped... Well, it doesn't matter now, does it? What I wanted isn't possible any longer.'' Fowler choked on his tears.

Emily draped her arm around his shoulders. "I know this whole ordeal must be terrible for you.''

"You have no idea. To have all my hopes and dreams destroyed. Just like that.'' Fowler snapped his fingers. "I tried to make you happy. To give you everything. If only you had stayed here with me. You would have been safe. None of this would have happened.''

"I couldn't stay here and continue being only half alive. And even if I'd stayed, I don't think I would have ever agreed to marry Charles. I wanted and needed real love."

"You wanted passion. The kind of passion a man like Mitch Hayden could give you." Fowler folded in on himself like a dying hothouse flower deprived of proper nourishment. Clasping his stomach, he cried. His slender body shivered. "How could you have let that man touch you? He's not worthy of you. He's not fit—"

"Please, Uncle Fowler, now isn't the time to discuss this. Charles is walking around a free man, and Mitch is in jail. Just tell me what you want me to do to help you. We can't afford to waste any more time."

"Yes, you're right, of course. Talking about your relationship with Hayden is a waste of time." Fowler glanced around the room, as if searching for something. "I misplaced my reading glasses. I had them on when I looked up Nikki's number so I could call you. What could I have done with them?"

"Don't worry about your reading glasses. We'll find them later." Emily placed her hands on her uncle's narrow shoulders. "Come with me now. Please."

"Go with you, my dear? Where?" Fowler gazed quizzically at her.

What was wrong with him? He was acting odd, as if...as if... No, please, dear Lord, no. Don't let him have a nervous breakdown. He doesn't deserve to suffer any more. And if he loses control and can't reason properly, how will we convince the police that Charles really did confess to him?

"We're going to the police station to tell them about Charles." Emily stared directly at Fowler.

"Yes. We must go."

Emily helped her uncle to his feet and led him out of the living room. Just as they entered the marble-floored foyer, Fowler halted abruptly.

"My reading glasses. We must find them before we leave. What if I have to sign papers at the police station? I can't see to read without those glasses." Jerking his head from side to side in an agitated manner, Fowler wrung his hands. "I can't leave without my glasses!"

"We don't have time to hunt for your glasses now, Uncle Fowler. If you have to sign anything at the police station, I'll read it to you and show you exactly where to sign your name. Please, let's stop wasting time."

"Yes, of course, you're right. We must hurry. We must get Mitch Hayden out of jail," Fowler said, allowing Emily to lead him toward the front door.

Suddenly the door swung open and Charles breezed into the foyer, smiling when he saw Emily. Fowler pulled away from Emily, placing himself between her and the other man.

Charles's sunny smile illuminated his face. "I came rushing over the minute you called, Fowler." Charles took a tentative step forward. Fowler moved to block his advance. "I'm so pleased...no, I'm ecstatic that you've finally come to your senses, my darling."

"What—what are you talking about?" Emily moved slowly backward, fear dictating her actions. What did Charles mean when he said that Uncle Fowler had called him? And what was he so damned happy about? She hadn't changed her mind about anything.

"I'm talking about your decision to marry me," Charles said, walking around Fowler and straight toward Emily. "When Fowler phoned and said you wanted me to meet you here, that you'd said you were through with Hayden, I could hardly believe my good fortune."

Emily glanced from a deliriously happy Charles to her uncle, whose odd little smile gave her a sick feeling in the pit of her stomach.

Emily gasped. Charles jerked his head around and stared at the man pointing a rather large, sinister-looking gun at him.

Zed and Nikki rushed inside the courthouse, both of them breathless by the time they reached Judge Anderson's courtroom. They had been delayed by a four-car accident on Highway 59. As Zed started to open the door, a uniformed policeman laid his hand on Zed's shoulder.

"You're Mr. Banning, aren't you?" he asked.

"Yes, I'm Zed Banning. Why?"

"I'm Officer Turner. Mr. Hightower wanted me to keep an eye out for you and let you know that he and Mr. Hayden are in the district attorney's office waiting for you."

"What's wrong?" Nikki asked. "Is the preliminary hearing already over?"

"Yes, ma'am."

"What happened?" Zed asked.

"It seems a witness showed up at the police station early this morning with some information that blew some mighty big holes in the case against Mr. Hayden."

"Where is the district attorney's office?" Zed glanced around, not at all familiar with the Baldwin County courthouse.

"I'll be glad to show you folks," the officer said. "But you might want to phone your office first. Your secretary has called twice and said it was urgent that you contact her."

"I don't understand why she didn't call me directly."

"She wouldn't leave a message, just said to tell you to phone her when you got here."

"Fine. Show us to the district attorney's office first," Zed said. "I'll call Sandra after I talk to Mitch."

"I suppose Emily is with Mitch and his lawyer," Nikki said, slipping her arm through Zed's as they followed the policeman.

Before they reached the office, Zed saw Mitch and Gerald Hightower walking toward them. Mitch didn't look like a man who'd just been set free. He looked worried.

"Well, I'll see you folks," the policeman said. "You won't need me for an escort now."

"Thanks," Zed said absently, then focused his attention on Mitch. "What happened?"

"A woman who'd had a romantic afternoon meeting with her boyfriend in the apartment directly across from Rod Simmons's came forward," Hightower said. "She confessed that her conscience bothered her, and even though telling the truth about what she saw might cost her her marriage, she couldn't let an innocent man be wrongfully accused."

"What did she see?" Zed asked.

"She saw another man enter Rod Simmons's apartment about thirty minutes before she saw Mitch arrive. Then a few minutes after Mitch showed up, she saw the other man leave,'' Hightower said. ''You want to know who we think the guy was? The witness gave us a pretty good description.''

Nikki gripped Zed's hand.

''She said the guy was about five-nine, slender, a slight stoop to his shoulders. He had thinning gray hair and wore wire-frame glasses,'' Hightower told them. ''She guessed his age to be somewhere between fifty-five and sixty.''

''Fowler Jordan!'' Nikki cried out.

''I've consulted with the Fairhope police, who are familiar with the harassment case and Ms. Jordan's friends and family,'' Hightower said. ''They say the description definitely fits Fowler Jordan.''

''Oh, my God, Emily must be devastated,'' Nikki said. ''Where is she? Gone to wash her face? If I know her, she's been crying—with joy over Mitch's being released and sadness over her uncle.''

''What do you mean where's Emily?'' Mitch grabbed Nikki's arm. ''Isn't she with you and Zed?''

''No, she...she came by herself. She left me a note saying she wanted to see you before the hearing.'' Nikki trembled uncontrollably. ''Oh, no!''

''Goddammit! I don't like this,'' Mitch said. ''Something's happened. I can feel it in my gut!'' Clenching his fist, he punched his stomach. ''When she didn't show up, I got an uneasy feeling. But when you two didn't show up, either, I figured she was with you and something had delayed y'all.''

''Mr. Banning?'' Officer Turner called out from a nearby office. ''Your secretary is on the line. I told her you were here.''

''I'll be right back.'' Zed gripped Mitch's shoulder, pressing firmly. ''Emily is all right. We'll find her. Just stay calm.''

Mitch met Zed just as he walked out of the office. ''I can't wait any longer,'' Mitch said. ''I've got to find Emily before...before—''

''She's gone to Fowler Jordan's house,'' Zed said.

''Dammit, why did she go to Jordan's house?'' Mitch grabbed Zed's arm. ''How do you know she's with Fowler Jordan?''

"Emily left a message with my secretary," Zed explained. "Emily said to tell you that if she didn't get here in time for the hearing, it was because she'd gone to Jordan's house and that she would be bringing her uncle here to Bay Minette so he could tell the police Charles Tolbert had confessed to him that he'd killed Rod Simmons."

"Oh, God! Why the hell didn't she just call the police?" Mitch slammed his fist into the wall.

Zed laid his hand on Mitch's back. "Don't go to pieces like this. Don't assume the worst."

Zed glanced over at Nikki, who stared back at him with big, round eyes.

"Mr. Banning?" Officer Turner stood a few feet away. "I called and checked the way you asked me to, and there's no Emily Jordan or Fowler Jordan at any police station in South Alabama."

"He's got Emily." Mitch gripped the lapels of Zed's jacket. "If he hurts her—"

"We'll go straight to Mobile," Zed said. "I'll hire a helicopter."

"Is there a problem?" Officer Turner asked.

"Yeah." Zed calmly covered Mitch's hands and loosened his grip on his suit, then he grabbed Mitch by the arm as he turned to the policeman. "Call the Mobile police and have them send some men out to Fowler Jordan's house. I don't know the address, but that shouldn't be difficult to find out. We have reason to believe that he may be holding his niece against her will."

Chapter 19

"Well, now that you're both here, I suppose we should move our little party into the living room." Fowler Jordan pointed the .44 Magnum toward the parlor.

"What's going on?" All semblance of happiness vanished from Charles's face, replaced by shock. "Why are you pointing that gun at us?"

"Well, let's just say that there's been a change in plans." Fowler grabbed Emily's arm, then waved his gun at Charles. "Get moving. Into the living room. Now!"

Emily thought that her uncle seemed to be more in control of himself at this precise moment than he'd been when he'd telephoned her—indeed, more in control of himself than she'd ever seen him. There was a sedate, unemotional aura about him.

Emily shivered. "Charles didn't confess to killing Rod Simmons, did he?" Bit by tiny bit, the fragments of a truth she didn't want to face began coming together to form one plausible explanation for her uncle's actions.

"What's she talking about?" Moving forward, Charles squared his shoulders and glared at Fowler. "Of course I didn't confess to killing Rod Simmons. I didn't murder that boy. Mitch Hayden did.''

"No, of course you didn't kill Rod," Emily said. "And neither did Mitch. But I think I know who did." The realization sent warning chills through Emily's body, creating a cold, deadly fear deep within her.

"If Hayden didn't kill Rod Simmons, who did? And what does that have to do with why Fowler has that gun?''

"Do you want to tell Charles or shall I?" Numbness claimed Emily as she stared at Stuart's uncle. The man who had sat at her bedside and comforted her after Stuart's death. The man who had loved her, supported her, encouraged her. The man who had willed her to live when she'd wanted to die.

Fowler Jordan laughed, the hearty chuckles rumbling from his chest and bursting into the atmosphere like frightening thunder. Charles's eyes rounded into big, brown circles of shock.

"Are you saying that Fowler killed Rod Simmons?" Charles's voice quivered.

Emily clutched the loose material on each side of her slacks, just below her hips. Dear Lord, was this really happening? Was it actually possible that her beloved Uncle Fowler was a murderer? "Yes, that's exactly what I'm saying."

"No, I don't believe it." Charles looked at Fowler. "Tell her that she's mistaken. You wouldn't—"

"Ah, but I would," Fowler admitted. "I'd do anything to prevent Emily from wasting her life on a man like Hayden."

"I don't understand," Charles said.

"It's quite simple, really." Fowler glanced from Emily to Charles. "I thought that if I killed Rod Simmons, I could eliminate two birds with one stone, so to speak."

Charles stared, bleary-eyed, at his mentor. "You really did kill that boy."

"My plan was for Mitch Hayden to be arrested. Which he was," Fowler said. "And I believed that once Emily realized Hayden truly was a murderer, she would come to her senses and cut all ties to the man. I thought she would return to us, Charles, and we could continue with our plans. I felt that, in time, she'd realize my choices for her were the right choices."

"But I didn't cut all ties to Mitch, did I?" Emily stared at Fowler, the man who had cared for her with such love and compassion after the fire, and wondered what had happened to him. How could he have changed so drastically from a kind, gentle man to a monster, capable of murdering an innocent man as a part of his misguided schemes?

"No, foolish girl that you are, thinking with your body's lust, you clung to your worthless lover." While holding the Magnum steady in one hand, he delved inside his coat pocket with the other and removed a handkerchief, then wiped the perspiration from his face. "I thought hiring those young thugs to break into your house twice and warn you against seeing another man— any other man than the one I'd chosen for you—would be enough. But no, you wouldn't heed the warnings."

"You set Mitch up for Rod's murder," Emily said, her voice deceptively calm. Her insides were a trembling mess. "You planned it all out, didn't you? You murdered that sweet, innocent boy because of me."

Fowler grinned. Nausea hit Emily squarely in the stomach, like a giant acidic tidal wave eating holes in a placid shore. She covered her mouth with her hand, muting her gasp of realization. This man wasn't the uncle who loved her. This man *was* a monster—a monster capable of destroying anyone and anything. That included Charles—and even her! A scream caught in her throat, trapped there by pure fear.

"You called and left a message for Mitch and you called me and disguised your voice when you told me that Mitch had gone to Rod's apartment. You wanted me to be there when Mitch was arrested. And you called the police, too, didn't you?"

"Guilty on all charges." Fowler's grin widened. His eyes actually twinkled with some inner pleasure. "It was so easy. Rod was such a pathetic weakling. And Mitchell Hayden. Ah, that stupid muscle-bound idiot played right into my hands. Hell, he even brought his own gun. I didn't even have to use my own. All I had to do was hog-tie and gag Rod and wait in the closet until Hayden showed up. You see my dear, everything would have worked out perfectly if you had just cooperated. But no, once again, you had to ruin all my carefully executed plans."

"Fowler, you're a sick man," Charles said. "Please, let Emily and me help you. We can call the police and then—"

"I'm afraid that calling the police right now isn't part of my new plan." Fowler chuckled. "Of course, after you've taken Emily hostage and I've shot you, and accidently shot Emily, too, in trying to save her from you, then I'll have to call the police and tell them what happened."

Emily could not believe that any of this was actually happening. But it was. And if she didn't think of some way to save herself and Charles, they'd soon be dead! Uncle Fowler had lost his mind.

"But you wouldn't harm Emily," Charles rationalized. "You love her. You've devoted the past five years of your life to her."

"You're quite right. I did devote my life to Emily. I loved her like the daughter I never had. All I wanted in return for all I'd given her was for her to marry you, for the two of you to live in this house with me and raise your children here. But she turned from you to another man. A man totally unsuitable for her. A man completely unworthy."

"I won't let you kill Emily." Charles spoke through clenched teeth, his face contorted with fear.

"I'm afraid I must kill Emily. It's the only way I can save her from herself. And regrettably, in order to make my plan work, I'll have to kill you, too. The police must be convinced that you killed Rod Simmons. I will tell them that you took Emily hostage, that you threatened her life and that I tried to stop you, killing you in the process. And unfortunately, I accidently shot Emily when I tried to rescue her from you."

Emily could not believe the cold-blooded plot her uncle had devised. Had she ever really known this man, or had his kind and loving demeanor been only a facade?

Charles moved toward Fowler. Emily tried to cry out to warn him not to confront Fowler, but her voice froze in her throat.

"You're not going to kill Emily." Charles advanced on Fowler, seemingly oblivious to the weapon in Fowler's hand.

Fowler fired his gun. Charles gasped. He stared at Fowler in disbelief, then slumped to the floor.

Emily screamed. Blood oozed from Charles's stomach. Emily turned her head, gasping for breath.

He had done it. He had actually shot Charles. And she was going to be next.

"Please...don't hurt Emily," Charles pleaded as the life drained slowly from his body.

Mitch, Nikki and Zed boarded the rented helicopter in Bay Minette less than ten minutes after the Mobile police had been notified about the possible danger to Emily Jordan. The police chief, a personal friend of Zed's, had promised not to waste any time sending two patrol cars out to the Jordan residence on Solomon Drive, and had promised to have a SWAT team on standby. Zed assured Mitch that everything possible was being done, but he could only imagine the torture his old friend was going through, not knowing if he'd ever see the woman he loved alive again.

In that split second after Fowler shot Charles, he focused all his attention on him. Bending down on one knee, he stared at him, then ran the tips of his fingers over his face. Charles groaned, dying but not yet dead.

Emily realized that Fowler wasn't paying any attention to her. Slowly, cautiously, she took one step backward, then another and another, keeping an eye on her uncle all the while. She continued moving backward, toward the French doors leading to the enclosed courtyard at the side of the house.

"I'm so sorry, my dear boy," Fowler told the dying Charles. "I regret that things had to end this way. It's all Emily's fault, of course. If she'd done as I expected her to, then none of this would have been necessary."

Emily slipped back against the French doors, reached behind her and grasped the crystal knob.

"I treated her like a queen." Fowler stood, shook his head sadly and sighed. "Poor girl. Poor misguided girl. I can't allow her to go on living. Not now. Now that she's in love with Stuart's murderer. Now that she's given herself to him."

Emily turned the doorknob, eased the door open a fraction and then opened it just a little bit more.

The doorbell rang. Fowler jumped. Emily froze to the spot.

"Who the hell?" Fowler asked himself.

The doorbell rang again.

Emily flung the French doors open and ran outside. Fowler raced after her, ignoring the ringing doorbell.

Emily hid behind a five-foot hedge that hugged the far back side wall of the enclosed courtyard. Her heartbeat hammered in her ears, obliterating every other sound.

"Come out, Emily dear, wherever you are." Fowler Jordan circled the courtyard. "There's nowhere to run, no way out."

Emily swallowed hard. He was wrong. There was a way out. Through the intricately carved cast-iron gate that opened up onto the driveway. But she would have to expose herself, put herself in the line of fire, to reach the gate.

She watched from her hiding place as Fowler scoured the courtyard, looking behind every bush, circling the two trees, overturning the patio furniture. Then he halted his rampage and stared directly at the hedge. He smiled.

"I know where you're hiding. Come on out. Now!"

Emily reached down, picked up a handful of pebbles and threw them at the opposite end of the hedgerow. She waited until Fowler began his search of the hedge at the far end, a good twenty feet away from her.

She crept along the hedgerow, then darted out and dashed to the gate. The moment she grabbed the latch, a shot rang out over her head, zinging off the cast iron.

Emily screamed, but she didn't look back. He was going to kill her, no matter what. She would rather die trying to escape than to wait for him to shoot her.

She unlatched the gate and swung open the door. Fowler fired again. Crying out in pain, she grabbed her shoulder where the bullet had entered and ran out of the courtyard and onto the driveway.

When Mitch, Nikki and Zed arrived at the Jordan house on Solomon Street, they found the Mobile police in charge of an explosive situation. A uniformed officer stopped them.

"What's going on here?" Zed inquired.

"Sir, I'm afraid I'll have to ask you and the others to leave the vicinity."

Paying no heed to the officer, Mitch rushed past him and headed across the street. If Emily was here, inside that house and in trouble, he had to go to her. Had to save her. Another policeman grabbed Mitch. Mitch reared back, drawing his hand into a fist.

"Don't, Mitch," Zed yelled. "I'll find out what's going on."

Lowering his fist to his side, Mitch glared at the officer, who held on to Mitch.

A dark sedan pulled up and parked directly behind the two police cars. A tall sandy-haired man in his late forties emerged, threw up his hand in greeting and walked toward Zed.

"Stay cool, Mitch," Zed warned. "Arnold Madden's here now and I'll find out what's going on." Zed turned to greet the new arrival. "Arnold, that's Mitch Hayden over there." Zed nodded toward Mitch and the officer just barely restraining him. "He's half out of his mind worrying about Emily Jordan. What the hell's going on here?"

"Release Mr. Hayden," Chief of Police Arnold Madden ordered the officer, who obeyed instantly, but stared at his commanding officer as if he questioned the man's sanity.

"Come here, Mr. Hayden, and I'll brief you and Zed on what's happened," Madden said.

Nikki rushed over to Zed. He slipped his arm around her waist. Mitch ran back across the street and stepped up on the sidewalk to stand on the other side of Zed.

"We don't know the whole story yet," Madden told them. "When our men arrived, we couldn't get anyone to answer the door, but we heard a gunshot."

Mitch cursed loudly. "If anything has happened to Emily, I'll—"

"When my men got inside, they discovered the body of a man in his early thirties. We found some ID in his wallet. His name was Charles Tolbert."

"Where is Emily and her uncle?" Zed asked.

"I'm afraid Mr. Jordan is outside in the courtyard, and he's holding his niece hostage."

Mitch's heart thundered in his chest. He trembled, knowing the truth. Bile rose from his stomach, coating his throat. He clenched his jaw tightly. Emily. Dear God in heaven! Emily was in the hands of a madman. A man she had loved and trusted.

Zed gripped Mitch's shoulder, but looked directly at the police chief. "What's been done to free Ms. Jordan?"

"The SWAT team is getting in place," Madden said. "And Fowler Jordan is talking to our officer inside the house."

Nikki gasped. Tears trickled down her cheeks. "Please, please don't let anything happen to Emily."

"We're going to do our best," Madden told her. "At this point, we have to assume that Ms. Jordan could be injured."

"I'm going in there," Mitch said.

Zed tightened his hold on Mitch's shoulder, then grabbed his arm and jerked him around so that they faced each other. "Let the police do their job. Once the SWAT team gets set, they can put a sharpshooter in place and he can take Jordan out."

"And what if Emily is hurt? What if he shot her?" Mitch asked. "What if the SWAT team can't zero in on Jordan? This house is on a corner lot and that walled courtyard faces the side street. Where are they going to get so they can take a shot at him? Huh?"

"They'll figure out something." Zed pulled Mitch several feet away and placed his hands on his shoulders. "If you try to storm the house, Chief Madden will have his men stop you."

"If Jordan was holding the woman you loved, what would you do, Zed? Would you wait around out here, hoping the SWAT team would get him before she bled to death? Would you wait to see if they could save her?"

Zed closed his eyes and clenched his jaw. Releasing his hold on Mitch, he spit out a crude expletive. Opening his eyes, he stared at Mitch. "You don't even have a weapon."

"If I can take Jordan unawares, I won't need any other weapon than my own two hands."

"How the hell do you think you're going to be able to sneak up on Jordan—that is, if you can get past the police?"

"Jordan will be placing most of his attention on the back entrance from the house and on that gate leading to the driveway," Mitch said. "He won't be paying too much attention to the wall itself."

"You're going to scale the wall?"

"Jordan has got to know that the police called in their SWAT team. So that means he's going to keep Emily in front of him and he's going to keep his back covered. He's telling himself that he can negotiate his way out of there."

"You could be committing suicide as well as endangering Emily's life by trying to rescue her."

"If I fail, you make sure they save Emily." Mitch clasped Zed's hand. "And make sure Fowler Jordan pays for what he's done."

"Think twice about what you're doing," Zed cautioned. "Hell, you're going to do it regardless of what I say. So, what can I do to help you?"

"Tell the chief that you've calmed me down and persuaded me to take a walk to cool off while we wait for the SWAT team."

"Okay. What else?"

"Make sure the chief keeps that officer in the house negotiating with Jordan. That might distract him long enough for me to get to Emily."

"God help you," Zed said.

"God help Fowler Jordan when I get my hands on him."

Mitch said a thankful prayer that Jordan's garage was unlocked. He lifted the door and scanned the dim interior, quickly spotting a fiberglass extension ladder hanging along the back wall. Emily's LeSabre was parked inside the garage.

Standing on an old trunk, Mitch eased the ladder off the hooks and stepped down onto the concrete floor. He spotted a length of wound rope hanging from a nail. He grabbed the rope. Dust particles swirled off the rope and into the air. The damn thing looked a hundred years old. No telling how long it had been in the detached garage. He slipped his arm through the loop and tossed the rope over his shoulder.

His best chance lay in a surprise attack. And he could accomplish that goal only if Zed had persuaded the chief to keep the officer inside talking to Fowler Jordan. Mitch had to have that distraction—that split second when Jordan would be vulnerable.

He laid the ladder against the eight-foot courtyard wall, inadvertently making a scraping sound. Damn! His heart beat at breakneck speed. He gripped the ladder with damp hands, climbing slowly, trying to be quiet.

When he reached the top, he peered below. Jordan had his back to him, and was focused on the house. Mitch tried to make out what Jordan was looking at, but the sunlight reflected off the panes in the French doors, preventing Mitch from seeing inside.

"I know what's going on," Fowler Jordan yelled. "I'm not stupid. Your damn SWAT team guys are here, aren't they, Sweeney? I heard more cars drive up out there. Well, you'd better get rid of them. Get everybody out of here, or I'll kill Emily now."

Thank God! Mitch thought. Chief Madden had kept Officer Sweeney in the house.

Jordan removed his arm from around Emily's waist and shoved her out in front of him, holding her by her bloody shoulder. She moaned. Mitch closed his eyes against the sight. Hot, sour liquid ran up his throat. He swallowed it. Jordan had shot her, the son of a bitch! She was bleeding, her blouse covered in red.

"Don't hurt Emily," Sweeney said. "Give me your exact terms and I'll talk to the chief and see if we can cut a deal with you."

"I want everybody out of here! Then I want a car. You can drive us. If I see anybody following, I'll kill her."

Mitch glanced down at the hedge below. The top of the hedge was a good three or four feet beneath him. Could he jump into the hedge, cushioning his fall, without Jordan hearing him? No way! He'd have to take his chances with the ancient piece of rope. He tied the rope securely to the cast-iron rail that circled the top of the brick wall, then dropped it. The end of the rope fell downward, a couple of feet curling on the ground.

Mitch eased himself over the wall, grabbed hold of the rope and began his descent. Halfway down the wall, his body partially hidden behind the hedge, he caught a glimpse of the man standing just inside the open French doors. The police negotiator. Jordan had called him Sweeney. He must have introduced himself before he started bargaining. Well, Sweeney wouldn't be expecting him. What would he do when he saw Mitch climbing down the wall?

Whatever you do, don't give me away, Mitch prayed. Don't screw up this chance to save Emily.

Sweeney saw him! Mitch sucked in his breath. Sweeney glanced away. Mitch let out his breath and eased down the rope and onto the ground.

"You tell the chief that there had better be a plane waiting for us. A plane to take us out of the country. I'll take Emily far away from this place. We'll start all over again. This time she'll do what I tell her to do."

"A plane to take you out of the country," Sweeney repeated. "If we provide you with a plane, we'll expect you to release Ms. Jordan."

Fowler Jordan laughed, the sound harsh and cold. "Absolutely not. She goes with me. What kind of fool do you take me for?"

Mitch peered through the hedge, and for the first time noticed that Sweeney was wearing nothing but his boxer shorts. What the hell? Jordan had not only made the officer discard his weapon, but he'd made him strip down to his underwear.

Emily swayed on her feet. Mitch called upon every ounce of willpower he possessed not to run out and grab her. Jordan shoved her into a nearby white wrought-iron chair, then stood behind her, holding his gun to her head.

Mitch searched for and found a sparse section in the thick hedgerow. Testing it with his shoulder, he realized this was the place to crawl through. But how much noise would that make? If he took the long way around, going to the end of the hedgerow, he ran the risk of Jordan catching sight of him in his peripheral vision. If only Sweeney would cooperate, make some noise, create a distraction. Mitch stood up and stared at Sweeney, who didn't look his way. Mitch kept standing there until Sweeney made eye contact. Only a split second, but he knew the guy saw him. But did he understand?

Mitch bent down, eased his shoulder into the hedge and waited.

"We really need to get a doctor in here to see about Ms. Jordan's shoulder," Sweeney said.

Mitch stuck his head through the hedge and saw Sweeney take a tentative step forward. Suddenly the man tripped and fell directly into the French door. One of his feet and one hand rammed into the glass panes, shattering them.

"What the hell?" Yelling, Jordan stepped away from Emily.

Mitch crashed through the hedge, ran the ten feet across the courtyard and jumped Fowler Jordan from behind. Emily turned her head and cried out, then slid out of the chair and onto the ground.

Mitch overpowered Jordan, sending them both to the ground. They rolled around, the Magnum still in Jordan's hand—the hand that Mitch gripped with all his might.

As they struggled for the gun, Jordan dragged it between their bodies. Mitch felt the barrel pressing into his stomach. He squeezed Jordan's hand, turning the gun, accidently forcing Jordan's finger against the trigger. The gun went off. Mitch froze.

Emily screamed. Mitch glanced around, looking for her. He saw Sweeney helping Emily to her feet.

Fowler Jordan lay on top of Mitch, a hard, heavy weight. Mitch rolled the man off him and onto the ground. Jordan coughed several times. A trickle of blood oozed from the side of his mouth.

"Mitch!" Emily cried out to him.

Mitch lifted himself up on his knees, his breath ragged, his chest hurting with every ounce of air he consumed. He stood, shaky on his feet, and walked unsteadily toward Emily. Sweeney released her. She rushed into Mitch's arms.

"It's all over, pretty lady. All over. You're safe." He circled her shivering body in an embrace.

Crying, Emily clung to him. "I was so afraid. I thought I'd never see you again, that I'd never get a chance to tell you that I believe you love me. Oh, Mitch—"

"Hush. Don't talk," Mitch told her. "Save your strength. You can tell me all about how you feel once we make sure you're all right."

Sweeney cleared his throat. "There's an ambulance outside waiting for Ms. Jordan."

Holding Emily close, Mitch looked over at Sweeney. "Thanks for distracting Jordan."

"That was a dumb fool thing you did," Sweeney said.

"Maybe. But it was what I had to do." Mitch lifted Emily in his arms and carried her across the yard. "How about opening the gate, Sweeney? I need to get my future wife to a hospital."

Emily's hospital room was filled with floral arrangements, but her favorite was the pale-pink roses Mitch had sent. Sitting up in bed, she rested her head on his shoulder. He hadn't left the hospital since he'd carried her in the day before. She rubbed her smooth cheek against the beard stubble covering his face.

"You need a shave," she told him.

"Yeah, and a bath, too. But I don't want to leave. I can't bear having you out of my sight."

"Nikki and Zed are coming back after they eat lunch. They'll stay with me long enough for you to get cleaned up."

Mitch cupped her face in his hands. "Just let me look at you, pretty lady. God, when I think about how close I came to losing you."

"We have a great deal to be thankful for, don't we? Just thinking about what Uncle Fowler did—"

Mitch covered her lips with his index finger. "Don't think about him. There's nothing you can do to help him."

"I know. It's just that I still can't believe Uncle Fowler was willing to kill me to keep me from being with you. And he murdered Rod and Charles." Emily covered her face with her hands and wept.

"I'm sorry he wasn't the man you thought he was." Mitch slipped his arm around her waist.

"I don't know what to think anymore." Emily lifted her tear-stained face. Mitch wiped the moisture from her cheeks with his fingertips. "It's as if Uncle Fowler was two different men. His obsession to have me marry Charles and spend the rest of my life under his protection must have driven him crazy."

"I understand about obsessions," Mitch told her. "I've been obsessed with you for a long time."

"And now you love me, don't you, Mitch? You truly love me." She made the pronouncement with conviction, knowing that if she wanted the happiness only Mitch could give her, she had to believe him. She had to take him on faith. Her near-death experience had taught her that she shouldn't waste time on doubts and uncertainties. When fate handed you a miracle, you didn't question it. You reached out and grabbed it. And said thank-you.

"Yes, I love you," Mitch said.

"Then after the funerals..." Rod's had been today, but the doctors had refused to release her so she could attend. She would have to make the arrangements for Fowler's and possibly for Charles's, too. He had no immediate family, only some first cousins in the northern part of the state.

Mitch wrapped her trembling body in his arms. She clung to him, knowing she was safe, assured that she could put the rest of her life in Mitch's hands and he would never disappoint her.

"Once I'm completely recovered and have made peace with what happened, I want us to plan a wedding," she said. "Nothing elaborate. Something simple and private, with just a few friends. With Zed as our best man and Nikki our maid of honor."

How had a guy like him gotten so lucky? Mitch wondered. He didn't deserve Emily. He'd never be good enough for her.

But who was he to question a gift from God? And that's exactly what their love was. A gift. The most precious gift this life has to offer. Silently, prayerfully, he made a sacred vow that he would love, cherish and protect Emily as long as they lived.

"No more doubts?" he asked. "You're going to take me on faith?"

"I realized something, you know. Yesterday, you saved my life," she said. "So, the way I see it, you repaid whatever debt you owed me. Now you don't have to marry me to make atonement. You don't have to pretend to love me if you don't. We're all squared away."

Mitch grinned. "Emily Jordan, I love you."

"Yes, I know you do," she said, and kissed him.

Epilogue

Mitch Hayden held his infant daughter in his arms, totally in awe of the precious new life that he and Emily had created together. Hannah Hayden, a pink satin bow nestled in her wispy blond curls, stared up at her father with eyes as ice-blue as his own and let out a cry.

"Hey, big girl, don't do that. Don't cry, sweetheart. Daddy'll make it all right."

Holding a large cardboard box in her arms, Emily entered the living room from the front porch. "I don't think Daddy can take care of the problem." Emily set the box down on the carpenter's trunk she used as a coffee table. "Hannah's probably hungry. It's past her feeding time."

Mitch held his daughter against his chest, cradling her tiny head with the back of his big hand. "What's Mama got in the box?"

"Here, let me take her," Emily said. "Open the box for me, Mitch. It's from Republic Books. I think it must be copies of my first Hannah book. When Hardy called last week, he said to be looking for them any day."

Mitch handed Hannah to her mother. Emily unbuttoned her

blouse as she sat down in the rocker they had placed by the front window. Glorious August sunshine poured inside, lighting the room and casting a pure, clean brightness over everything, including Emily and her baby.

After pulling a knife from his pocket, Mitch ripped into the box and lifted out a slender hardback book, the jacket depicting a dark-haired little girl dressed in a sailor suit and straw hat, so popular in the early twentieth century. Smiling, he held up the book for Emily to see; then the sight of his daughter at his wife's breast took his breath away. Emily sang quietly as she rocked. Hannah laid her tiny fist against her mother's breast while she nursed greedily.

Swallowing hard, Mitch cleared his throat. "It's copies of your first Hannah book, all right. They look great, honey."

"Take out two copies," Emily told him. "I want to sign them and have them ready to give Nikki and Zed tomorrow before the christening."

"The month of August is going to be busy for us," Mitch said. "First Hannah's christening, with Nikki and Zed as godparents, and then Nikki and Zed's wedding, with us as best man and matron of honor."

"Too bad Hannah isn't old enough to be a flower girl." Emily smiled as she gazed down in adoration at her child. "But I'm just thankful Nikki waited until after Hannah was born so I wouldn't have to be an enormously pregnant matron of honor."

"You would have been a beautiful enormously pregnant matron of honor."

"You just say that because you love me."

Laughing, Mitch stood, laid the book on the trunk and turned back to Emily. Leaning over, he kissed Hannah's rosy cheek.

"Did you ever imagine we could be so happy?" Emily asked. "We've been married nearly two years. We have a beautiful daughter. I've just published my first book, and as Banning Construction's new vice president, you'll be running Zed's whole construction empire while he's away on a two-month honeymoon."

"Zed has done a lot for me. I can't imagine what my life

would be like now if he hadn't come to Arkansas and saved me from myself."

Emily lifted her hand to his face, cupping his chin. "I can't imagine my life without you and Hannah," she told him. "I love you both so very much."

"You and Hannah are my life," Mitch said.

And Emily Hayden believed her husband, the stranger who had entered her world over two years ago and given her a new and gloriously happy life.

They had survived so much heartbreak and tragedy in their lifetimes, but for the past two years, since they'd married, they had stood together, strong and invincible, against the outside forces that could have destroyed them.

Emily tried to remember the loving uncle who had cared for her so devotedly for five long years, the uncle who had forced her to live when she wanted to die. Even now, after two years, she found it difficult to think of Fowler Jordan as the same man who had murdered two other human beings in such a cold, calculated way.

Emily knew she could never forget the past—not completely. It would always be a part of her, just as it would always be a part of Mitch. But the past was behind them, and that's where it belonged. Yesterday. A faded memory that could never harm them again.

Emily sighed, then looked at Mitch and smiled. Her husband. The father of her child. The man she loved. The stranger in her heart was a stranger no more.

* * * * *

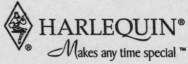

Take 2 bestselling love stories FREE

Plus get a FREE surprise gift!

Special Limited-Time Offer

Mail to Silhouette Reader Service™

3010 Walden Avenue
P.O. Box 1867
Buffalo, N.Y. 14240-1867

YES! Please send me 2 free Silhouette Intimate Moments® novels and my free surprise gift. Then send me 6 brand-new novels every month, which I will receive months before they appear in bookstores. Bill me at the low price of $3.57 each plus 25¢ delivery and applicable sales tax, if any.* That's the complete price, and a saving of over 10% off the cover prices—quite a bargain! I understand that accepting the books and gift places me under no obligation ever to buy any books. I can always return a shipment and cancel at any time. Even if I never buy another book from Silhouette, the 2 free books and the surprise gift are mine to keep forever.

245 SEN CH7Y

Name	(PLEASE PRINT)
Address	Apt. No.
City	State	Zip

This offer is limited to one order per household and not valid to present Silhouette Intimate Moments® subscribers. *Terms and prices are subject to change without notice. Sales tax applicable in N.Y.

UIM-98   ©1990 Harlequin Enterprises Limited

The World's Most Eligible Bachelors are about to be named! And Silhouette Books brings them to you in an all-new, original series....

World's Most Eligible Bachelors

Twelve of the sexiest, most sought-after men share every intimate detail of their lives in twelve never-before-published novels by the genre's top authors.

Don't miss these unforgettable stories by:

Dixie Browning

MARIE FERRARELLA

Jackie Merritt

Tracy Sinclair

BJ James

RACHEL LEE

Suzanne Carey

Gina Wilkins

VICTORIA PADE

Susan Mallery

MAGGIE SHAYNE

Anne McAllister

Look for one new book each month in the **World's Most Eligible Bachelors** series beginning September 1998 from Silhouette Books.

Silhouette®

Available at your favorite retail outlet.

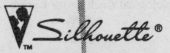